ALWAYS BE MINE
Trickle Creek
Book 3

ELENA AITKEN

Chapter One

CRAIG

"NO! NOT LIKE THAT."

Meredith ripped the brush out of my hand and hurled it across the kitchen with more strength than I would have thought possible for a five-year-old.

"You said you wanted braids." I inhaled deeply and willed myself to remain calm as I retrieved the brush from where it only narrowly escaped smashing into the potted plant my sister had brought over to 'brighten the place up'.

"Daddy, I said I wanted *French* braids." Meri's nose crinkled up while her lips pressed into a formidable pout.

I ignored the wilted leaves of the plant, added a mental note to the already extensive to-do list in my brain, and crouched in front of my daughter. "Meri." I did my best to sound stern. "You can't throw things, kiddo. You know better."

She dropped her head and rubbed at her eyes. "Sorry, Daddy."

I couldn't stay mad at her. Meri was a great kid, almost always. Mornings could be hard on both of us.

"I don't know how to do French braids, kiddo. But I promise I'll watch a video later and learn, okay?" I wasn't entirely sure when I'd squeeze that into my already hectic day, but when it came to Meri, I knew I'd find the time. "Would you settle for a high ponytail today with a ribbon that matches your shirt?" I didn't bother saying anything about the bright-purple shirt she was wearing for the second day in a row that probably should have been in the wash last week. I'd learned to pick my battles.

I pressed my index finger to the tip of her nose, and just as I'd hoped it would, her frown turned into the sweet smile I loved to see.

"Yes to the pony," she said. "No to the ribbon. None of the other girls wear ribbons anymore, Dad."

"Duh." I shrugged elaborately and once more resumed brushing out Meri's hair. "I knew that. I was just testing you."

Meri rolled her eyes with way too much sass for such a little girl. "Silly, Daddy."

As casually as I could, I pushed the jar full of ribbons that, less than six months ago, Meri had insisted on wearing in her hair almost every day. I'd ordered dozens of them so she'd have one to match every outfit. I'd hoped I'd have a few more years before the obsessing about trends started. She wasn't even six years old. Did it really matter what the other girls were doing?

I didn't bother voicing the question aloud; I already knew the answer.

Somehow, I finished Meri's hair without any further incident and sent her off to find her book bag. "We're running late, so hurry, okay?"

She flashed me a bright smile. "Don't forget to bring the class snack." Her voice trailed down the hall as she went in search of her backpack.

"Snack?" I spun in a slow circle in the middle of my kitchen, the breakfast dishes still on the table, a half-drunk cup of coffee on the counter. "Class snack?" I moved to the stack of papers that were pinned to the fridge by magnetic clips and fanned through them until I came to the calendar that listed the snack schedule for Meri's kindergarten class for the year and— "Dammit."

"Jar!"

I bit back another adult word, fished a handful of coins from my pocket, and dumped them in the jar on the windowsill that, for some reason, I'd agreed to when Meredith came up with the idea to keep the adults in her life from saying too many *adult* words around her. I would blame my siblings, if there was time.

There wasn't.

There never was.

LUCY

Welcome to Trickle Creek!
Smile! We're happy you're here.

Of course, in all the times I'd thought about what it would be like to finally visit Trickle Creek, I'd never once imagined I'd be here alone. A strange mixture of anger and sadness washed over me as I glanced at the empty passenger seat next to me.

But as quickly as the feeling came, I banished it.

I refused to be sad about Ross. Not anymore.

Even if it was my boyfriend—correction, *ex*-boyfriend— who was the reason I was going to the super small town in the middle of the mountains in the first place. He never quit talking about what a special place Trickle Creek was and how much I would love it here. He never got around to taking me, but that didn't mean I couldn't go on my own.

And I *would* love it here. Without him.

I stared a little longer at the oversized wooden sign on the edge of town, and for the first time, questioned every single one of my decisions over the last few days. I'd taken a leave from my job, found someone to sublet my apartment in downtown Vancouver for a few months, and packed up my car with everything I could fit, putting everything else in storage or donating it before driving ten hours into the mountains.

Alone.

And it felt great. Mostly.

"What do you think, Garfield?" I scratched my giant tabby cat's ears. The cat, who had been curled in a big fluffy ball for most of the drive, lifted his head and answered me with a loud meow before resuming his nap. "I agree," I said with a laugh. "It's time for a fresh start."

Not that I was even sure it was a fresh start I was after. My decision hadn't been well thought out at all. It was more of a gut reaction to pack up and leave, but I didn't regret it. At least not yet. And really, it wasn't like I'd rented a house or anything. I had a short-term rental booked for a few weeks. After that, I'd decide what I wanted to do next. One step at a time.

There were probably a thousand little towns that would've been a better fit than the one Ross had promised me he'd take me to one day, but it had been the first place I thought of when I opened my laptop the night before to start my search.

And then I'd lucked out when it came to finding a short-term rental that wouldn't eat up all my savings and would let me bring Garfield, so I jumped on it. It wasn't until I told my best friend where I was going that I realized it might not have been the best choice.

"You're going *where?*" I could practically hear Mandi's disbelief through the phone.

"Trickle Creek," I repeated. "But you can't tell anyone. Especially—"

"Pick somewhere else."

I closed my eyes and shook my head despite the fact she couldn't see me. I'd called Mandi at work, which was risky enough considering Ross could have answered the call. After all, my ex also happened to be the owner of the restaurant I'd managed for the last eighteen months, and my abrupt departure had thrown all the staff for a loop, which meant Ross was spending more time there trying to keep his business from collapsing now that I was gone. *Good.* He deserved the stress.

It also meant that Mandi had received a sudden but much-deserved promotion from her role as assistant manager.

"I already paid for two weeks." I swallowed hard. "I leave in the morning."

"Damn, Lucy. Just like that?"

"What else would you have me do?" I had to fight back tears. I hated that I'd already cried so much over a man who didn't deserve it. I hated a lot about how I'd behaved when it came to him. I hardly recognized myself anymore. "I need to get out of here."

"I get it." Mandi's voice softened. "But you could go somewhere else. I know you guys always talked about—"

"It's already done. And that's not why I chose it."

"If you say so."

Mandi knew me too well. Plus, she'd had a front-row seat to the rise and fall of what, up until recently, I had been so sure would be my last relationship. I'd been so sure we were going to get married.

"You can't say anything to—"

"As if I would." No doubt Mandi was rolling her eyes. "It's about time you finally saw him for who he really is."

"He's still your boss."

She scoffed. "So? He's still a piece of shit. Honestly, Lucy, you know I love you and I think you're amazing, but I really don't understand how—"

"I have to go, Mandi. But I'll text you when I get there, okay?"

"One more thing, Lucy. Please promise me you'll do something to get him out of your head. Go on a date, kiss a stranger, hook up with a random—"

"I'm *not* hooking up with anyone."

"Ah ha!" I could practically see her wicked grin. "You didn't say no to a date or a kiss."

"You know I'm not kissing any strangers."

Mandi laughed. "Don't knock it till you try it."

I hung up on my friend and put the car in gear. Despite myself and the situation I found myself in, at least the call had done one thing.

I was smiling again.

CRAIG

I glanced at the clock on the wall. We were going to be late. There wasn't even time to stop at the Bean Bag to buy muffins. I knew I wasn't going to win any Father of the Year awards, but out of options, I dug through the pantry and unearthed three boxes of nut-free granola bars. It would have to do.

"Come on, Meri." I poured my mostly cold coffee into a travel mug, balanced it on top of the stack of granola boxes, scooped it up along with my portfolio of papers and forms for the shop, and headed for the front door. "We're going to be— oh."

"I'm right here."

I couldn't help but laugh to see her—backpack on, ready to go, holding the front door open. "Thanks, kiddo. Lock it behind you."

It had snowed again overnight, but there was no time to shovel. Even if I'd wanted to. Which I didn't. It was the end of April, and I was over it. The ski hill still had snow, which was good for the tourists and the diehard skiers who weren't quite ready to put away their winter gear. But as far as I was concerned, I was ready to officially welcome spring.

Even after all the snow had melted in town, it wasn't unusual to get a few random storms well into April or May. That was the fun of living in the mountains. With any luck, the spring sun would melt it all away before I had to deal with it. Just in case it didn't, I made a mental note on my very long to-do list, to pick up some more sand. I'd used up the last bit after the last time I'd forgotten to shovel.

It wasn't that I forgot; I just had an irrational hope that since we were approaching the ski hill's official closing day, the snow, too would disappear.

I deposited my pile into the front seat of my Jeep and slipped in behind the wheel. "All buckled?" I asked, checking Meri's reflection in the rearview mirror.

"You know it."

My heart swelled at my sweet little girl. Yes, she could be a terror on occasion—mostly in the mornings—but she was my entire life. Being a father was, without a doubt, the hardest thing I'd ever done. But it was also the best thing. Ever.

There wasn't a single day that went by that I wasn't thankful for the choices that brought me Meri. It wasn't at all how I'd seen my life turning out. But I wouldn't trade our dynamic duo for anything.

It only took a few minutes to drive to the elementary school, but I heard all about how Jeremy's mom made carrot cake cupcakes with little icing carrots on them for his snack day and just how delicious they were. I snuck a glance at the boxes on the passenger seat. She wasn't going to be happy. But I'd make up for it next snack day.

When we arrived at the school, the second bell was already ringing. "You'd better hurry," I told her as I held her car door open. Meri tugged her backpack on, and I handed her the stack of granola bar boxes with what I hoped was a bright smile.

"Dad." She dragged out my name. "No way." Meri crossed her arms over her little chest. "I can't take those. Not again."

"They're yogurt-dipped."

She rolled her eyes.

"Sorry, kiddo. Really, I am. Next time we'll make cupcakes, okay?"

"Promise?"

"You know when I make a promise, I keep it. Especially when it comes to you."

I knew she wouldn't be able to argue with that. No matter how crazy things got, Meri came first. Always.

"Thanks, Dad."

I dropped a kiss on the tip of her nose. "Have a—"

The ringing of my cell phone through the car's Bluetooth speakers cut me off. "Go," I said to Meri. "You're going to be late. Tell Miss Schafer it's my fault you're late."

Meri giggled and turned to skip into the school, but not before adding, "I always do."

The smile fell from my face. I really needed to figure out a way to get a little more organized. Juggling the responsibilities of owning and running a business, along with being a single dad to a very busy little girl, was a lot. A real lot. But I could handle it. I had no other choice.

My phone was still ringing through the speakers when I got back behind the wheel. Without looking at the caller, I pressed the button to accept the call.

"I almost gave up on you."

"Hi, Charli." I smiled at the sound of my big sister's voice. "I was just dropping Meri off at school. What's up?"

"I just heard from William Evans. It's time for another family meeting."

William was the family lawyer, and the man in charge of administering our late father's estate, which, at this point, meant calling me and all my siblings into his office to give us the next stipulation of Dad's will. So far, both Chase and Charli had jumped through their assigned hoops.

There were three of us left, and it didn't surprise me to hear it was time to hear what Asher's requirements would be. As the thirdborn, it was his turn.

I exhaled slowly and pulled the Jeep away from the curb, making the short drive to the center of town. "I'm totally swamped, Charli. Can I skip this one? We all know it's Asher's turn next, and I support what everyone thinks is best. I just—"

"I'm going to pretend I didn't hear that." Charli's voice lost her usual friendly, light tone. She meant business. "Meet at the big house at two."

"Two?" I was about to protest with a million reasons why two was an awful time for me, but before I got the chance, Charli spoke again.

"See you there, brother." The friendly tone was back. "Don't be late."

LUCY

The speed limit slowed, the trees thinned, and a moment later, I turned the corner into Trickle Creek.

Tiny, well-kept houses lined the snow-covered street I drove through. I'd been surprised to see snow so late in April, but it didn't look like it would stay. The ski hill that loomed as a fixture over the town looked as if there was still plenty of snow, but I was pretty sure I'd seen a few tulip or daffodil heads poking out here and there as I drove. Still, it was a far cry from the full blooms in the gardens back home.

Home.

Vancouver wasn't home anymore. At least not for a while. It was stupid to let one man drive me away from the only city I'd ever lived in. But it wasn't just Ross. It was everything. It was who I'd become. I didn't even recognize myself anymore. It was time for a break.

I followed the directions from my GPS as the robotic voice guided me past the little houses to a busier, slightly more commercial-looking part of town. My rental was in the 'heart of Trickle Creek', the listing had said. It was a small apartment over an ice cream shop in the plaza—a pedestrian-only shopping area. It had looked cute and clean in the photos.

My phone guided me to a large parking lot, but there was no ice cream shop in sight.

I put the car in park and flipped through my phone to read the detailed instructions.

You will have to park in public parking and walk through the plaza. The bright-blue door to the suite is located beside the Sugar Shack.

"Okay, Garfield. I guess this is it."

Truthfully, it wasn't much at first glance. The parking lot sat at the back of a long row of short buildings that all looked to be joined together in a bit of a mishmash. I spotted an arched walkway with lights strung along the top between two buildings and a Welcome sign hanging in the middle. I guessed that was the entrance to the plaza.

It looked like it might be a bit of a walk to my temporary home, so I decided to take as much as I could in the first go. After living the last few years in a third-floor walkup, I'd become pretty good at being a *one-tripper*. And although the amount of stuff I had packed in my car was clearly going to require more than one trip, it didn't mean I couldn't do my best.

I pulled my purse across my body, gathered up one of the smaller boxes in one arm, and lifted Garfield in the other. Fortunately for me, he was a pretty sedentary cat who was more than happy to be carried.

I'd only barely made it through the arched walkway into the pedestrian-only plaza when I realized I may have overestimated my carrying capacity. The box started to slip, and when I adjusted my grip to keep it from falling, Garfield protested by digging his claws into my shoulder.

"Ouch. Dammit!"

Startled, I loosened my grip, and the cat chose that exact moment to embrace independence. He leapt from my arms, landing on the brick cobble. Fortunately, Garfield looked just as startled to be on his own as I was. He froze in terror. But then, from somewhere behind me, I heard a dog bark.

"Garfield, no!"

It was too late. I could only watch, my arms still full, as Garfield turned and ran faster than I'd ever seen him move—in the opposite direction.

Chapter Two

CRAIG

"I'M REALLY SORRY, Craig. I wish I could give you two weeks, but—"

"It's okay."

It wasn't. It wasn't even close to being okay that one of my best employees had shown up for his shift only to let me know that it would be his last . But it's not like there was anything else I could say. "It sounds like the restaurant will be an excellent opportunity."

"It will be. Thank you for understanding."

I gritted my teeth and forced a smile. "Of course."

It *was* a good opportunity for Tom. Not only would the restaurant at the golf course be able to pay more, but there would be tips involved as well. As much as I prided myself on being a good boss and making the Sugar Shack a great place to work, I couldn't compete with the tips that the golf course offered.

It would just mean I'd have to work a few more afternoon shifts than I would have liked until I could find a replacement for Tom. At least it was shoulder season and not nearly as busy as it would be when the summer tourists started flocking to Trickle Creek soon.

Fortunately, I still had the Help Wanted sign in the back room. I grabbed it, along with a roll of tape.

It had warmed up a little since the last time I'd been outside, which, according to the watch on my wrist, had been hours ago. It was already after lunch. I'd worked right through it. The work never seemed to end. I'd had no idea an ice cream shop would be so much work. Or stress.

I'd been researching other avenues of revenue to expand into other markets and although I'd found a few promising things, they all required time and money. I still had some savings, but I was sorely lacking the time and energy it was going to take to add something new.

One problem at a time.

I sighed and ripped off a piece of tape from the roll at the same moment something slammed into the side of my leg.

"What the—"

On the ground next to my leg, looking a little stunned from the collision, was a massive orange cat. It was twice the size of my sister Charli's cat, and way too far from home to be Lilly.

Quickly, I slapped the tape on the sign and bent to grab the cat. I wasn't a particular fan of cats, but surrounded by forest and all the wild animals that tended to live in the forest, Trickle Creek wasn't the type of town where the fluffy guy should be running free.

"You're a big guy, aren't you?" I hefted the big cat into my arms. Judging by his size, he was definitely not a stray.

"Don't body-shame him."

Startled by the voice—never mind the comment—I turned around to see a petite brunette with a ridiculous number of things in her arms, walking toward me as fast as she could considering the load she carried. "Excuse me?" I was equal parts amused and confused.

"He's just big-boned," she said. "And very fluffy. Don't make him feel bad about his size."

There was no way I could hide my surprise at the words coming from her mouth. "You're not serious?"

"No." She shook her head and, for the first time, cracked a smile. "His name is Garfield. He's huge and almost always avoids exercise of any kind." She shot the cat a look, and I couldn't help but chuckle. "Thank you for grabbing him. He got spooked and my arms are full."

"I see that."

I shifted Garfield to my other arm and reached out to take the box from her. "Where are you headed with all this? I'll give you a hand."

"I'm going…" She glanced around and turned in a slow circle before looking at me again with a smile that brightened her very pretty face. "Here."

"Here?"

"Well, there." She gestured with her now-free hand to the bright-blue door that was inset just a little bit from the Sugar Shack. "I rented out the unit above this ice cream shop."

Interesting.

Like most of the old buildings in the plaza, there was a small apartment above the storefront. When I bought the building, it had been used for storage, and I hadn't thought much of it. When Chase found out about the space, he'd offered to set me up on a short-term rental site to bring in some extra passive income. Vaguely, I remembered agreeing to it, and because I was already so busy I barely had time to sleep, Chase told me he'd handle the first rental for me.

Now that I was thinking about it, there were a handful of

unread text messages—and maybe a voicemail or two—from my brother that I hadn't gotten around to checking.

"Is that right? With a cat?" I was definitely going to have to talk to Chase about that. I couldn't imagine having pets in the rental property being a good idea.

"Right? I got so lucky."

She moved to the bright-blue door and punched in a code on the keypad. There was a beep, followed by a click. "I'm in."

I watched her set down her things inside and flick on the light. "Thank you for your help. I overestimated how much I could hold."

Her laugh was contagious, and I found myself completely mesmerized by the sound of it.

"I can take him now."

It took me a moment to realize she was referring to the cat still in my arms. "Oh. Of course." I shook my head as she stepped forward and took Garfield from me.

"Thanks again." Garfield cuddled into her arms, immediately more comfortable. She looked me in the eyes but didn't make a move to leave. In fact, she stepped forward, closing the distance between us.

"Welcome to town." I offered a friendly smile. "My name is—"

The rest of my introduction was lost as she pressed her lips to mine in what had to be the most unexpected kiss I'd ever had. Yet, not entirely unwelcome.

Her lips were soft, and she smelled of lemons. Instincts kicked in, and my arms came up to hold her. But before I could, she'd stepped back and broken the kiss.

"Sorry." She touched her fingers to her lips. "I don't really know why I did that. I just..." She shrugged and blew out a breath. "Thanks again."

Before I'd even registered what had happened, she'd gone inside and closed the door. I stood in the plaza, stunned, for a few moments before shaking my head and turning away from the blue door.

"What…did that…" I looked around in search of a hidden camera—or more likely, my siblings who'd set up some sort of elaborate prank to get me back into the dating world. I wouldn't put such a move past my nosy sisters.

But there wasn't anyone in the plaza watching me, waiting to jump out and yell, *Gotcha!*

My phone rang sharply, and when I saw my eldest sister's face on the screen, I laughed. "I knew it." I answered the call, still chuckling. "What did you have to do to get her to do that?"

"Get who to do what?"

"The girl. And the cat. She—"

"I don't know what you're talking about." Charli cut me off. "Craig, you're late. We're all waiting for you."

"Shit." I glanced at my wrist and saw the time. "The meeting."

"Yes. The meeting."

"I'm sorry." I started to walk. "I'll be there as soon as I can."

I ended the call and jogged through the plaza toward the parking lot. I'd think about the woman and the random kiss later. When I had time.

But that was the problem.

There was never enough time. Not for anything.

LUCY

Had I seriously just done that?

The cat still in my arms, I leaned up against the door and squeezed my eyes shut in an effort to pull myself together.

I'd just kissed a random stranger. Worse. A *really* cute random stranger who had just helped me.

Could I get any more awkward?

Obviously, it was all Mandi's fault. Still, I knew I should apologize to the man.

I released a breath and was about to open the door to do just that when I heard a cell phone ring, followed by the stranger's voice.

"I knew it. What did you have to do to get her to do that?"

Mortified, I squeezed my eyes shut again. I was only making a bad situation worse by eavesdropping, but I couldn't force my legs to move.

"The girl. And the cat. She—"

There was a pause, followed by, "Shit. The meeting." And then the sound of boots as he walked away—my opportunity gone.

"Well, that's one way to make an entrance in town."

Garfield mewled his agreement, and we headed up the tiny staircase into my new temporary home.

The apartment was small but cozy. The furnishings were pretty basic, but it was clean and had everything I'd need for the next few weeks.

Hopefully, that would be long enough to figure out what I wanted to do next. If not, I'd deal with that when the time came.

After a few more trips to my car—this time without Garfield—I got everything inside. There'd been no sign of the cute guy as I'd unloaded my car, and I couldn't decide whether that was a good thing or not.

It didn't take me long to unpack, and with the rest of the day stretching in front of me, I wasn't sure what to do with myself. I hadn't thought much beyond getting out of Vancouver, and I definitely hadn't thought about what I might do once I got wherever it was that I was going.

I had some savings, but not much. My salary as a restaurant manager didn't stretch very far once I'd taken care of rent and bills. I was going to need a job of some sort if I planned to stay away longer than two weeks.

My gaze drifted out the window to the plaza below. I'd noticed a Help Wanted sign in the window of the ice cream shop on one of my many trips to the car.

I was a bit overqualified to scoop ice cream, but a job was a job. With nothing else to do, I pulled out my laptop and settled into the overstuffed chair by the window to update my résumé.

I was almost finished updating the details when my phone rang.

"Hi, Mom."

"Lou Lou."

I rolled my eyes at her nickname for me.

"I got your message. What's this about you going on vacation?"

"Not a vacation, Mom. I told you I was—"

"Going away."

I swallowed back my impatience. Audrey Willis had a way of only hearing what she wanted to hear. "No, Mom. I said I was *leaving town*."

"Right. That's what I said."

I put my laptop on the coffee table and pinched the bridge of my nose. "Right, well. I'm sorry I didn't have a chance to come by and see you before I left but—"

"You're already gone?"

I winced at the hurt in her voice. As frustrating as she could be, my mother loved me very much. I could probably work a little harder to be a better daughter. Truthfully, I hadn't even *considered* her until I was almost in Trickle Creek. I'd fired off a quick text message when I'd stopped to get gas.

"I'm sorry," I said quickly. "It was all kind of last minute, to be honest. Something came up and I just needed to go."

"But it's *not* a vacation?" Worry laced her words. "What's going on, Lou Lou? Where are you?"

"I'm in a little town called Trickle Creek. It's really cute and quiet at this time of year."

"Trickle Creek?"

My mistake dawned too late.

"Wasn't that the place you said that boyfriend of yours was going to take you?" Before I could say anything, she continued, "Yes. It was Trickle Creek."

I could practically see her nodding and smiling to herself.

"Don't tell me you let him take you on a holiday before you'd let me meet him. I keep telling you, it's not normal for a mother not to meet her daughter's boyfriend after so long. Why don't you—"

"We broke up."

My choice of words was woefully inadequate considering what had actually happened, but she definitely didn't need the details. Audrey would lose her mind if she knew the truth about that relationship—which only reaffirmed that I'd done the right thing by ending it once and for all.

"I can't say I'm surprised."

"What?"

Of all the reactions I'd expected, righteousness hadn't made the list. "What do you mean?"

"Lucy." My mother blew out a breath. "Think about it. If a man cannot make it a priority to meet his girlfriend's family after over a year, then it's clear she is *not* a priority."

I couldn't argue with that, but I almost choked when she added, "Either that or he's married."

It took me a moment to recover, and I hoped my voice sounded normal when I finally spoke. "Well, it doesn't matter. We're not together now."

"Well, that gives you a chance to find a new young man who is more suitable for you."

Right.

The last thing I wanted was to date.

But then my mind flashed back to the look on the man's face after I'd kissed him. I knew exactly what Mandi would say, right after telling me how proud she was. She'd tell me to *get him into bed* if I really wanted to move on.

That wasn't my style. But then again, kissing random strangers wasn't my style either, and I'd just done that.

Maybe it wouldn't be so bad to do things a little differently.

I swallowed hard against the lump in my throat and shifted the conversation to safer ground—my mother's social life.

Thankfully, there were no follow-up questions about my relationship status or what I was doing in Trickle Creek, as she gleefully launched into updates about her week.

I zoned out and put the call on speakerphone, mindlessly scrolling social media while murmuring the occasional "oh yes" and "that sounds great."

Social media was a bad habit I couldn't seem to shake. Looking at other people's perfect lives—with their handsome husbands and gorgeous children posing on the porches of pristine homes—only reminded me of everything I didn't have. And worse, everything I used to think I *would* have with Ross.

I was no longer delusional about the future I wasn't going to have with him. I hadn't been for quite some time. Not since the first time I'd broken up with him two months earlier. Deep down, I'd known that was the end.

The next photo I scrolled to proved it.

Ross almost never posted anything personal on his social media. *Almost* never.

"Mom?" I cut her off mid-story about a neighbor's garden. "I have to go. I'm sorry. I'll call soon."

I didn't wait for her response before ending the call and giving my full attention to the screen.

Ross looked as handsome as ever. Maybe even more so. He

was in a T-shirt and shorts. It was a combination I'd rarely seen him in. I realized now it was because I almost never saw him on weekends. Our relationship at the restaurant had been kept very, very professional.

But that wasn't what made my heart clench.

Ross had his arms wrapped around a beautiful blonde.

His hands rested on the swell of *her pregnant belly*.

And his warm, loving smile was directed at her.

His wife.

Chapter Three

CRAIG

I WAS ALMOST thirty minutes late by the time I pulled up in front of the big house, the same house I'd grown up in, aptly named because it was the biggest house in Trickle Creek, situated just outside of town, high on a hill with acres of untouched forest surrounding it.

I moved quickly through the halls to my late father's office, stopping only to take a breath and run a hand through my hair before I pulled the heavy wooden door open.

The moment I stepped inside, every head turned to face me.

"Nice of you to join us."

Asher, my older brother, the middle child, and the one who always seemed to have some kind of chip on his shoulder, was the first to comment.

I ignored the sarcasm in his voice. No doubt Asher was nervous. It *was* his turn to hear his fate as dictated by our father, who'd seen fit to teach us all lessons beyond the grave with the special stipulations he'd included in his will.

So far, Chase, our oldest sibling, who'd left town the first chance he had as a teenager, had been brought back to Trickle Creek and had learned that, despite thinking the opposite, he was, in fact, a valuable part of the family. He'd also fallen in love with Annie Darling during the six months he'd been forced to stay in town.

I smiled at them both as I picked my way across the room.

My big sister, Charli, had been next. She'd been forced to take an investment and double it in only six months. It had been a lesson in believing in herself, which she now very much did, as did her new fiancé, Symon Scott. They'd been best friends growing up. Everyone else could see how much they'd always loved each other. Now, fortunately, they could too.

I kissed Charli on the cheek before taking a seat next to my youngest sister, Kat. She was the baby of the family and arguably the sibling I was closest to.

"Sorry, I'm late," I whispered.

"Better late than never." She winked. "I'm glad you're here now. These things are so nerve-racking. I mean, I know our turn is coming soon but it's the waiting that's killing me."

"We still have time." I squeezed her arm. "Nothing will be—"

"Now that we're all here, maybe we can get started."

William Evans, the family lawyer, cleared his throat at the front of the room. Next to him sat Steven Larson, who'd been our father's assistant and right-hand man for as long as any of us could remember. He, along with William, had been instrumental in helping us navigate our father's will and deal with what was a massive estate.

"Sorry."

I sat up straighter and addressed the room as I apologized again. "I really am sorry I'm late."

A few murmurs and nods followed. Asher made a grunting

noise from his chair closest to our father's desk, ready to hear his fate.

William started to read the legalese, and my mind drifted to my to-do list, which now included finding a new employee. Then there was the matter of my short-term rental, and my first tenant, the very pretty brunette whose name I'd failed to ask for, even after she'd kissed me.

The kiss.

There was the kiss to think about.

Oh yes, I could definitely think about that kiss for a little bit. It had only lasted seconds, and maybe it was just the shock of it, but there'd been a spark that shot through me at the touch of her lips.

Of course, it could be that I was out of practice when it came to kissing in general. I literally couldn't remember the last time I'd—

Kat nudged me sharply in the ribs.

I jerked upright and shot her a look. I was about to protest until I saw the look on her face.

"What?" I mouthed.

Kat rolled her eyes. "Did you hear any of that?"

I considered lying for half a second, but there was no point. I was only at the meeting because it was required. Ultimately, it didn't matter what the next stipulation of our father's will was. It wasn't as if any of us believed Asher wouldn't follow through with whatever it was. As the only Carlson child working for the family business—or, in Asher's case, running the whole thing—he had the most to lose.

Our father, Michael Carlson, had been a very successful businessman who'd come to town and basically saved Trickle Creek from financial ruin by seeing the potential in a new industry when the mining industry closed down. That new industry was tourism, and with the opening of the ski resort and a world-class golf course, it didn't take long for Trickle Creek to see a massive revitalization.

After he died, Asher had slipped into the role of CEO of Carlson Corp and as far as any of us were concerned, he was doing an excellent job with it.

Which was why no one was overly concerned about whatever lesson it was that their father wanted him to teach him from beyond the grave.

"Sorry," I admitted with a shrug. "I was thinking about everything I need to do."

It was a white lie, but this wasn't the moment to tell Kat that a strange but beautiful woman had just kissed me, unprompted.

Well, you might want to put listening to the reading of the will on your to-do list," Asher snapped. "Unless you plan on being the one to let us all down."

I twisted in my seat to look at him. Asher usually looked stressed out and way too serious for his age, but right now he looked even more stern than usual.

"What are you talking about?"

When Asher only shook his head and looked away, I turned to Chase.

"This one's for you, man," Chase said simply.

"What?"

A chill crawled down my spine. I turned forward. "It's not my turn," I said to William and Steven. "It's Asher's turn."

"There are no *turns*, per se." William made air quotes. "I'm only following the directions set out by your father. And it was made clear that this next condition be directed toward you, Craig."

I shook my head. I hadn't heard a single word William had said before that, but even without knowing, it didn't matter.

Whatever lesson Dad wanted to teach me, I didn't have time.

I literally didn't have one more second in my day.

The timing couldn't be worse. Whatever the stipulation was, there was no way I was going to be able to do it. I was already stretched too thin. One more thing would snap me in half.

"No."

The already quiet room became even quieter.

After a moment, it was William who spoke. The weight behind his words hit like a hammer.

"Are you officially declining the terms and conditions of your father's latest stipulation? Because if that is the case, I must remind you that the entirety of your father's estate, including the house and property, as well as one hundred percent of the holdings in Carlson Corporation, will be donated to the charities he previously—"

"No!" Kat jumped to her feet. "He's *not* saying that."

She turned to me, eyes wide. "You're not really saying that. Are you, Craig?"

Was I?

Every set of eyes in the room was focused on me, waiting for my answer.

I swallowed hard.

Maybe I should have asked William to reread the will. Buy myself a minute.

But it didn't matter. Not really.

LUCY

Determined not to stay cooped up inside feeling sorry for myself, I left my phone in my apartment—lest I be tempted to do any more doomscrolling—and headed outside into the plaza. I needed to explore my new surroundings. And a few groceries wouldn't hurt.

Immediately, I was struck by the chill in the air. It was the end of April. I wasn't ignorant to the fact that not all parts of the country were as temperate as Vancouver, but yet, somehow, I hadn't expected Trickle Creek to be so cold. I was definitely going to need a warmer jacket.

Summit Style, the first shop I popped into, had exactly what I needed. On a clearance rack at the back of the store, I found the last jacket in my size. A puffy but warm coat in a bright purple that I never would have normally considered—but dressing like an eggplant seemed like a better option than freezing. I grabbed a knit cap and mitten set in cream wool with matching purple flecks and made my way to the front of the store. At least it was all on sale.

"I know it's chilly today," the young woman at the till said. "But there wasn't any snow down in town at all yesterday."

"Really? I find that hard to believe."

She laughed. "That's life in a ski town. It took me some getting used to, too. One day it's spring and you're thinking that summer is right around the corner, and the next…boom! Winter wonderland."

I shook my head in wonder. "We definitely don't get this in Vancouver. All I know is, it's cold."

"Hopefully you won't need any of this much longer."

She rang through my purchases and, at my request, cut off the tags.

I'd be wearing everything immediately.

"I think the forecast is calling for one more big dump of snow."

"Really?" Maybe I'd chosen the wrong town after all.

She didn't hide her laughter as she handed me the jacket first. "There's a reason the ski hill doesn't shut down until the very end of April. Most of the time, the spring skiing conditions are excellent right up to the day of the Spring Splash. And often into May."

I shook my head as I slipped the coat on. Instantly, I was warmer. "You just said a lot of things that don't make any sense. Spring skiing? I thought it was a winter thing. And what exactly is a Spring Splash?"

"Are you sure you're only from Vancouver?" she teased. "I thought all Canadians knew about skiing."

I couldn't help but smile. "Not this one." I shrugged. "I'm a city girl, born and raised. And to be totally honest, I've never been to a ski hill. At least not for skiing."

Many years ago, my mom took me to Whistler on a summer vacation. We'd ridden a chair lift to the top, where we hiked around and took in the views. My mom had been a lot more impressed than my twelve-year-old self had been. Especially considering I would much rather have been at the mall with my friends.

"Well, if you have a chance you should check it out. Spring skiing is really the most fun."

I gave her the side-eye.

"It is," she insisted, laughing. "My name is Krysta Nelson, by the way. If you mention my name at the ski school, they'll hook you up with Kane. He's my twin brother, and the best instructor there is on the hill. Besides myself," she added with another chuckle.

Her good humor was contagious, and my bad mood from earlier began to slip away.

"Thank you, Krysta. I don't know if I'll give skiing a try yet. But I will be around for a bit."

"Really? How long?"

She handed the cap across the counter, and I tugged it onto my head in a way I hoped made me look as cute as some of the women I'd seen walking around earlier.

"Honestly? I don't really know. I have my short-term rental

for a few weeks, but I might start looking for something more permanent. I don't really feel like going back to Vancouver right away."

"You needed a change." Krysta nodded as if she knew exactly what I was thinking—which it seemed like she did. "I totally get it. Kane and I were the same way. We moved here from out East to teach ski school when we were nineteen and never left. Trickle Creek can be a bit magical."

"Magical." I nodded as if that made sense, but I hadn't even been in town twenty-four hours. As far as I was concerned, it was going to take a magical town to make me forget about the mess I'd left behind on the coast.

"You'll see." Krysta took my credit card with a wink. "If you give it a little bit of time, you're never going to want to leave."

I couldn't think of anything to say. Instead, I took my credit card back along with the receipt and tucked them both into my wallet. "It was really nice meeting you, Krysta." I grabbed my mittens and turned to leave. "I hope to see you again."

Krysta laughed. "You know where to find me. And if you do decide to try skiing, don't forget—"

"Ask for Kane."

"You bet."

I walked out of Summit Style in a remarkably better mood than when I'd gone in and continued through the plaza until I reached the grocery store at the far end, just off the main plaza.

Twenty minutes later, loaded down with two large paper bags, I made my way back through the plaza toward my apartment. I wasn't sure whether it was the fresh air or the dozens of friendly people I'd run into since stepping outside, but I felt much better about my decision—rash and not thought-out as it had been—to be in Trickle Creek. I had a good feeling about the small town, and I had hardly even begun to explore it.

Maybe I *would* take Krysta up on her suggestion to have a ski lesson. It wasn't something I'd normally do, and wasn't that the point? And I never had actually found out what the Spring Splash—

Before I could finish my thought, my foot slipped on a patch of ice, and before I knew what was happening—or could even think to try to break my fall—my groceries flew from my arms and I landed on my back.

Hard.

Chapter Four

CRAIG

BY THE TIME I saw the woman slip, it was too late. I'd been so lost in my own thoughts, and my latest of far too many stresses, I hadn't even noticed until I heard her let out a holler.

Using caution over the slippery ice, I ran over to where the woman had fallen. I dropped to my knees, and something in my gut twisted as I realized it was the same pretty brunette from earlier. "Are you okay?"

Without waiting for an answer, I pulled off my jacket, balled it up, and gently placed it under her head. Her eyes were closed, and she wasn't moving. I took a moment to assess her. Earlier, she'd only been wearing a sweater. Now she was practically swallowed up by a ridiculous puffy purple coat, and a knit cap covered her dark hair.

I reached for her hand and squeezed. "Are you okay?" I asked again.

This time, the woman's eyes fluttered open.

"Don't move. You might have broken something."

She blinked and shook her head. "I'm fine."

"You went down hard." I silently cursed myself. I'd been too distracted earlier to sand the sidewalk. "I'm so sorry. I'll call an—"

"I'm fine," she said again. "I don't need an ambulance. I need to get up."

I moved so I could slip my arms under her. "Nice and easy," I said as I lifted. "Just go slowly and sit for a minute in case you hit your head."

"Honestly, I'm fine."

"Do you know your name?"

Her lip quirked up in the corner, and she raised an eyebrow. "Do you?"

"Fair point."

"I'm Lucy. And I just knocked the wind out of myself." She reached for her head. "I'll probably have a bruise, but I don't think I hit my head."

"Hi, Lucy. It's nice to meet you."

She offered me a shy smile.

"I'm Craig."

"Hi, Craig." She blushed and looked away.

Was she embarrassed about slipping and falling? Or the kiss earlier?

"Does anything hurt?"

"Just my pride." She straightened the cap on her head and blew out a breath.

"Still," I said. "I'll collect your groceries. Just sit. Please."

She tried to protest again, but I placed a hand on her leg. "Please," I said again. "I really do feel responsible. Let me help."

Reluctantly, she nodded, and convinced she wasn't going to move—at least for a moment—I stood to collect her groceries.

A few minutes later, I returned with her bags. "I think I managed to save everything, except for a few eggs."

"Thank you," Lucy said. "I feel so stupid."

I set the bags down in order to help her up. She was light in my arms. Lighter than I expected. I lifted with a little too much vigor, and she launched up from the sidewalk and into my arms. Reflexively, my hands went to her hips to brace her. Even through the ridiculously puffy purple coat, I could feel the gentle curves of her body as she first tensed at my touch and then relaxed.

Once more, we were face-to-face. My thoughts flashed back to the quick kiss we'd shared earlier. More than anything, I wanted a do-over. This time I'd kiss her back. Properly.

"Sorry," she muttered.

"No." I reluctantly released her when I was sure she was steady on her feet. "You have nothing to apologize for. I shouldn't have—"

"It's fine." She wiped at her face with her mittened hands. "I feel like you're making a habit of rescuing me today. First the cat and now…" She shrugged. "Thank you."

"It's my pleasure. And it's nice to officially meet you, Lucy." I extended my hand for a much safer handshake.

She reached for my hand, then suddenly pulled back and took her mitten off. "Sorry, I'm kind of new to mittens."

I laughed. "New to mittens? Don't tell me you're from—"

"Vancouver."

I laughed even harder. "I was going to say California. But yes, Vancouver makes sense. I guess you don't have much of a reason to wear mittens there."

"Not at the end of April." She joined in my laughter. "And even then, not really very much, to be honest."

"Hopefully you won't need them much longer." I bent to pick up her bags. "This won't last."

"That's what I hear." She reached for her bags. "I can take those. Thank you."

I hesitated. "I'm happy to take them up for you. I don't want you to fall again."

"Unless there's ice inside, I won't be slipping again."

I released the bags to her, albeit somewhat reluctantly. "It was nice to meet you, Lucy. I'm sure I'll see you around. I'm actually your landlord, for lack of a better word."

She glanced toward the bright-blue door that led to her rental apartment and back at me. "You are? You didn't mention that earlier."

"I didn't get the chance." I raised an eyebrow.

"Right." Lucy gritted her teeth and nodded. "Sorry about that. I wasn't…I mean, it didn't mean anything. I don't know why I did that."

I waved away her protests. "I'd already forgotten about it."

If she could tell I was lying, she didn't say so.

"Well, I'm still sorry."

Her smile was genuine, and I couldn't help being drawn to it. Something about the woman pulled me in and made me want to spend even more time with her. Which was ridiculous. Now, more than ever, I didn't have time to even entertain the idea of a woman in my life. Not in any capacity.

What I needed to be doing was figuring out what the hell I was going to do about my father's request. No. His father's *demand*.

"If there's anything I can help you with, please don't hesitate to ask." I took a step back. "I hope you enjoy your stay in Trickle Creek."

I was about to turn away when she asked, "Craig? Actually, there is one thing. Do you know anywhere close by where I can use a printer? I have a résumé I need to print out."

"A résumé? Absolutely." I pointed to the opposite end of the plaza. "Just past the end there, down Rotary Drive, you'll find the post office, town hall, and the library. The library has some community-use computers and printers you can use."

"Great. Thanks. I want to apply for the job at the ice cream shop here, but I didn't even think of—"

"The ice cream shop?"

She nodded.

"Do you have any experience?"

"With ice cream?" She shrugged. "Not particularly. And to be honest, I'm a little overqualified. But if I plan on sticking around for a while, I should probably—"

"When can you start?"

LUCY

I found the library without a problem, printed a few copies of my résumé, and was headed back into the heart of the plaza, watching my step on the ice this time, when my phone vibrated in my pocket.

MANDI:

Got a minute?

For you?

Always.

A moment later, my phone rang, and Mandi's face appeared on the screen. "Hey," I answered with a smile in my voice. "I don't usually hear from you in the middle of the day."

There was a brief silence on the other end of the phone, followed by a sigh.

"I'm sorry to have to tell you this, Lucy, but—"

"I already know." My good mood evaporated, and I moved to a bench and sat. "You're calling to tell me about Ross and…" I couldn't bring myself to finish the sentence.

"The baby."

I nodded.

"You knew?"

"I saw it on Instagram," I admitted.

"Instagram? Lucy? Why would you—it doesn't matter." Mandi blew out a breath. "I'm sorry, Luce. I know you—"

"I didn't love him."

It was a lie, and we both knew it. I had loved Ross. He'd broken my heart when I'd discovered the truth. For days, I wasn't sure how I'd ever be able to get out of bed again. Let alone go to work. I'd used all my vacation time in bed crying.

"I was hoping to tell you before you found out another way," Mandi said. "It's all so gross, and she came into the restaurant the other day."

"What?" That caught my attention. In the entire time I'd worked there, she'd never once stepped foot in the restaurant. Or if she had, I hadn't known about it, nor had I known who she was.

Which was the whole problem. I hadn't known.

"No. I don't want to know." I shook my head. "I don't want to know anything. It's fine. I'm fine. I'm over it." I straightened my shoulders. "I'm over *him*."

I forced a neutral expression onto my face, despite the fact that Mandi would be able to see right through it.

After a moment, Mandi nodded. "Okay. I won't say another word, except I do need to ask about your plans work-wise."

"Work-wise?"

"Yeah. I know you're on a little holiday or whatever you're calling it, but when you come back…are you…well…"

"Just say it." I tried not to sound impatient.

"Well, I don't know if *she* knows about what happened."

"She doesn't."

"Well, then this is coming straight from Ross. He told me to let you know that you probably shouldn't think of coming back. Apparently, with the baby on the way, he's trying to make changes."

I rolled my eyes, and tried to pretend it didn't hurt that I was the change. "I don't think I could go back anyway."

"There's more."

I sighed. "Of course there is."

"Apparently Ross married into the Flynn family, of the Flynn Group."

The Flynn Group owned the majority of Vancouver's hot-spot restaurants and nightclubs. Mandi didn't even have to finish what she was going to say before I knew.

"So I've been blackballed."

"I'm sorry, Lucy. It wasn't your fault, none of it. I'm sure he's only acting like this because his pride's hurt. He thought he could get away with it forever."

And he would have, too. If I hadn't discovered his secret.

"It's fine."

But it wasn't. I'd worked hard to build my career and my reputation in the industry as an excellent manager. I was good at my job. Really good. I'd never planned to go back to work for Ross, but I'd never considered that I'd have a hard time finding work anywhere else.

"I'm sorry, Luce."

"Really, it'll be okay." I sat up and inhaled a breath of fresh mountain air. The folder with the printed résumés sat in my lap. "I actually just got a new job."

It was only a little white lie, because I didn't technically have the job yet, but there was no doubt I would have it. I just needed to give Craig my résumé first.

"You did? Where? Doing what?"

I hated lying to my best friend, so instead of digging myself in any deeper, I did the next best thing. "I'll have all of the details for you soon. But I actually need to rush off to a meeting with my new boss right now and if I don't get off the phone, I'll be late."

If Mandi knew I was full of shit, she was too good of a friend to call me on it. "Okay," she said instead. "I can't wait to hear all the details."

Me either.

"I'll call you soon. And, Mandi?" I took a breath. "I took your advice, and I kissed a guy."

"What? No way?"

I knew that snippet of information would send my friend into a nosy spiral.

"Who? What does he look like? What's his name?"

"I'll tell you, I promise." I winked. "But not right now. I've got to run."

I ended the call and tucked the phone into my purse as I realized the truth. I couldn't tell Mandi who I'd kissed because, unbeknownst to me when I'd done it, I'd just kissed my soon-to-be boss.

Dammit.

One thing was for sure.

I definitely had a type.

CRAIG

I hadn't actually hired Lucy on the spot. That would have been beyond unprofessional.

As it was, I was treading in dangerous territory because every time I spoke to her, I couldn't stop looking into her bright-blue eyes or picturing our brief kiss and imagining another.

But if she wanted to drop off her résumé, it certainly couldn't hurt. And I did need someone to replace Tom, who'd been quite happy to grab his things and head out the door to his new career opportunity as soon as I returned from the meeting.

I had only been in the shop for a few minutes before the bells over the door chimed with the arrival of customers. I'd begun to offer fancy hot chocolate and other hot drinks for the winter season, and although they'd proved to be a big hit with the tourists, it wasn't enough to make up the difference in the colder seasons, but it was a start.

I had just finished making the last of the drinks when once again the bells over the door rang. This time, instead of customers, it was my youngest sister Kat with Meri, whom she'd picked up from school to give me a few minutes to clear my head.

Not that I'd had that chance yet.

My daughter ran full speed toward me. "I had the *best* day, Daddy."

I picked her up and swung her around before setting her down and bopping one finger on her nose. "Of course you did. What was so special about today?"

"Not the snacks." She rolled her eyes with so much sass that I had to swallow back my laughter. "But it was okay because Savi's mom brought in cupcakes in ice cream cones for her birthday. Have you ever seen cake in an ice cream cone, Daddy? How come we don't have those here?"

I looked to Kat, who only shrugged. "Maybe it's something we could offer for special occasions. I'll ask Savi's mom how she makes them." Meri seemed satisfied by that. "Is that why today was such a great day?"

Meri looked at me as if I had three heads. "Yup. Why else would it be great?"

I laughed at my daughter. "Why don't you go put your bag in the back and wash up? Bring your coloring stuff out here and you work with me for a bit, okay?"

I turned to my sister. "Thanks for picking her up for me, Kat. Today has been…well…"

"You know I don't mind." My little sister crossed her arms over her chest. "And I know you weren't expecting that today. None of us were."

"Not even a little bit." I dropped my head. "The timing is just so…"

"Perfect?"

I glared at my sister. "I'll remind you of that when it's your turn. And the timing is far from perfect. The last thing I need right now is one more stress on my plate."

"Thank you for agreeing to do it, Craig." She crossed the floor and put a hand on my arm.

As if I had any other choice. None of us did. The only one of the siblings we'd all actually doubted would follow through had been Chase. Our eldest brother had spent most of his life living apart from us, and even longer feeling as though he didn't belong in our family. If anyone was going to blow off our dead father's demands, it would have been him.

"And for what it's worth, I don't think you should be looking at it as a stress. It's actually kind of the opposite."

I gave her the side eye.

"I know you have a lot going on right now. You always have a lot going on. Maybe this isn't such a bad thing."

"Not a bad thing?" I forced myself to keep my voice down as I spun around to face my sister. "You are kidding me, right? He wants me to hire a nanny, Kat. A *nanny*?" The word was acid on my tongue. "Do you know what that means?"

She shrugged a little. "It means that you're finally going to get some help."

"I don't need help." I all but hissed the words at her. "I've never needed help. I can't believe that Dad would…" My anger softened. "I can't believe Dad thought I did."

Kat put her hand on my shoulder. "Craig, it doesn't mean that Dad thought you couldn't do it on your own."

"That's exactly what it means, Kat." She shook her head, but I wouldn't hear it. "He didn't think I could do it on my own." I sucked in a breath and looked up at the ceiling. I had deep emotions about this latest development, but letting them out in the middle of the shop with my daughter in the other room wasn't going to happen.

"Craig, it's not like that at all."

"Don't worry, Kat. I'll do it. I said I would, and I will. I'm not going to let you down."

What I didn't say was that I was never going to feel the same way about my father again. That damage had been done the moment William Evans had read the stipulation.

Craig Carlson, you are required to hire and have in your employ for a period of no less than six months, a primary care professional, otherwise known as a nanny, to care for Meredith Carlson.

At first, after William had reread the stipulation, I was numb, because it didn't make any sense. From the moment Meredith had been placed in my arms, I'd devoted my entire life to my little girl. Every single thing I did, the choices I made…they were all for her. Even opening the Sugar Shack had been for Meri. The ice cream shop was a way to provide for her while being there so I could avoid an endless stream of babysitters. I prided myself on being an excellent father. To hear that my father not only thought I needed help but was *ordering* that help had been a blow, to say the least.

"I'd do it if I could, Craig."

I looked at my sister. Her pretty face was twisted into a frown, and she looked as if she might cry. It was easy to forget that we were all affected by our father's loss and his crazy stipulations dangling over our heads.

"I know you would, Kat." I pressed my lips together and nodded a little. Kat already helped with Meri more than she should. Kat had her own hair salon in the plaza, which was always busier than she had time for. Plus, she should be out dating and having fun. Not babysitting her niece.

Even if she could help, it wasn't allowed, and William Evans had been sure to remind us of that. *There is to be no help from your siblings. That includes in a professional capacity. You will have to hire an independent party.*

"You don't need to do this on your own, Craig," Kat said now. "I can help you find someone suitable."

"I did not have a child for someone else to raise, Kat." I inhaled and rolled my shoulders back. "I knew what I was getting into when I signed up for this life. It's not anyone else's responsibility to take care of my daughter except my own."

"I know that. We all know that. But you don't really have a choice right now."

She was right, and that pissed me off more than anything else.

"You are an amazing father." Kat nodded slowly, her red ponytail swishing. "A nanny isn't a parent replacement. It's an enhancement. Think about it. She can do the things you don't have time for, or don't want to." Kat took a step closer and whispered, "Like making cupcakes for snack day instead of sending granola bars for the second time in a row." She nodded smugly. "Oh yes, I heard all about it."

I glanced behind me, where Meri had gone into the back room.

"She'd be able to do the after-school pickup. Do homework

with Meri and make a hot dinner instead of fish sticks every night."

I shot my sister a glance.

"Yup," she added. "I've heard about that, too."

She wasn't entirely wrong. There definitely were a few things that would be helpful about a nanny.

"It's not forever," Kat said. "It's only for six months. Summer is right around the corner, and that's your busiest time. Meri isn't going to sit in the corner and color forever, you know? If you ask me, the timing couldn't be better right now."

I groaned and scrubbed a hand over my face. I hated it when my little sister was right.

Six months.

Summer *was* busy, and Kat wasn't wrong. Meri deserved more than afternoons spent at the ice cream shop when I couldn't give her the attention she deserved, followed by frozen meals and rushed mornings that always seemed to turn into a fight.

Plus, I didn't have a friggin' choice in the matter.

The jingle of the bells pulled my attention.

Lucy, still in her ridiculous purple coat, but sans bags of groceries, or large orange cats, walked through the doors. "I hope I'm not too early." Her smile was warm, if not a little unsure.

Kat turned, got a look at Lucy, and turned back to me with big eyes and raised eyebrows.

I didn't even want to know what she was trying to communicate with that look.

"You're right on—"

"You're right on—"

"I *love* your jacket!" Meri appeared from the back of the store and made a beeline toward Lucy. "Purple is my very favorite color. See?" She grabbed at her T-shirt and held out the hem. "I have purple, too."

Lucy dropped to a crouch in front of Meri. "We're purple twins. You have excellent taste."

Kat's eyes got even wider as we both watched the little scene play out in front of us. Without looking away, she jabbed an elbow into my ribs.

I scowled in my sister's direction and took a step forward. "Lucy?" I waited for her to turn toward me. "You're hired."

LUCY

"I'm…" I glanced away from the little girl and her big smile. Slowly, I rose to standing and looked at Craig. "I'm what?"

"You're hired." Craig wiped his hands together and grinned broadly.

A petite redhead woman next to him shook her head, a small smile on her face, which only added to my confusion.

"But I didn't interview yet. And I told you I didn't have any experience with ice cream."

"Ice cream?" the redhead almost choked.

Craig ignored her and focused on me. "It doesn't matter." He smiled confidently, as if the matter was settled.

But it was far from settled. I still had a ton of questions.

Like what my hours might be and how much I was getting paid. Not that the answer to either of those questions mattered. Not really. It's not like I had anything else to do during the day, and I *did* need a job. Even if it was just scooping ice cream.

Still. Never in my life had I been hired for any job without at least a basic interview.

"Craig. Seriously." The redheaded woman rolled her eyes, jabbed Craig in the ribs with her elbow, and crossed the floor toward me. "Hi," she said. "I'm Kat." She held out her hand.

"And I'm sorry for my brother. He's had kind of a big day. Obviously, his managerial style could use a little work." She turned and shot her brother a look. "This is Meredith."

"Hi," I greeted the little girl first. "I'm Lucy."

"Everyone calls me Meri." Very seriously, Meri held out her hand for me to shake. "Do you have anything else that's purple?"

I pretended to think about it for a moment. "You know what? I don't think I do."

"That's okay. You have a purple jacket." Meri held up a pencil crayon. "I'm going to draw you." Before I could respond, she ran away with her art supplies and climbed up to a table in the corner by the window.

I couldn't help but smile after her. I didn't have a lot of experience with kids. But Meredith was a cutie, with just the right amount of sass.

I liked her.

"Your daughter is super cute."

Kat shook her head and laughed. "I agree. She is super cute, but she's not mine."

Confused, I looked to Craig, who simply nodded.

"Oh."

It was far from an adequate thing to say considering I'd kissed the man the first time I'd met him, which was something I never would have done if I'd known he was married with a family. A red-hot blush crept up my neck as I surreptitiously glanced at his left hand.

No ring.

Interesting.

Not that it made a difference. No matter how attractive he was. And he was—all six feet of him, with his flop of sandy-blond hair and deep-green eyes that made my stomach flip when they were focused on me.

Nope. Not even the fact that I couldn't stop thinking of

that silly little kiss I'd laid on him would make a difference. It wasn't happening. He had a child, which meant there was a mother to that child somewhere, and, as of a few minutes ago, Craig had officially become my boss.

No, thank you. I wasn't going down that road.

Not again.

I winced at the thought. What happened with Ross hadn't been my fault. But that didn't make me feel any better about it.

"She's mine," he said, as if it needed any further explanation.

"She's cute," I repeated needlessly.

"And…" He shrugged and gave me a bashful look. "I know this is going to sound a little strange, but that's actually why I hired you."

The situation was getting more confusing by the moment. I looked between Craig, Kat, and then Meri before finally facing Craig again. "Excuse me?"

"I know you were applying to work in the shop here, but you said yourself you were overqualified to scoop ice cream."

"Uh huh."

"Oh boy." Kat chuckled but didn't make any moves to leave until Craig shot her a look. "Why don't I take Meri in the back to find a snack?"

"Good idea."

Kat didn't bother hiding her laughter as she held out her hand for Meri, who grabbed it readily at the promise of a cookie.

"Good luck," Kat called out over her shoulder as she went.

I didn't know who it was aimed at, but my senses were on alert.

"What exactly is the position you're hiring me for?" I asked the moment they were out of the room.

Craig gestured to a nearby table, where I took a seat.

He took a deep breath. "It turns out that I'm in the market

to hire a nanny, and when I saw you with Meri, it just seemed like—"

"A what?" I shook my head, unsure I'd heard him properly.

"A nanny."

"A nanny?"

"A nanny."

"A—"

"Yes." He stopped me from repeating myself yet again. "I know it's not what you were thinking when you told me you were going to apply for a job, but there have been a few developments in my life in the last few hours, and now I need a nanny for the next six months."

"Six months?"

He nodded. "It would only be a temporary position, yes."

"Temporary." On some level, I was aware that I was probably coming off as a simpleton with all my parroting, but I was having a very difficult time processing what was happening. I hadn't thought much beyond a few weeks, let alone six months. Sure, taking the job at an ice cream shop might have bought me a month or two to figure out what I was doing, but *six months*? As a *nanny*?

There were a million reasons I should get up from the table and walk out without saying another word. I didn't know these people. I didn't know their story or owe them anything. Never mind the fact that I had absolutely no experience with children whatsoever. I hadn't even really been a babysitter when I was younger. In fact, the only thing I really knew about little girls was that once upon a time, I myself had been one.

"I haven't even met your wife yet."

"I don't have a wife."

"Meri's mom," I said quickly. "I haven't—"

He shook his head, but his face was blank and unreadable. "Meri doesn't have a mom."

I blinked.

"I…I don't have anywhere to stay." The objection slipped from my mouth without thought. Why hadn't I just said thanks, but no thanks? I didn't need to make up excuses. I could just say no. "The rental is only for two weeks and—"

"No problem." Craig sat back in his chair.

A huge smile lit up his handsome face. He had a dimple on his right cheek. It was the last thing I should have noticed at that moment, but I couldn't seem to look away as he said, "I own the suite upstairs, remember? You can stay as long as you want."

I shook my head. My mouth opened and shut wordlessly.

"Look." The smile slipped from Craig's face as he leaned forward and took my hand in his.

The touch was completely unexpected, but as soon as his skin touched mine, heat raced through me, and I found myself settling.

His hands were big and strong and warm. There was something comforting about him; despite the fact that I hardly knew the man, I felt good around him. And that wasn't a small thing. Not lately.

"I know this probably sounds totally crazy."

"It really does." I nodded. "Did you even look at my résumé?"

He pressed his mouth into a thin line and shook his head. "I don't really have a lot of time to get this done." He blew out a breath.

"I can save you the trouble then. I don't have any experience with children. I'm a restaurant manager. I've worked at a variety of Vancouver hot spots. The closest thing I've come to being a nanny is juggling the dramas of a staff full of twenty-year-olds who are all either dating each other, or sleeping with their best friend's boyfriends, or—"

"Really? They do that?" Craig looked amused.

I nodded. "Trying to balance feuds and friendships within the staff is the hardest part of the job. It's like a reality show." I chuckled and then remembered what we were talking about. I pulled my hand away from his, but instantly wished I hadn't. "But that doesn't mean I have any experience with a…I don't even know how old Meri is."

"She's almost six." Craig smiled warmly. "She's just finishing up her first year of kindergarten in June. So, you'll have the summer when you'll have to be with her all day. But until then, on the days when she's at school, you're welcome to enjoy the town or do…well, whatever."

"I didn't accept the job." But I knew I would. After all, I had nothing else to do, and Meri did seem like a pretty sweet kid. Besides, apparently, I'd decided to do things differently than I normally would, and it didn't get any different than working as a nanny. And staying busy would be the perfect way to get over everything I'd left behind. The best kind of distraction.

"I don't know what the average salary for a nanny is, but I'll pay you…four thousand a month?"

"Four thousand?"

"And free rent."

"Free rent?"

"Do you always make it a practice to repeat everything said to you?"

Damn, he was sexy when he laughed.

And that was probably the biggest reason I should have refused the job. From the moment I'd met Craig, I'd been drawn to him, and it had nothing to do with the spontaneous kiss I'd planted on him. It was something more.

And that could be nothing but trouble.

Still, the pros outweighed the cons. And it wasn't like I had a lot of options, either. Apparently, there was nothing to go back to in Vancouver. At least not right away. Maybe after a few months, things would calm down and I could try to get a restaurant job again. But that wasn't likely to happen for a while. I didn't have any other options.

Against my better judgment, I held out my hand. "You have a deal."

Chapter Five

CRAIG

"WAIT." My oldest sister, Charli, shook her head and held up her hand. "Back up. You did *what?*" She looked across the kitchen table to Kat, who sat with a cup of coffee in front of her and a smug smile on her face. "He did *what?*"

"He hired a woman to be Meri's nanny without even knowing her last name, let alone looking at her résumé."

Charli slapped both her hands on the table and stared at me. "You did not."

"He did." Kat nodded. "The best part is she hasn't even been in town for a full twenty-four hours."

"No references?"

Kat shook her head. "Not from Trickle Creek anyway."

I sighed heavily. I was beginning to regret having my sisters over for Saturday morning coffee. Not that I had a choice, considering they more or less told me they were coming over. I cleared my throat, but the women were too engrossed in their discussion of my life to pay any attention to me.

"I would ask if she was cute, but when it comes to Craig…"

"That's more of an Asher thing," Kat finished for her. "I don't think Craig even knows how to date anymore."

I shot her a look and for a second was tempted to tell them about how Lucy had kissed me. Fortunately, I thought better of it.

Charli nodded knowingly. "Definitely more of an Asher thing."

"Definitely."

I had heard just about enough. I pushed my chair back as loudly as I could, stood, and pressed both of my palms down on the table between my sisters. "If you two are done dissecting my decisions, I would like to point out that I do know her last name. It's Willis. Plus, I got her references and her résumé, and they all check out. Besides, if you recall, I did not have much of a choice in the matter."

Both women gave me a slight nod.

"Besides, Kat met her, and she can tell you that Lucy is a very nice woman and she's great with Meri."

They looked at each other and shrugged.

It was Kat who broke first. She laughed and patted my arm. "Calm down, Craig. You know we're only being annoying because we care."

"As long as you recognize that you're annoying," I grumbled and moved toward the coffeepot. If I was going to get through the day, I was going to need a lot more coffee.

Truthfully, not that I'd ever admit it, let alone to my sisters, but more than once in the last two days since I'd spontaneously hired Lucy, I'd second-guessed myself. I wasn't the type of guy who made rash decisions. Ever. Especially when it came to my little girl.

Meri was my entire world and had been from the moment Donna had announced she was pregnant. Donna was a college student from Australia who'd taken a gap year from school to spend a ski season in Trickle Creek to have fun and work at the ski school. We'd met at the bar one night after a day on the slopes. The attraction had been immediate and hot. But neither of us expected anything more.

I was only twenty-four when Donna presented me with the positive pregnancy test. We'd been careful, but nothing was a hundred percent, and just like that, my entire life changed.

It wasn't at all the way I'd planned, but I always wanted a family, and instantly I'd been thrilled at the idea of having a baby. However, I was the only one. Donna had never wanted children. It had never been part of her plan, and she made it very clear that wasn't ever going to change. Thankfully, she agreed to stay in Canada long enough for the baby to be born, with the understanding that she would sign over full custody to me. Less than a week after Meri was born, she returned home.

My father and my siblings had struggled to understand how a mother could make that decision, but I respected it. Donna had made the very unselfish decision to give me full custody. She knew then, as everyone else had come to understand, that it was better for Meri to have one parent who was a thousand percent in, than two, with a mother who was resentful and unhappy.

Being the only parent had been challenging, but I wouldn't have traded it for anything. Everything I did was for Meri. Including hiring Lucy.

My inheritance was her inheritance, too. And if I didn't hire a nanny to satisfy my father's demands, it would disappear. I cared too much about her future to let that happen because of my own stupid pride.

Besides, Kat was right—another thing I didn't want to admit—Meri deserved to take cupcakes to school for snack day and have a home-cooked meal. Or two.

"Did you really hire her without looking at her résumé?" Charli's question shook me from my thoughts.

Slowly, I returned the coffeepot, added a spoonful of sugar, and turned to face my sister. "I did." She opened her mouth, but before she had a chance to object, I continued, "It was a gut instinct."

"A gut instinct?"

Kat shook her head and reached for the box of muffins she'd picked up from the Bean Bag on her way over. My little sister was enjoying watching me squirm. When I looked toward her for assistance, she only winked and took a bite of a muffin.

"Yes." I sighed. "She was actually applying to work in the shop temporarily, but when she came in…" I glanced at Kat, who still wasn't offering any support. "She started talking to Meri, and she was just so good with her that I thought, why not? There's no guarantee that I'd find a better candidate and why not get started and jump in right away? The sooner we get this over with, the better, right?"

Despite the fact that I was feeling a certain way about my father at the moment, Michael Carlson had been one of the most generous men any of us had known. He'd not only been incredibly giving to his family, but also to the entire town, and was credited by many to have single-handedly saved Trickle Creek by bringing in and encouraging the tourism industry when the mine closed years earlier. I got my own work ethic and my head for business from my father. He'd also been an extremely loving dad and grandfather, and he was missed dearly.

"I'm not saying that getting started isn't a good idea," Charli said, "but I think it's usually a good idea to check references for the person you're hiring and…maybe a criminal background check."

I couldn't disagree. "That's why she's not starting until Monday. I needed a few days to do all that." I wasn't completely irresponsible. "So far, everything's checked out really well. Everyone had nothing but good things to say about her."

"And she's new to town?"

"She was actually only here for a visit." Of course, Kat chose that moment to speak up. "She's staying in Craig's short-term rental."

Charli's eyes grew wider than I thought possible.

"And she's super cute." Kat winked before shoving another piece of muffin in her mouth.

"Oh? She's cute?"

I tipped my head and shot both my sisters a look. "When have you ever known me to care about that?"

They exchanged glances, and it was Charli who said, "It must have been about six years ago now."

"Before Meri was born."

"Way too long."

Kat nodded in agreement. "*Way* too long. And Lucy is very cute. I think this will be a very interesting six months."

I took a large swallow of my lukewarm coffee. "I don't know about interesting, but I hope it will be good for Meri. You know that's the only thing that matters. I need to get through this and move on. Then everything will go back to normal, and it will be someone else's turn to get tortured by Dad from beyond the grave."

"Normal?" Kat wrapped up the rest of her muffin and stood. "I kind of think the entire point of what Dad's trying to do here is to shake up your *normal*." She blew me a kiss before I could argue. "I'm going to go say goodbye to my niece before I head out."

We watched her leave, and when she was gone, I shook my head. "The jury's still out on whether this is a good idea or not."

"It will be." Charli chose a pastry from the box but almost

immediately pushed it away. She was in her first trimester of pregnancy, and judging from what I observed, pretty much unable to eat most of the time. "You're not the only one Mom taught to trust their gut." She smiled knowingly at me.

I hadn't said anything about our mother, but Charli knew. Our mother had encouraged all of us to tune into our instincts. *Usually, your gut reaction is the right one*, she'd say. It wasn't always easy to remember that advice, but there were times, like when Lucy had walked into the shop for the first time, when it was impossible to ignore.

"I hope you're right."

Charli stood and crossed the room to give me a kiss on the cheek. "It's going to be okay, brother. All of it. I've been through it, remember?"

Charli had been the second one to receive her *orders* from our father's will. Her task had been to take a small investment and double it in a matter of six months. It turned out to really be a lesson in believing in herself, which through the process of taking Alpenglow, her hobby flower farm, and turning it into a year-round flower business, she had.

"I know it might not seem like it right now, and I know if anyone had tried to tell me this when I was in the middle of it, I wouldn't have believed them either, but Dad really did know what he was doing. Trust the process and really open yourself up to it. You never know what could happen."

I knew she was talking about the fact that not only did she learn to believe in herself, make a success out of her business, and fulfill our father's request, but she'd also fallen in love with her childhood best friend and superstar skier, Symon Scott, subsequently gotten engaged, and they were now expecting their first child.

"With all due respect, sis. Marriage and more babies aren't in the cards for me. I know you and Kat would love nothing more than to romanticize every situation, but in this case, it's not happening. Meri is my priority, and I'm doing this for her. To protect her inheritance. That's the only reason."

Ultimately, that's all it came down to. Meri. It was the only reason I did anything I did. And this was no different.

It didn't matter what Charli or Kat or any of them said. I didn't need to be open to the process or even try to understand why our father did what he did. I just needed to get through it. Preferably with as little disruption to my little girl as possible.

Which meant that even if I did think Lucy was ridiculously cute with her big blue eyes, sexy soft lips, and what seemed to be an endearing amount of clumsiness, and even if I had on more than one occasion toyed with the idea of dating again one day if I ever got a spare moment, it wouldn't be with my daughter's nanny.

LUCY

I was questioning all my life choices.

Especially the latest one that had led me to be standing on the top of a mountain, with two boards attached to my feet.

"I don't know about this." I turned to the man next to me, but Kane flashed me the same brilliant smile that had convinced me, against my better judgment, to agree to a ski lesson.

"Trust me." His voice was soothing, and when he placed a gloved hand on my shoulder, I surprised myself by doing just that.

"Okay."

Okay? Who was I?

It wasn't just the impromptu ski lesson, although that was a huge part of it. But I'd only been in this new town for a few days, and already I was making decisions that I would never have made in a million years if I were in Vancouver.

The jury was still out on whether or not that was a good thing.

No. It was definitely a good thing.

All the decisions I'd made in Vancouver, at least in the last few months, had done nothing but get me in trouble. So really, what was the harm in doing things differently?

From the moment I'd agreed to take the nanny job, which was something I never would have seen coming, I made a decision to embrace the unexpected. At least for the next few months. It wasn't as if my life could get any more screwed up than it already was. It was obviously time for something new.

Like, apparently, learning how to ski for the first time at thirty-one years old.

"It's really quite easy." Kane started to speak. "Remember what I taught you down on the beginner run?"

I nodded. "I think we should go back to the beginner run."

"Sure thing." He laughed, but there was no malice in it. "But there is only one way down the mountain."

"The chairlift?" I pointed behind me to the lift we'd just come off.

"No." Kane turned my arm gently so it pointed down the hill. "Down."

The panic began to well up inside me once again, but Kane continued to talk. "But first," he said. "Take a minute to appreciate this."

I shook my head but took a deep breath before looking out to where he was using my hand to point.

Just like that, the fear vanished as I sucked in a breath. "Wow."

"Right?"

I nodded. "It's…"

"Pretty spectacular, isn't it?"

It really was. It was a perfect day, with a bright-blue sky stretching out in front of me. We were on the top of the mountain with a view of the town below and another mountain range just beyond. I had never seen anything quite like it.

"See? Skiing isn't all that bad, is it? And honestly, you're lucky to have such great snow this late in April."

"I don't think I've ever heard anyone say that I was lucky to have snow in April." I looked at my instructor, whose broad grin was impossible to resist. I found myself smiling and agreeing with him. "But you're right," I said somewhat truthfully. "It is beautiful."

"Let's get down this, and I'll buy you a drink to celebrate." Kane winked at me.

Despite the chill in the air, I felt a rush of warmth, but I didn't have time to dwell on the fact that he may or may not have been flirting with me. Because a moment later, Kane was prompting me to *push off and pizza pie.*

I did as I was told and much to my surprise, started sliding down the hill, just the way I had earlier on the beginner slope.

I made a few easy turns before Kane declared me advanced enough to try *French fries.*

Dutifully, I followed the tracks he made ahead of me and did my best to turn where he did. I only fell twice, and neither wipeout was as dramatic as I feared.

"I told you you could do it." Kane held up a gloved hand for a high five when we reached the bottom.

I looked behind me at the hill I'd just skied down and back to Kane, who'd taken his helmet off. "I can't believe I just did that."

"And you did it really well." His smile was warm.

Was it a little warmer than before?

"Now, how about that drink?"

He *was* flirting with me.

And really, was that so bad? What did they say about the best way to get over someone?

But getting over Ross was more complicated than that, because it wasn't just the end of the relationship that I had to come to grips with. It was who I'd become. Who he'd turned me into that I was struggling with.

The smile fell from my face, and I shook my head a little. "I'd love to, Kane."

"But?" He tipped his head and raised his eyebrows.

He really was good-looking…

"But…I just got to town, and I start a new job on Monday." It might be an excuse, but it was the truth. "And I really need to get everything ready for my first day. Maybe another time?"

"I'm going to take you up on that."

His bright smile was back, and I couldn't help but smile, too. Kane seemed like a genuinely nice guy, and I definitely needed a little more of that in my life.

We said our goodbyes, making promises to see each other again.

It wasn't until after I was back in my apartment, Garfield purring on my lap, that I pulled out my phone and pulled up my social media account. Normally, I would post a photo of myself on the ski hill with a hashtag like: #learningnewthings #skibunny #mountainlife

But I couldn't bring myself to type the words. Instead, I navigated almost by habit to his profile and that photo that had confirmed I'd made the right choice by leaving town—and him —behind.

I met Ross when I'd accepted the job as manager of his restaurant in downtown Vancouver. My first impression of him was that he was handsome, smart, and successful.

And my boss.

Which meant he was off-limits. There'd been no flirting or anything inappropriate for months, but as we worked closely together, the glances and lingering touches seemed to increase in frequency, until finally one night, as I was finishing up my closing duties in the back office, Ross leaned over the table where I was adding up the receipts from the evening and kissed me.

After that, he asked me out on a dinner date, and then another and then…well, I fell hard and fast for him after that.

It took almost ten months before I realized my happy ever after with Ross was never going to happen.

Just thinking about that day when Ross had left his cell phone on the coffee table while he showered, and I saw the pretty blonde face light up on his screen with the name "Wifey" and a heart emoji across the top made me sick to my stomach.

"Who's the blonde?" I'd asked when he stepped from the bathroom, a towel around his waist. And then, before he could lie to me, I added, "Wifey."

The smile fell from his face, and that's when I knew.

"Lucy, it's not what you think."

"I think you're married."

He didn't speak right away.

"Ross? Are you married?" I looked at his left hand but there was no ring. There'd never been a ring.

He saw where my eyes traveled. "I've never worn it."

That was the moment it became real. Even when I'd seen the caller ID. Even when he didn't immediately deny it. I'd hoped it wasn't true. It couldn't be true. Ross wasn't married. He was my boyfriend.

"How long have you been married?" I shook my head before he could answer and stood up. "It doesn't matter." I thrust the phone at his chest. "Get out."

I felt like I was outside of my body. Somehow, I was still standing when I couldn't feel my limbs at all.

"Lucy." He juggled the phone in one hand and tried to hold up the towel with the other as he moved toward me. "I love you. It's not—"

"Get out, Ross." I clamped a hand over my mouth before a sob could slip out and ran to the bedroom.

That was the first time I broke up with Ross.

I exhaled slowly, banishing the memory from my mind. I stroked Garfield's soft fur and scratched behind his ears the way he liked until he was purring so loud that I laughed. "You're the only man I need in my life, right, buddy?"

The cat mewled and adjusted his weight on my lap.

"I definitely don't need a liar and a cheat, do I?" I didn't need Garfield to agree to that one. I already knew the answer to that.

I'd spent weeks in bed after breaking up with him. Going over and over our months together. How had I not known he was married? Why couldn't I see it? I did not date married men. I wasn't that person. But I was. And I hated him for putting me in that position.

When I finally dragged myself out of bed and went back to work, I'd done my best to avoid him, and for a while, I convinced myself that I could still work with him.

I'd only been back at work a few weeks when Ross showed up at my apartment with flowers. He declared his love for me and spun story after story about how his marriage had been dead for years, and they didn't love each other anymore. He promised me that he'd ended things with his wife. "It's only you, honey. It's always been you. I swear."

And like the purposefully ignorant woman I had chosen to be, I let my blinders slip back into place, but only momentarily.

Fool me once, shame on you.

I let him pull me to him and wrap his strong arms around

me. I could still remember the way his arms felt around me as he held me and whispered reassurances in my ear.

Fool me twice, shame on me.

When he moved to kiss me, something stopped me. I turned my head and pulled away. "Prove it."

"Pardon?"

"Prove it," I said again. "Prove you're not with her."

He chuckled and took a step back. "What do you…why would you…"

"Because you made me the other woman, Ross." I straightened my spine. "That wasn't fair. Not to her and not to me. I'm not that kind of person. I feel sick about it." I had spent many sleepless nights imagining how his wife would feel if she'd found out about us, and even more than Ross's betrayal, that had broken my heart. I would never purposefully hurt someone like that.

"I screwed up." Ross took a step toward me, but I crossed my arms over my chest. "But all that's over now."

"So prove it. Call her. I need to hear it from—"

"What?" His face twisted into an unrecognizable mask of anger, and that's when I knew with one hundred percent certainty. "We're not *calling* her. My word should be good enough. I just told—"

"It *should* be good enough." Sadness and realization seeped through me. "But it's not. Not anymore." I reached past him to open my front door. "Goodbye, Ross. I won't be the other woman."

He stared at me, his mouth open. "Lucy. You're being irrational. Think about it. You need me."

"I don't."

"I need you, Lucy."

"Go home, Ross." I swallowed hard. "To your wife."

In what may have been the wisest decision Ross had ever made when it came to me, he walked out of my apartment without another word. A few days later, I was packed up and on the road.

"Never again." I exhaled slowly. "Right, Garfield?"

He offered a loud purr in support.

I hit the button with my thumb to unfollow and block Ross's profile, and the picture disappeared from my screen.

Chapter Six

CRAIG

I SCANNED the list in front of me one more time. I'd spent most of the night before putting it together, but I was fairly certain I'd forgotten something anyway.

I'd never left anyone who wasn't family in charge of Meredith before. Ever. And even then, I rarely used my siblings as a babysitter. To be fair, there was very little reason I would ever need anyone to watch my daughter for me, considering I had no life outside of her and the shop.

"It's going to be fine." I spoke aloud to the quiet kitchen and took a deep swallow of my coffee. I'd gotten up almost two hours earlier than I usually did because I wanted to be prepared when Lucy arrived. I had no idea what to expect from a nanny or how to even *onboard* one.

For the tenth time that morning, I considered calling the whole thing off. Maybe I should have given myself more time to prepare. The list wasn't comprehensive enough. I'd definitely missed something. Starting Lucy so early in the morning was probably a bad idea. I—

A knock on the back door stopped the runaway train of thought. I looked up to see Lucy, looking very cute despite the early hour with her hair in a ponytail on the top of her head and a bright smile on her face, through the window. She raised her hand in a little wave, and I gestured for her to come in.

"Good morning." I couldn't help but smile when she was around. I stood and moved toward the cupboard to get her a mug. "Coffee?"

"I actually don't drink coffee."

I froze, my hand on a mug, and turned slowly to face her. "How do you not drink coffee and still manage to function? Are you sure you're not an alien?"

She laughed and the sound filled the small kitchen. "Hardly. But I do like tea, if you have some."

I didn't have to look. "I don't. This is definitely a coffee house. Sorry." I made a mental note to pick up some tea for her the next time I was at the store.

She shrugged and her gaze landed on the list I'd left on the table. "Is this for me?"

I topped up my mug and joined her at the table. "It's just a few things I thought about last night. To be honest, I don't really have any experience with any of this."

"Well, that works out because I don't either."

I knew she was only trying to make a joke, but it stopped me. I really didn't need any more doubt in my mind about what I was doing.

But then again, her references had checked out. Even if none of them had anything to do with childcare.

Trust your gut.

My mother's advice. It had been too long since I'd listened to my intuition. The last time was when I'd made the decision to be a single dad, and that had turned out to be the very best decision of my entire life.

I looked at Lucy as she studied the list I'd made. I watched as her brows wrinkled together a little. I took in the way she tapped her finger against her temple as she read.

Yes.

My gut told me this was a good thing. I needed to trust it.

The only other option was to go through a nanny service to find a candidate, and that could take months, with no guarantee that they'd find anyone better suited. Besides, both my sisters were on call in case anything went sideways—which it wouldn't—but it made me feel better knowing they were there.

"Do you have any questions?" I nodded toward the list.

"Yes." She looked up at me, her blue eyes wide. "Lots."

"Lots?"

"Oh yeah." She slid the paper away. "I mean, I don't really know much about how this all works, but…I do think I should know things like what Meri's favorite foods are. What types of things she likes to do after school. Maybe, who her friends are."

"Oh."

I'd written down the names and phone numbers of my brothers and sisters, the family doctor and the school. I'd noted the start time and pick-up times for school every day, and I'd even remembered to write down what days Meri needed to bring a snack. But I hadn't considered any of the details Lucy was asking about.

"I didn't even think about—"

My voice caught in my throat when Lucy placed her hand on my arm. "I'm teasing," she said with a smile that lit up her face. "I'm sure Meri and I are going to be just fine, and we'll figure out all the little things together. It's going to be fun."

I looked at my arm, and her hand resting there, but didn't pull away. When was the last time a woman besides my sisters touched me like that? Too long to even begin to remember. And even longer since I'd felt that flip in my stomach.

I swallowed hard and pulled my arm away. The last thing I

needed on top of everything else going on was to feel any kind of flips when it came to Lucy.

"Look at the time." I glanced at the clock on the microwave. "It's time to wake up the little princess now. And you'll see firsthand how chaotic the morning can be."

Lucy tipped her head in question. Or was it doubt? The last thing I needed was for her to second-guess this entire arrangement before it even began.

"Ninety percent of the time, Meri is a total sweetheart."

"And the other ten?"

I grinned. "Let's just say that every once in a while, I get a vision of what her teen years might be like." I winked and gestured for Lucy to follow me down the hall to Meri's room to start the wake-up process.

Lucy watched from the door while I flipped the switch on the wall, flooding the room with bright light before pulling the curtains to the side. "Rise and shine, kiddo."

The little figure piled under a mountain of stuffed animals groaned and flipped over. "Nooo."

I'd hoped for Lucy's sake that maybe this would be one of the mornings when Meri jumped out of bed with a smile on her face, but it only took a few seconds to realize that wasn't the case. Oh well, maybe it was best for Lucy to witness the darkest side of my little princess right off the bat.

"Come on, Meri. We don't want to be late for school again. Besides, we have a special visitor today."

Mid-groan, Meri stopped, and I watched as her little head lifted from her pillow in curiosity. I'd spent the weekend telling my daughter about how Lucy was going to be spending more time with us and hanging out with her before and after school. She'd been excited about the *purple lady* when we discussed it. I hoped she remembered that excitement now, or it would be a very long morning.

"Good morning, Meri." Lucy walked across the room,

dodging the toys that had been left out the night before. I watched as she crouched next to the bed and lifted an elephant from the pile of stuffies on Meri's bed. "This little guy is so cute. What's his name?"

It was the right thing to say. Meri popped up instantly and began to introduce Lucy to each of her plush animals. I tried not to look at my watch, but we'd already spent too much time talking in the kitchen, and despite my best efforts, we were once again running late.

As if she'd read my mind, or maybe the low-level anxiety in the room, Lucy shifted gears easily. "How about after school, you can tell me all about them and maybe we can have a tea party with your favorites."

"They're all my favorites," Meri said with complete seriousness.

"Of course they are. Now, why don't we get ready for school while your dad gets some breakfast ready?" Lucy glanced in my direction for confirmation, but I was already nodding as a smile crept across my face.

Yes. I'd made a very good decision.

***

LUCY

I'd been a little concerned when Craig mentioned that Meri could be difficult in the morning, but any worries I had dissolved almost immediately when we started discussing her stuffed animal collection.

The rest of the morning went more or less smoothly as I helped Meri choose her outfit for the day—it was purple—fed her a quick breakfast, and then, with what I gathered was a normal chaotic situation, rushed around at the last minute, grabbing everything she'd need for a day of school.

I tagged along for the drop-off and made a few notes on where to park and what some of the teachers' names were, before Craig finally handed me a key to the house and disappeared, leaving me to my own devices for the day.

I didn't have to be back at the school to pick Meri up until two-thirty, so I headed back to the house to start making lists.

Craig and Meri's house was small but comfortable. And from the little I'd observed, in need of some major organization.

Sure, we'd been able to get Meri dressed and fed before school, but everything about the process was chaotic and stressful. It was true that I didn't have any experience as a nanny or even running a household beyond my own one-bedroom apartment for me and Garfield, but what I *did* have experience in was managing a busy restaurant and a staff of forty. I was an expert in organization and systems.

And that was exactly what I was going to introduce into Craig and Meri's life.

First up, the kitchen.

I stood in the middle of the room and took a moment to assess the situation before putting in my earbuds and cranking up my favorite playlist.

A few hours later, I'd reorganized most of the cupboards and the pantry. I created a space to put Meri's snacks and easy-to-grab items for her school lunches on one of the lower shelves as well as part of the fridge. I rounded up all kinds of loose papers and notices that had been sent home from the school and put them all in a clip on the fridge after clearing off all the expired notices, coupons, and other random papers.

It was only one room, but I was already proud of myself. With more time to kill, I wandered into the living room and rounded up some of Meri's stray toys that had made their way out of her room and a sweatshirt I assumed to be Craig's.

The little girl's room would be a joint project, I decided. It was way too big of an undertaking to tackle on my own, and I had a feeling that Meri would have very strong opinions on where and how her toys should be stored.

There was a spare room across the hall from Meri's that didn't look like it was used for much more than storage.

At the end of the short hallway was a door to the bathroom and across from that, Craig's room. I hesitated before setting foot inside. It felt like a violation of my new boss's privacy to enter his bedroom, yet he hadn't told me anything was off-limits and I did need to return his sweatshirt.

I twisted the knob and the door opened. I had no idea what I expected to find in the man's room, but it wasn't the empti-ness I was greeted with.

There was an unmade queen-sized bed against one wall, with a long dresser against the other. No photos or pictures adorned the walls, and besides the one framed picture of Craig and Meri when she was a newborn, there was no other decora-tion of any kind in the room.

In fact, there was very little decorating of any kind in the house at all besides the pink and purple explosion of little-girl-ness I'd found in Meri's room. In the living room, there were a few photographs of Craig and Meri together, and one framed shot of what I assumed was Craig's family at Christmas. I'd been expecting to find some sort of evidence of Meri's mother somewhere in the house, but there was nothing.

"Hello!"

The voice jolted me from my thoughts, and I quickly slipped from Craig's room into the hallway. "Oh." I spun around—and jumped back as I slammed directly into a hard chest. "I'm—"

"Sorry." The man held up his hands, and I pressed myself against the closed door, my hands up in a defensive stance. My heart raced.

"Who are you and how did you get in here?" He looked

vaguely familiar, like I'd seen him before, but I wasn't about to take any chances.

The man started to laugh, but fortunately took a step back before I had to use my self-defense moves on him.

"I'm sorry," he said again. "I'm Asher. I'm—"

"Asher!" a familiar female voice yelled. "What are you thinking, scaring Lucy half to death?" Kat, Craig's sister, appeared at the end of the hallway. She crossed her arms and shook her head. "Sorry, Lucy. This is my brother, Asher."

Of course. He looked familiar because he was in the family photo I'd seen in the living room. Now that I knew he was Craig's brother, I could see some resemblance. But only some. Where Craig's smile was soft and welcoming, Asher's was cocky. Which was why I only slowly lowered my arms.

"Come on." Kat grabbed the man's arm and tugged him down the hall.

"You were in Craig's room, huh?" He wiggled his eyebrows at me. "Find anything interesting in there?"

"You're an ass." Kat smacked him and finally managed to yank him away.

As soon as I had space, I took a breath. Craig had warned me he had a big, somewhat meddling family, but I had *not* expected them to just walk into his house and scare me half to death.

"I'm really sorry, Lucy," Kat said when she joined me in the living room. "We did knock but no one answered."

"It's fine." I shook my head a little. "I was just tidying up and—"

"You didn't find anything good in there, did you?" Asher asked smugly. "I can't imagine you did. He lives like a monk. It's got to be the most boring bedroom in the world." He looked at Kat. "Except maybe for yours."

"Enough." Kat smacked him again. "We just wanted to come say hi and see if you needed anything. Honestly, we did try to knock, but usually we just walk in, and I didn't even think it might scare you. Really, I'm sorry."

"It's fine." I shook my head and led them to the kitchen, offering lemonade. Kat accepted, Asher declined.

"Something you should know about this family," Kat said after a sip. "We're kind of all up in one another's business. I guess that's also kind of an apology. Because you're going to have to deal with all of us."

"Some of us are more difficult than others." Asher winked.

"Is that an attempt to flirt with me?"

Kat nearly spat out her lemonade. The shock on Asher's face was honestly worth it.

"It's obvious he wasn't used to being called out. It took him a moment, but he smiled easily. "I guess it is."

"Well, it's not a very good one."

Kat howled with laughter.

"Okay," Asher admitted. "It wasn't my best effort, but I had to take a shot. It didn't work, did it?"

I pressed my lips together and shook my head. "Sorry."

"Nice try, bro. But she's clearly out of your league."

Asher shrugged. At least he took it well. The last thing I wanted was to offend anyone—but I wasn't about to lead anyone on, either. That's not why I was in town.

"It's not you," I said honestly. "But I'm really not interested in dating at all."

"I feel like there's a story there." Kat put her empty glass in the sink. "But don't worry, I'm not going to push," she whispered to me. "We should be going." She dragged Asher toward the door. "If you need anything, Lucy, please ask. I own the hair salon in the plaza."

"Thank you." And I meant it. I liked Kat. And even with his forwardness, I liked Asher too. It was easy to see how much this family loved each other.

"I'm sure you'll meet the rest of us soon," Kat added.

"They're probably all dying to meet the woman who's special enough that Craig would leave Meri in her care."

That wording snagged in my mind. "What do you mean?"

"Craig's, well…I don't know how to say this…" Asher pretended to think. "A bit of a control freak."

"That's the pot calling the kettle black," Kat muttered. "It's actually a miracle Asher took five minutes from the office to come here today."

"Hey." He shrugged. "You said it yourself—everyone is dying to meet the woman who changed Craig."

Again, that hung heavy. I hadn't changed Craig. I hardly knew him.

"Okay, it's true," Kat said, shoving him toward the door. "It *is* a miracle you're here, Lucy. It's not that Craig is a control freak, it's just more that he thinks he can do everything himself. So…hiring you was a big deal."

"Not like he had a choice."

"What?" I stared at Asher, but he only raised his eyebrows.

"Anyway," Kat cut in quickly, "we're all really glad you're here."

I tried to smile, but inside, I could feel the ground shifting again. The circumstances of my hiring were already strange—and now they were getting stranger. I was starting to get the distinct impression that I was part of something bigger than simply a nanny job.

And as if I didn't already have enough on my plate, I was very quickly starting to feel like I was in over my head.

Chapter Seven

CRAIG

"THIS IS NOT GOING to work out."

I tossed the folders I was holding onto the huge mahogany table in front of us and watched as they slid almost to the other side before my older brother stopped them with a slap of his palm.

"Yes, it is."

"No." I shook my head, fully aware that I was acting like a child. "It's not. She hasn't answered my last text message."

Chase didn't even try to hide his laughter. "How long has it been?"

I swallowed hard and looked away.

"And how many texts have you sent her so far?"

A low growl rumbled from deep in my chest, but Chase only laughed harder.

"Give her a break, man. You can't go total papa bear on her on the first day."

I hated to admit it, but my brother had a point. I flipped my phone facedown. I *really* hated to admit it.

"I know this is strange for you, Craig. But—"

"You really have no idea."

Chase shrugged one shoulder. "Fair. I've never been in your situation. But you have to trust that it will work out. Besides, isn't she just home alone right now? Meri's at school, isn't she?"

I could see him trying not to chuckle again. I glared, and Chase wisely swallowed his laughter.

"Should we refocus?"

The only thing I wanted to do even less than sit around and wait for Lucy to respond to my most recent text was continue going over the details of my business with Chase. But it would take my mind off what may or may not be going on in my house, and it was a necessary evil.

Before Chase had moved to Trickle Creek, he'd been a top-notch business consultant in the city. He generally worked with bigger companies than the Sugar Shack, but when he'd offered to take a look at things for me and see where we might be able to make improvements, I'd been smart enough to recognize the opportunity.

"What I've seen so far isn't bad at all." Chase opened the folder I'd shoved in his direction. "Your numbers look pretty healthy, all things considered."

"All things considered?" I tipped my head at his choice of words. "What does that mean?"

Chase looked up and leaned back in his chair. We'd chosen the big house dining room table for our meeting since there was more room to spread out and, because the shop was closed on Mondays, I didn't need to be there.

"What it means is that you're running a seasonal business in a year-round town."

"I know that." I shook my head. "But I'm open year-round."

"Sorry." Chase flashed a bright smile. "I'm not being clear.

You *are* open year-round, but you're offering ice cream in the middle of winter."

I bristled. I was proud of my shop and the growth I'd had over the last few years. Maybe taking Chase up on his offer to help was a bad idea after all.

"I offer fancy hot chocolates and some coffees in the winter, too."

He tapped on the folder. "They make up a very small percentage of sales. *Very* small. In fact, I'm willing to bet that once I dig into the numbers a bit further, you might even be experiencing a loss on these drinks."

"A loss?"

Chase nodded. "Remember, you're only a few doors away from the Bean Bag. If people want coffee, they're going to the coffee shop, not the ice cream shop."

He had a point. Again.

I sighed, already weary of the conversation. "And what do you suggest then?"

"I thought you'd never ask."

I watched while my big brother pushed his chair back and walked to the other end of the room, where he pulled a folder out of his leather case.

"What's that?"

"The plan."

"The plan?" I eyed the folder suspiciously. "Have you been working on this for a while?"

Chase shrugged and dropped the folder in front of me. "It's what I do, brother. I take companies and make them better. These are just a few ideas. But I think you'll like them."

I didn't bother opening it before sliding it away. "I don't know, Chase. This is all a lot right now. I need to—"

"It's okay to accept help."

My head snapped up. "What are you talking about?"

"I know you think you can do everything on your own. And I'm just—"

"I do not." I swallowed hard against the protests bubbling up inside me, because Chase was right. I *did* think I could do it all on my own. Because I *could*.

"That's why you're so calm about the whole nanny thing." Chase raised his eyebrow. "Because you're so good at accepting help?"

I was not impressed by his sarcasm. "That's different and you know it."

"It's really not."

I shook my head. It was *very* different, but I wasn't about to fight him about it. Not today. "What's your idea then?" Reluctantly, I pulled the folder toward me and flipped it open.

"I thought you'd never ask."

I leaned back in my chair and crossed my arms as Chase started talking. But it didn't take long before I dropped my defensive stance and actually started listening. Despite my poor mood, and the fact that Chase was right and I did have trouble accepting help, it turned out my big brother actually had a few good ideas.

More than a few.

Soon, I was reaching for the folder in front of me. Inside were spreadsheets with projections detailing Chase's idea.

"So, you think that if we diversify, that will help level out our off-season sales?"

"I know it."

"You're awfully confident." I looked up at him.

"I told you," Chase said. "This is what I do, Craig. I ran the numbers. And sure, there's some margin for error, but if I've learned anything over the years, it's that numbers don't lie."

I scanned the paper in my hand again. "These numbers are pretty good," I admitted.

"I thought you might like that." Chase took his seat across from me again. "And really, you *are* called the Sugar Shack... why shouldn't you offer even more sugar? It just makes sense."

"I do offer all kinds of candy. There are literally shelves of it."

"I mean, *high-end* sugar. Things that will appeal to adults. I don't think jelly beans are doing it."

"Okay. I can't deny that." I dropped the papers. "So you think that by offering freshly made chocolates, fudge, and treats, it'll be that simple?"

Chase nodded. "I mean, it isn't *quite* that simple. After all, you'll have to learn to make chocolate or hire someone who can. But yes, once you jump that hurdle, it is that simple. Chocolate knows no season."

"Good point." I laughed. "But how do you suggest we find a suitable candidate? Because I do not think I'd be a very good chocolatier, and I already have staffing issues." I made a mental note to check my email for applicants to replace Tom. "And I still have to staff up for the summer."

"This will be a different type of position." Chase tapped the table. "I don't think it will be much of a problem attracting the right candidate from the city. Especially if we throw in the use of the apartment over the shop as a benefit."

"The apartment?"

"The one above the Sugar Shack. Remember? I told you I would set it up for the first renter, but then you needed to take over."

I nodded vaguely and reached for my phone again. There had been emails and texts from Chase about the short-term rental apartment. "I remember." I didn't sound convincing, even to myself. "That's actually where Lucy is staying right now."

"Lucy? As in the woman you just hired to be your nanny?"

I nodded and flipped the phone over. Still no response. I

glanced at the time—she should be on her way to pick Meri up from school soon.

"She can't stay there, Craig."

My fingers hovered over my keyboard, ready to text her again, but I decided against it.

"Craig." Chase rapped on the table.

"What?"

"Did you hear me? She *can't* stay at the apartment."

I shook my head. "Right, you said something about offering it to the chocolatier candidate. But that's hypothetical. We didn't really decide on any of that. And even if we did, that gives us time to—"

"Not really. I may have already found someone who will be a really good fit. But—"

"You did?"

Chase shrugged. "I mean, I can still get out of it, but I don't think I should."

I dropped my head to the table and groaned. I knew hiring the chocolatier was the right move. My gut told me so, even if Chase's projections hadn't been so clear.

"No. Don't get out of it. But find a different place for them to stay."

"I really don't think that's possible, Craig. She can't stay there. Not past next week anyway."

I sat upright and stared at him. "But she *has* to."

Chase shook his head. "Not possible. If you want to move forward with this chocolatier idea, you need the space. Vacancy rates are at an all-time low in town. It's the only way to attract the right candidate. She can't stay there."

"She has to. I just hired her, Chase. Six months starts today."

For the first time that day, my brother didn't offer any solutions.

Unable to sit any longer, I left my phone on the table and

paced to the far side of the room. "Where is she going to stay? Here?" I waved my arm around the giant dining room. The big house was…big. Lots of empty rooms.

"Don't you have a spare room?"

"What?" I spun around. "No!"

"It makes sense, Craig. She's going to be taking care of Meri before and after school, right? And what about weekends when you're at the shop? Having her live with you might just make it—"

"Absolutely not."

There was no way. Under no circumstances could Lucy live under the same roof as me. I'd never lived with a woman before—not even Meri's mother. It was enough of an adjustment having her help with my daughter. But her living there too? What about privacy? What about hers? I only had one bathroom. What if I saw her in a towel? Or walked in on her in the shower?

No. It couldn't happen.

"Don't tell me you're worried about living with a woman."

Did Chase have mind-reading abilities?

"Of course not," I lied. "That's ridiculous. I just don't want to have… what if she's… just no."

He laughed. "That's right. Kat did mention that Lucy was pretty cute. This makes perfect sense now."

"She's not—okay, she *is* cute. But that has nothing to do with anything."

My phone beeped, giving me the perfect escape.

LUCY:

Everything's great. Just waiting for Meri at school.

Everything's great. Just waiting for Meri at school.

I tapped out a quick reply and tucked my phone into my back pocket.

"You know I'm right, Craig."

He watched me with a smug expression.

"About the chocolate? Sure. But you're not right about Lucy. She can't live with me."

Even as I said it, I knew it was going to happen. Because as much as I hated to admit it, Chase was right—again.

It made sense.

And there was no way I could tell him the *real* reason I didn't want her living with me:

I was attracted to the nanny.

And I wasn't going to admit that to anyone.

LUCY

I finished responding to Craig's latest text message and tucked my phone into the pocket of my backpack. I wasn't annoyed by his almost constant check-ins—at least, not *very* annoyed. It had to be strange to hire a nanny for the first time. Especially one who had no actual experience with children and had quite literally applied for the job by not actually applying for it at all.

So, yes. I would be patient with Craig's constant messages until he was a little bit more comfortable with the situation. Besides, he *was* my boss.

It was a beautiful day, with only a little bit of chill in the air, and to my surprise, the snow had all melted, so I had decided to walk to the school to do the pickup instead of driving the short distance. I'd left early, unsure how long it would take me, but now I still had a few minutes before the dismissal bell was set to ring.

Normally, I would've flipped through my phone, scrolling mindlessly through social media, but for the first time in a long time, the idea held very little appeal. Instead, I dug my phone out of the backpack once more and pressed the button to connect to my best friend.

"Hey. You caught me before work."

"You're working an evening shift now?"

"I'm working all the shifts." Mandi laughed. "I don't think anybody realized just how much work you did around here. We miss you."

I was pretty sure that wasn't true for everyone. "I'm sure you're filling the void just fine."

"How's the new job? You didn't even tell me what restaurant you're at. Do they even have that many places to eat in Trickle Creek? I've never actually been, but—"

"Yes." I cut her off. "There are restaurants here. A few really nice ones, actually." Instead of cooking for myself, I'd spent the last few evenings exploring the eateries of Trickle Creek. True, there wasn't nearly the same selection as there was in downtown Vancouver, but what I'd experienced, I'd really enjoyed. "But I'm not actually working at a restaurant."

"No way. I thought you were a lifer in the restaurant world."

So had I. Once.

"Things change." That was putting it mildly. "And you're never going to believe this, but I actually took a job as a nanny."

Mandi made a noise somewhere between a cough and a laugh. "Wait. I don't think I heard you right. You took a job as a what?"

"A nanny."

There was silence on the other end of the phone.

"Mandi?"

"Like a nanny for kids?"

"Just one," I clarified. "But yes."

"Have you ever actually been around a child before, Lucy?

I mean, I'm not trying to sound rude, but…what the actual fuck? A nanny?"

I'd expected a reaction from Mandi, but not quite so much incredulity. "Is it really that hard to believe?"

"Yes."

"Okay. Fair. I guess it's a little different from what I was doing before."

"Just a little."

I laughed. "Honestly, Mandi. That's a good thing. I needed a total change. These last few months…well…"

"I know." Her friend's voice softened. "I know it's been hard, Lucy. I hate him for what he did to you. What kind of piece of shit—"

"Please. It's fine."

"I'm sorry. I'm just glad you're rid of that piece of shit. Now you're free to start fresh with a whole new career and a whole new man in the mountains."

New man? Out of reflex, I shook my head even though she couldn't see me. Before I could object, Mandi moved on.

"Tell me about the new job."

I spent the next few minutes filling her in on all the details of Meredith, including how we'd bonded instantly over the color purple the day we met.

"You've got to send me a picture of this purple jacket." Mandi laughed. "I can't picture you in anything but black."

It was true. My city wardrobe had consisted primarily of black with the occasional white blouse. I'd already visited the second-hand store in town, and after one trip there was considerably more variety in my closet.

"How are the parents?" Mandi asked. "The little girl sounds sweet. Hopefully, they aren't too difficult to deal with."

"Actually, he's not. Besides a lot of text messages, so far, Craig seems pretty chill." I left out the part about him being ridiculously handsome with a smile that did something to my insides every time it was aimed in my direction.

"*Him*? What about a wife? Doesn't this little girl have a mother?"

"Actually, no." My gaze drifted across the playground as cars lined up in the carpool lane and parents gathered near the door. "I don't know the whole story yet, but Craig's a single dad. There are a bunch of siblings, though, and they all seem really close. The Carlson family is kind of a big deal in town."

"A single dad, huh? What does he look like?"

"What?" I knew exactly where this was going. "No. It's not like that."

Too late.

"Craig, you said…" Mandi's voice sounded farther away. I knew I'd been put on speaker as she was no doubt searching social media. "Craig Carlson?"

Damn. That didn't take long.

"He's gorgeous, Luce. Oh my! They all are. Damn. And his little sister…"

"Anyway." I cut her off. "I should probably let you go. The school bell is going to ring soon."

"Oh no you don't. You cannot end the call like this. Now that I know you're the nanny for this hunk—"

"He's my boss, Mandi. That's the last thing I need, remember?"

She made a hissing noise. "Okay, I can't argue with that. But tell me about that kiss."

I almost dropped the phone. "Kiss?"

I totally forgot I'd told her about that.

"You said you took my advice—which is always a good idea, by the way."

I rolled my eyes.

"But you didn't give me details. Who did you kiss? What's

his name? What does he look like and more importantly, when are you going to go out with him?"

"I…umm…that's the thing…I…"

"Oh shit."

I shook my head even though she couldn't see me. She knew me too well. "No. It's not like—"

"It's him. Isn't it?"

I dropped my head into my hand but didn't say anything.

"Lucy! Did you kiss your boss?"

"I didn't know," I finally said. "This was before I knew there was a job or a…well, before I knew anything. I just decided to take your advice, which I now think is awful advice, actually. Anyway, I didn't know, and it was before I got hired, so now that I know who he is and that he's my boss, nothing is ever going to happen."

I wasn't sure whether I was trying to convince Mandi or myself.

After a moment of silence, she released a long breath.

"Please don't say anything." I squeezed my eyes shut.

"I was only going to—"

"Mandi."

"You don't even know what I'm going to say."

"Sorry, I—"

"I was going to suggest you run yourself a hot bath, close your eyes, grab a vibrator, and put a whole new fantasy in your head."

"Mandi!"

"What?" Her laughter filled the phone. "You need to get that piece of shit ex out of your head, and your mind is a powerful thing, Lucy. Don't underestimate it."

"I appreciate the advice, Mandi." I rolled my eyes again.

"Don't roll your eyes at me." She laughed again. "Seriously, Lucy. Now that I know you've already kissed him, it changes everything."

"It doesn't change anything, Mandi. He's my boss."

"And?"

I froze.

She didn't mean it. Not like that. I knew she didn't. Still, it stung.

"Oh." She realized it instantly. "I didn't mean it like that. I was just—"

The dismissal bell rang, cutting her off.

"I've got to go." I disconnected the call and stuffed my phone into my backpack before slinging it over my shoulder.

It didn't matter what I said. Or if Mandi meant it that way or not.

Because, it *did* change everything.

Chapter Eight

LUCY

I'D BEEN at my job almost a full week, and although I was still getting used to the early mornings—which were very different from my days working at the restaurant where I'd sleep in after late nights—it was all going much smoother than I would have guessed.

The house was still dark when I pulled my car next to Craig's Jeep in the carport at the back of the house. I let myself in with the key he'd given me and took a minute to get the coffee started and put the kettle on for tea. After the first morning, Craig had stocked his house with four different kinds of tea for me.

He was usually in the kitchen waiting for me by the time I arrived, but when the water had boiled and he still hadn't made an appearance, I figured he must have slept in. Not that it made any difference to me. I'd been watching his morning routine all week; I didn't think it would be much of a problem to get Meri ready.

I flipped on the light in the hallway as I made my way to Meri's room. Craig's door was still shut at the end of the hall.

Slowly, I turned the door handle and entered Meri's room with only the light from the hallway.

She was sleeping under a pile of stuffed animals, her little face only barely visible. It was such a sweet sight, I paused and soaked in the moment before sitting gently on the edge of the bed.

"Good morning, sunshine." I spoke softly as I brushed the hair away from her face. "It's time for a new day."

Meredith's eyelids fluttered open. "Lucy?"

"Good morning." I smiled broadly. "Did you have a good sleep?"

Meri nodded and slowly stretched her arms over her head, causing some of her stuffies to fall off the bed. "Is today Friday?"

"It is." Now that she was awake, I moved to the curtains and opened them halfway to let some of the light of the new day in. "Do you remember what that means?"

Meri was sitting up now. "It means fabulous, fun Friday."

I laughed. She hadn't wanted me to leave the night before, so I'd reminded her that because there was only a half day of school on Friday, we'd be able to do something extra fun after school. "That's right. But you have to get up and get your day started before we get to the fabulous fun Friday part. Did you pick out your outfit last night before you went to sleep?"

She jumped out of bed and went straight to her dresser, where she'd laid out an outfit. "It's not purple, but it's my second favorite color."

"I like green, too. It makes me happy."

"Me too."

"Okay, kiddo. Get dressed and meet me in the kitchen for breakfast. Do you want toast with scrambled eggs or yogurt and granola?" I was quickly learning that it was easier to offer her a choice of two acceptable things than to give her open-ended options.

"Granola."

"Granola, please?"

"Please."

I winked. "You got it. See you in a minute."

I flipped on the light as I slipped from the room. I took one more quick glance behind me to make sure Meredith hadn't been distracted by her stuffed animals before I stepped out into the hall and ran smack into a hard chest.

CRAIG

Reflexively, I reached out and grabbed Lucy to keep her from stumbling as she ran into me. I hadn't meant to get in the way. In fact, I hadn't meant to eavesdrop at all outside of Meri's bedroom door, but when I came out of the shower and heard voices, I'd been drawn to her room and had been quickly mesmerized by the gentle way Lucy had woken my daughter.

It made me feel some kind of way watching the way she was with Meri after only a few days and the way Meri responded to her...it was...

"Sorry, I—" The words died on Lucy's lips as her eyes traveled up my body to my face.

It was only then that I remembered I was half naked, only wearing a towel wrapped around my waist. A towel that was getting dangerously close to slipping off completely.

I took a quick step back, releasing my grip on her and securing my towel. "No," I said quickly. "I'm sorry. I wasn't trying to eavesdrop, I was just—"

"You were listening?" Her brows furrowed.

"Oh." I shook my head. "Not like that. I mean, not because I was checking up on you or anything." The last thing I wanted was for Lucy to think I was second-guessing her or unsure about what she was doing. Especially after what I'd just witnessed. "I was just…I'm sorry. I'm just running late this morning and…thank you for waking her up."

"No problem." The smile that lit her up returned to her face. "Sorry I ran into you. I seem to be making a nasty habit of running into you Carlson men in this hallway."

She laughed, but I looked at her sideways.

"Your brother," she explained and dismissed it with a shake of her head. "The other day. That's how I met Asher." She waved her hand. "Anyway, I better go get breakfast started and let you…"

Was it my imagination, or did her eyes dip down the length of my body?

"I'll let you get dressed."

Brother?

Kat had filled me in on how they'd come over to say hi to Lucy on her first day. It seemed that she'd left out a few details of their visit.

I clenched my teeth as a surge of caveman jealousy washed through me at the thought of Lucy pressed up against Asher's chest in any way. My brother needed to keep his distance when it came to Lucy. I didn't want Asher and his playboy ways anywhere near her.

"Yes. Of course." I stepped to the side and let her pass when what I really wanted to do was reach for her and pull her up against my naked chest to kiss that sexy smile. The thought shot into my brain so quickly that it rendered me immobile. Still dressed only in a towel, trying to make sense of where these unfamiliar thoughts were coming from and what the hell I was going to do about them, it took me a few minutes to pull myself together long enough to retreat to my bedroom and get dressed.

LUCY

Somehow I managed to make it to the safety of the kitchen before I leaned up against the fridge and took a deep breath.

He'd been practically naked. His towel slipped. There were water droplets in his hair.

Deep breath, Lucy. I forced myself to take a breath and then another one.

He's your boss. Your boss. He's not a man. He's your boss.

Boss.

Yes. I forced myself to fixate on that word.

It didn't matter how I was feeling inside after our close encounter in the hall. And the fact that he smelled like peppermint with just a trace of something sweet, almost like cotton candy, didn't matter. Not at all. That was a detail that had no bearing on my relationship with my *boss*.

"Pull yourself together, Lucy," I muttered under my breath and forced my mind into safer territory, like breakfast and putting together Meri's school snack.

I'd managed to slow my heart rate and put the image of Craig's bare chest out of my head—mostly—by the time Meri raced into the kitchen. "Ready for breakfast, kiddo?"

I slid the bowl of granola in front of her, and Meri dug in while I made myself a cup of the tea Craig had stocked for me. I poured Craig a coffee and added sugar to each of our cups moments before he joined us in the kitchen.

"You're amazing."

"It's just coffee." I smiled but avoided his gaze.

"No. I don't just mean the coffee." Craig used his head to

motion toward Meri. "I mean with her. How did you do that earlier?"

"Do what?"

"Get her to wake up like that? I swear, when I do it, my normally sweet little princess becomes some sort of demon-possessed. But with you, she was…"

"Lovely?" I laughed when he nodded his agreement. "I could say I got lucky, but I think it's all in the approach. Some people don't like to be jarred awake, but like to wake up gently. I've noticed that when you do it, you go in full steam, flipping lights on and pulling covers back." I shrugged like it wasn't a big deal. "I went with the opposite approach."

"Well, it worked." He shook his head approvingly. "Admittedly, mornings aren't my favorite. It doesn't help that I've never been a morning person either."

"Well, I'm happy to help."

I reached past him for a napkin, but he grabbed my hand and held it for a moment. I sucked in a breath and willed myself not to react despite the fact that my heart was still racing from our close encounter in the hallway and now, with his hand on mine, it felt like it might burst straight out of my chest.

What was happening to me?

Slowly, I turned to look him in the eye.

"Thank you." His voice was soft, his gaze intense. "It's really amazing how Meri has responded to you."

"No problem." I swallowed hard. "I'm just doing my job."

Job. Boss.

He. Is. Your. Boss.

He was still touching me, and the contact wasn't helping me get the image of his hard, naked chest out of my brain. How *did* he get so friggin' ripped?

I took a step back and wrapped my free hand around my tea mug to keep it from shaking.

Maybe Mandi was right, and I should entertain the idea of a little release? It might settle me down a little.

Not that thinking of a release or anything even remotely sexual while Craig was still inches away from me was helping the situation at the moment.

It most certainly was not.

I left my tea on the counter and started to gather things for Meri's school snack.

"Speaking of your job…"

I spun around. "Is everything okay?"

"Oh. Of course." Craig held up his hand. "You're doing a great job. I just said so, remember? It's just that there was something I needed to talk to you about."

Something in his tone stilled me. "Anything bad?"

"Oh no." He shook his head and took a sip of his coffee. His eyes danced around, and he wouldn't meet my gaze.

"Craig?"

"Honestly." He looked up then. "You're doing great, really. Meri loves you."

I nodded.

"It's just…" Again, he looked down and stumbled over his words. "It's been a week and today is Friday."

"All day." I narrowed my eyes and took a breath in. If Craig had been any other guy, I would have sworn he was about to ask me out on a date. Which was crazy, because he was my boss, a fact I was continually trying to remind myself of. But there was no way he would—

"I was wondering if—"

"I have a date."

I blurted out the words, and Craig looked up, confused.

"A date?"

I nodded but didn't offer any more information.

"Oh," he said after a moment. "Okay. Yeah. That makes sense."

But it didn't make sense, because he ran his hand through his hair and turned away, and the moment he did, I had the realization that he wasn't going to ask me out after all.

My face flushed a hot red, and I was thankful he couldn't see my embarrassment because in an instant, I'd made everything painfully awkward *and* I'd lied to my new boss.

Chapter Nine

CRAIG

LUCY WAS GOING ON A DATE. Of course she was. She was a smart, attractive young woman with a brilliant smile and killer personality.

It made sense that she was going on a date.

But with who?

It was the who that had been driving me crazy all day long. Who had managed to capture her attention? What was he like? Was he good enough for her? Would he treat her right?

And why did I care?

"What do you think of that one?"

I looked up from the plate of chocolate confections Chase had put in front of me and stared at my big brother blankly.

"Well?"

"Well, what?"

Chase crossed his arms and rolled his eyes. "Well, what do you think of that one?" He reached over and pointed with an unnecessary level of exaggeration to the coconut-dusted chocolate.

"It's good."

"Good?"

I shrugged. "Yeah. It's good."

My brother blew out a deep sigh and put his hands flat on the table in front of him. "If you don't want to do this today, just say so, because I'm sure I could find a dozen better ways to spend my time."

"Sorry." I ran my hands through my hair, tugging on the roots before releasing it with a shake. "I'm a little distracted today."

"Really? I hadn't noticed."

"But I'm ready now." I pulled the tray of confections closer to me. "Let's do this." I picked up a round milk chocolate ball with a coffee bean pressed into the top. I lifted it to my lips. "It's just that I don't know who it is."

"Who what is?" Chase tilted his head in question.

"I mean, I should know who. Right?" I held the chocolate aloft and stared at Chase, waiting for an answer. "That's reasonable, right?"

"I have no idea what you're talking about, Craig." Chase shook his head. "Or should I say, who we're talking about."

I looked at the candy in my hand and took a breath. It didn't matter who she was dating. It was none of my business. Lucy was allowed to have a life outside of work. And that's all Meri and I were—work. It didn't matter that every time I looked at her, I remembered the kiss we'd shared and the way it had lit up my body, despite the fact it had ended almost before it began. It didn't matter that I found myself looking for reasons to text her or call her during the day just because I wanted to hear from her. Or that coming home from work to see her with my daughter had very quickly become the highlight of my day.

No.

None of that mattered.

It couldn't.

"It doesn't matter." I refocused on the chocolate. "This one looks good. I like the coffee—she doesn't drink coffee. Did you know that?"

Chase groaned and pulled out a chair and sat heavily across from me. "Who doesn't drink coffee?"

"Lucy."

My brother swallowed back a laugh. "I should have known."

I dropped the chocolate. "What do you mean by that?"

"Never mind." Chase shook his head. "So, Lucy doesn't drink coffee. I won't hold that against her. But what's all this about who that you're going on about? Who should you know?"

I debated the pros and cons of confiding in my brother. It probably wasn't a good idea to say anything at all to any of my siblings, but my best friend Andy was busy with his own life in Vancouver, and Chase was sitting right there. "I should know who she's dating, don't you think?" The question was out of my mouth before I could reconsider.

And judging by Chase's low whistle and wide eyes, I probably should have reconsidered. "You want to know who Lucy's dating?"

"Never mind." I looked down at the table but then instantly looked up again. "I know I shouldn't care. It shouldn't matter, right?"

"Well, I—"

"But she is spending time with my daughter, so don't you think that means I should know who she's spending time with?"

"I don't know if—"

"It speaks directly to her character." I jumped up from the table and paced to the window of the shop that looked out onto the plaza. "And if she's going to bring this guy around Meri, I think that gives me a right."

"Whoa. Slow down."

I spun on my heel and stared at my brother.

"You're saying that Lucy has a boyfriend and is bringing him around Meri?"

"What? Boyfriend?" The word hit me like a brick to the chest. I really did need to get a hold of myself. "I didn't say that. I don't know if he's a boyfriend or not, I just…" I blew out a breath and inhaled slowly in an effort to calm myself.

"You like her."

"I like her as a *nanny*. She's doing a great job with Meri."

"You're sure that's all it is?"

No. I wasn't sure. But I could very quickly see that it would be easier if that's all it was.

"Yes," I lied. "That's all it is."

Chase was silent for a moment, but finally he nodded. "That's good. Because you don't need it to get awkward when she moves in next week."

"Next week?"

Again, my brother groaned. "Don't tell me you forgot?" He held up his hand. "No. Don't tell me that because I don't want to know and it doesn't matter. But Mya is moving in next week, so sort it."

"Mya?"

"I don't know what's wrong with you, little brother, but you need to pull it together. I told you about Mya. She's the choco-latier I hired. Part of the agreement was a place to live. Lucy needs to move out. You have a week to break it to her." He shook his head. "Or maybe I should say, you have a week to wrap your head around it and be sure that things aren't going to get awkward with your nanny because you can't afford to lose her. You know that, right?"

Lose her?

She'd only been in our life for a week, but I'd already noticed the difference in Meri. She loved having Lucy around and the way she'd woken Meri up that morning...it was incredible. Never mind the meals she was cooking and the organization she'd already tackled in our home.

And her smile.

Her presence.

The way the energy changed when she was in the room.

No. I couldn't lose her. Not when I was just starting to find her.

"I can't lose her."

I hadn't realized I'd spoken aloud until Chase grabbed my arm and looked me dead in the eye. "Because you need to fulfill Dad's requirements, Craig. *That's* why you can't lose her."

Shit.

"I know." I shrugged off his touch. "Don't worry. I know what's important."

I wouldn't lose Lucy, because I was going to keep my feelings to myself.

LUCY

A date probably might have been a better option than going back to my empty short-term rental on a Friday night.

Despite what I'd told Craig, the only date I'd arranged was cuddling on the couch with Garfield. And the moment I'd changed into my sweats, poured myself a glass of rosé, and the big orange tabby cuddled up in my lap, I knew I'd made the right decision.

Not that there'd been a lot of options on the table.

I'd only been in Trickle Creek for just over a week, and

besides Craig, Meri, and their family, the only other people I'd met were Krysta and Kane.

For a split second, I entertained the idea of calling Kane and taking him up on his offer for a drink. Ultimately, as much as I might have liked a little male attention, and despite my best friend's theory that I needed to have some rebound sex to put Ross out of my mind once and for all, the idea just didn't appeal.

At least not enough to convince me to get off the couch, get dressed, and put makeup on.

"It's hard work looking after a five-year-old, Garfield."

The cat purred in response, and I scratched him under the ear. "But she's super cute, and I think you'll really like her." The cat looked up at me and mewled. "I'll bring her by next week so she can meet you. But until then, it's just me and you this weekend."

The moment the words came out of my mouth, I groaned and took a gulp of my wine. "This is what my life has come to. Friday night, drinking wine alone with my cat. No offense, buddy."

To prove he understood, Garfield leapt from my lap and headed into the kitchen in search of food.

I watched him go before finishing my wine with one final slug and was in the process of deciding whether I should pour myself another, or get dressed and go out, lest I turn into a crazy cat lady after all, when my phone chimed with an incoming text.

Sorry to bother you on your date.

Craig.

Like a switch had been flipped, my body warmed and a smile slid across my face. It was ridiculous.

You're not bothering me.

Not at all, but I wasn't about to tell him how pathetic my Friday night really was.

The Spring Splash is tomorrow up at the ski hill. It's a lot of fun with live music and a competition. Do you have plans?

My face flushed. Saturday was my day off. Was he asking me out? Before I could think of a response that would straddle the line of what I wanted versus what was appropriate, another text came through.

Meri wanted me to remind you.

Of course. Meri.

I flipped my phone upside down on the coffee table without answering. Of course, he wasn't going to ask me out. Craig was professional. He was my boss and just because I was feeling things I shouldn't, didn't mean he was. Not at all.

Maybe there was something wrong with me? First with

Ross. And now with Craig. I needed to pull myself together. The last thing I wanted to do was screw up my new job. Especially because I didn't have anywhere else to go. There was certainly nothing waiting back in Vancouver for me. And more importantly, I liked the new job. Meri was a sweetheart and although I never would have expected to find myself as a nanny, I was surprising myself with how much I was enjoying it.

I didn't want to mess it up.

Maybe calling Kane wasn't a bad idea after all. He'd made it clear that he was interested, and he was a nice guy. And very attractive. There were worse ways to spend a Friday night. Besides, maybe it would help me clear my head.

I reached for my phone again.

It certainly couldn't hurt.

———

His hands traveled up the length of my naked body, leaving a trail of fire in the wake of his touch.

A moan slipped from my mouth as he pressed his lips to my stomach and looked up into my eyes. "You are absolutely delicious, babe."

I squirmed a little and his strong hands clamped down on my hips, holding me in place as he once more resumed his attention on my body. His mouth dipped lower between my legs. His tongue found my core and I cried out. But I wanted more. I needed more.

So. Much. More.

I tried to lift my hips to bring him closer to me, but he held me firmly in place as he torturously flicked my clit with his tongue. Slowly at first, and then faster until I was ready to burst.

Just when I was sure I wouldn't be able to hold off any

longer, he lifted his head. I groaned, and he grinned. His lips quirked up in a wicked smile. "Patience."

"No." I shook my head and squeezed my eyes shut, desperately trying to buck my hips up to him. "I need you. Please."

He chuckled a little as his fingers danced across my hot skin, his fingers brushing between my legs. "Patience," he repeated.

But it was not the word I wanted to hear.

He pulled himself up until he was directly over me and looked deep into my eyes. "It'll be worth it," he murmured before kissing me slowly. "I promise."

I believed him, and after that kiss, I would have waited my entire life for him if that was what he wanted. But I didn't have to, because only moments later, he was kissing me again, his hands moving quickly now, touching every part of me.

My own hands reached up and slid down his muscled back to his ass, where I sunk my fingers in and urged him forward.

Instead of teasing me further with promises of later, this time his hot, hard length pressed at my core. I opened my legs for him, closed my eyes, and lifted my hips to meet him.

This.

This was what I'd been waiting for. Wanting from him. From the moment I'd laid eyes on him, I'd known. It was this moment. We—

My eyes snapped open.

The room was dark. I was on the couch.

Alone.

Shit.

It took me a moment to get my bearings and remember where I was: on the couch, in my rental apartment. My phone beeped again, lighting up on the cushion next to me. That must have been what had woken me. I flipped the phone over, ignoring the message, and squeezed my eyes shut again in favor of trying to recapture the dream, but the moment was gone.

I groaned and pressed my head into the couch cushion behind me as Garfield jumped up into my lap.

"Maybe I should have texted Kane for that date after all." I scratched the cat behind his ears. "What do you think, buddy?"

The cat mewled in response and kneaded his paws into my leg, which wasn't helpful, but the most I'd be able to expect from him.

"I agree," I said. "It wouldn't be right, would it?"

I sighed and dropped my head back again. I didn't need Garfield or anyone else to agree with me, because I already knew the answer. Mandi was right—a little sexual release might be exactly what I needed, but there was no point in taking Kane up on his offer. It wouldn't be fair.

Because it wasn't the sexy ski instructor I'd been fantasizing about.

Oh no.

The man in my dreams who knew just how to touch me and how to kiss me was the same man who made my stomach flip when I was wide awake.

And that was the whole problem.

That man was off-limits.

Very off-limits.

Chapter Ten

CRAIG

I'D TRIED. I'd *really* tried. But it had been a week since Lucy told me she was going on a date, and I still couldn't get the thought out of my head. It was ridiculous, really, because even if I was interested in Lucy that way—which I wasn't—she was allowed to have a life, and that life was none of my business.

Which was why I needed to stop thinking of it.

But I couldn't.

Every time I tried to focus on work, my thoughts drifted to Lucy and the date she'd been on last weekend. It was driving me crazy that I didn't know who it was. More than once, I'd considered that she might have gone out with Asher, but just as quickly, I put it out of my head. I couldn't let myself go down that road because if I did, I was pretty sure I'd kill my brother.

And when I'd run into Asher at the Spring Splash the weekend before, he hadn't made any indication that he'd been out with Lucy. Knowing Asher, if he had gone on a date with her, he'd be sure that I knew about it.

Lucy hadn't shown up to the Spring Splash festivities, even after I'd texted to invite her. Sure, I probably should have just asked her. But I didn't want her to think I was crossing any boundaries and—

I groaned and dropped my head into my hands. Why was everything so weird with her? Or more specifically, why was *I* so weird with her? I was acting like…well, I couldn't figure out what I was acting like because I'd never acted so strange before. *Ever.*

"Hey, brother."

My head shot up as Kat walked through the doors of the ice cream shop.

"Tough day at the office?" She winked, but I couldn't find it in me to smile.

"It's just been…" I shook my head clear as my youngest sister pulled up a chair at the table.

"Hey." The humor dropped from Kat's voice. "You aren't worried about the shop, are you? Annie was telling me that you and Chase had discussed diversifying, and I know that's probably stressful, but Chase knows his stuff and you're in good hands."

I wasn't even remotely surprised that Kat already knew my plans to add more candies and treats to the shop. There were no secrets in our family. More the reason to keep my thoughts about Lucy to myself.

"It's not that." Truthfully, I hadn't been able to concentrate much on the projections or details Chase had presented to me last week, which was a whole different problem I should probably dedicate some time to.

"Is it Meri? Is she—"

"She's great, too." I smiled at the thought of my daughter. "More than great, really. She's really taken to Lucy. I sometimes forget that it's only been a few weeks. They have their own little routines already, and I'm always hearing Lucy this and Lucy that."

"That's awesome. She's really going to love it when Lucy moves in, hey?"

"When she—"

"Yeah." Kat raised one eyebrow. "I was under the impression she was moving into your spare room because the chocolate maker person Chase hired was moving into the suite upstairs."

Shit.

I'd been so wrapped up in my own thoughts about Lucy I'd completely forgotten about how our living situation was going to change. And worse, I hadn't even talked to her about it.

"Right." I dragged out the syllables of the word.

"Craig?"

"Um…here's the thing."

"You didn't tell her."

"I didn't tell her."

"What?" Kat's eyes widened in disbelief.

"I know. I know. I meant to, I just…" There was no way I could explain to her that I'd been so distracted by my sexy new nanny that I'd completely forgotten about the very not-so-small detail that she was going to need to move out of her rental and into my house in less than forty-eight hours.

And that was going to bring with it a whole different set of problems.

Like sharing a bathroom. *Lucy, naked in my shower.*

What did she wear to bed? I guessed it was just a simple tank top with panties. But maybe it was something silky? Or nothing at all?

What if she wanted to bring her date home? *No. Just…no.*

I balled my hands into fists on top of the table and shook my head.

"Craig? What the hell?"

I shook my head clear, flattened my hands on the table, and looked at my sister. "It's been a bit busy. But I'll talk to her."

"Nothing like leaving it till the last minute. Doesn't she need to move this weekend?"

"Sunday."

"Sunday?"

"Repeating me isn't helping." I pushed up from the table and tucked the chair back in before gathering my things. "I've had a lot going on. It totally slipped my mind."

Kat pressed her lips together and shook her head.

"I'll talk to her as soon as I get home," I said in my sister's direction before turning to Kristie, my long-running employee and new right hand since Tom left. "You're good here? I need to head home."

"You know it. Don't worry about a thing."

Easy for her to say. She wasn't about to go home and tell my ridiculously hot nanny—whom I couldn't stop thinking about and couldn't afford to lose—that she needed to move into our house in less than two days.

Kat joined me at the door and together we stepped out into the warm spring day.

"While you're talking to her, maybe you should—"

"Oh no." I held up a hand. "Whatever you think I should do, the answer is no. This is going to be awkward enough."

Kat flipped her hair over her shoulder. "Why would it be awkward?" She didn't wait for an answer before she shook her head and continued. "I was just going to say that I think you should invite her over for family dinner on Sunday."

"Family dinner?"

Over the last few months, the Carlson clan had resumed the habit of a weekly family dinner, often at the big house, where we could reconnect and come together as a family. It was loud and chaotic, and there was no way I was going to bring Lucy into that. Especially when this weekend was going to be hard enough.

"Come on," she pushed. "She spends so much time with Meri that she's practically family. We should all get to know her better. It'll be fine."

I took a deep breath in through my nose. It would most certainly not be fine, but there was no way I could tell my sister the reason I didn't want to invite her to the family dinner was the same reason I didn't want her to move into my house.

I was starting to have feelings for Lucy.

Feelings I couldn't afford to have.

LUCY

I had dinner cooking in the slow cooker on the counter, two loads of laundry done and folded, and Meri had already completed her printing assignment from school.

If anyone had told me a month ago that I would find myself in a small town, playing house with a little girl who wasn't mine, I would have laughed in their face. Of all the ways I'd seen my life playing out, cooking, cleaning, and looking after a child who wasn't mine didn't even make the top twenty.

Despite how unexpected my new job was, I could honestly say that the last few weeks had been some of my favorite in a very long time. Meri was a sweetheart, and the two of us had taken to each other right away. It was a much quieter pace of life, but as far as I was concerned, a much-needed change.

"Lucy! I'm ready!"

Meri appeared, dressed head-to-toe in her full snowsuit in the kitchen. She had a scarf wrapped around her head and face, mittens on her hands, and to finish off the look, running shoes on her feet.

I bit back a laugh. "What exactly are you ready for? Running away from a snow monster in the middle of a blizzard?"

Meri laughed. "No, silly. For building snowmen. You said when I was done cleaning my room, we could go outside."

"I sure did say that. But I think you might be a little overkill. I know we got another dump of snow…" I circled her slowly, pretending to think. "I guess I'd say you're both over-dressed and underdressed. But good job getting ready."

I hadn't fully believed people when they'd told me it wouldn't be unusual to get another big dump of snow, but when I'd woken up to see a thick layer of white stuff, I got an idea.

I unwound her scarf and handed her a knit cap instead. "It's pretty warm out there already. We might not even need hats. But just in case."

Meri nodded seriously.

"And maybe your fleecy jacket would be a better choice than the parka. But leave the snow pants on so you can sit in the snow." I tapped my finger against my lips. "And the running shoes have to go. You need your winter boots for sure. We don't want cold wet toes ruining our build, do we?"

"No way!"

"Go grab boots, kiddo. I have a surprise for you when we get out there."

"A surprise? What is it?"

"It wouldn't be much of a surprise if I told you already, would it?" I winked. "The faster we get out there, the sooner you'll know. Besides, the snow is melting quickly. We don't have long."

That was all it took for Meri to run out of the room and make the changes to her wardrobe. I laughed with a shake of my head and grabbed the *surprise* from the counter where I'd just finished preparing it.

My phone dinged with an incoming message.

Craig wasn't texting me quite as frequently as he had been those first few days, which was probably a good sign considering he clearly trusted that I could do a good job watching his daughter. Still, I couldn't help but hope it was him who'd sent me a message.

It was my mother.

> Did you have a chance to try those recipes I sent?

I turned, snapped a picture of the slow cooker on the counter and sent it to mom.

> Beef stew is cooking right now. Thanks. So far they've all been big hits.

After the first day or two on the job, when it became clear that Meri and Craig lived mostly on frozen food like fish sticks and chicken fingers, I reached out to my mom for some tried-and-true favorites. I myself had never been much of a cook, especially working in the restaurant industry for most of my adult life. I'd relied pretty heavily on quick and easy foods, or whatever I could convince the chef at work to make me.

But that didn't seem like the healthiest choice for a growing girl, and **I** surprised **myself** by discovering how much **I** was enjoying cooking and finding recipes that the little girl enjoyed.

> I'm glad. The stew was always your favorite. Let me know how it turns out.

I didn't have the heart to tell my mother that I wasn't enjoying the meals I'd been cooking with Craig and Meri. Every single night before I left, Craig would invite me to stay for dinner, but I always had an excuse to make my escape. It wasn't that I didn't want to spend more time with them; it was quite the opposite, really. And *that* was the problem. I was enjoying my time with both Meri and Craig a little *too* much.

Craig was funny and kind, and the way he interacted with his daughter was amazing. He was always so interested in hearing every detail about Meri's day. And when he spoke to me, he was equally invested in our conversation, too.

I tried to keep their conversations that weren't about Meri to a minimum. It was easier to keep things between us on a strictly professional level. Especially because the thoughts I was having about my boss were anything but professional. And then there was the small matter of how amazing he'd looked wearing just a towel around his waist.

I still didn't know anything about Meri's mother. There were no pictures of her in the house at all, nor had there been any mention of her. It was strange. Surely if she'd died, there'd be at least one photo of her? And if they were divorced, presumably she'd still want to be involved in Meri's life in some way.

I could probably just ask Craig, but there'd never been a good time. I didn't want to say anything around Meri and because I was actively avoiding any situation that would have me alone with my ridiculously perfect man of a boss, that didn't leave a lot of options.

Except speculation.

But even in my wildest imagination, I couldn't think of any woman who would choose *not* to be with Craig and his doll of a daughter.

"Lucy! I'm ready for my surprise."

"Coming!" I hollered down the hallway before turning my attention back to my phone quickly.

Will do.

I replied quickly.

Gotta run, Mom. Love you.

I tucked my phone away before once more grabbing the surprise I'd prepared for Meri and headed outside. I couldn't wait to see the little girl's reaction.

Chapter Eleven

CRAIG

WHEN I GOT HOME, Meri and Lucy were not in the kitchen the way they'd been every evening before.

"Hello. I'm home."

I dropped my things on the counter and moved through the room into the living room. They weren't there either. Confused, I called out again, but when there was still no answer, I pulled my cell phone out, ready to call Lucy, when I caught a flash of movement out the picture window that faced the street.

Lucy and Meri were dressed in fleecy jackets and mittens, but no hats. They'd had a huge dump of snow the night before, but I knew from experience that this late in the season, it wouldn't last long. Which was why it took me by surprise to see Lucy and Meri in the front yard, working on a snowman they'd positioned in the shadows next to the large pine tree that towered over the bungalow.

Meri had a spray bottle in her hands and was moving

around the bottom of their construction with it, leaving splashes of purple all over.

"This looks fun." Still dressed for work, I stepped out the front door and joined them.

"Daddy!" Meri dropped the bottle and ran to me.

My heart swelled as I scooped up my little girl and swung her around before setting her on her feet again.

"What do you think? Isn't she pretty?"

My eyes locked on Lucy, who smiled broadly. "She's beautiful."

She ducked her head and looked at the ground. It was only then that I noticed my daughter was pointing at the snowman.

"She's a princess."

"Wow." I focused completely on Meri, who dragged me by the hand toward her as soon as I'd set her down. "I came in the back way, so I didn't see her, but she's amazing."

"We're going to put a crown on her when we're done, but I still have to make her head pink."

"Pink?" I glanced at a row of spray bottles lying in the snow.

"Princess paint," Meri said seriously. "It was my surprise."

I looked to Lucy, who shrugged. "Colored water. Kind of a nice touch, don't you think?"

"I think it's perfect."

I offered her a warm smile, but she quickly looked away again. I couldn't help but feel like I was doing everything wrong with this woman. I didn't want her to feel uncomfortable around me. Especially with the news I had for her. I opened my mouth, but unable to come up with anything else to say, I closed it and focused my attention on my daughter again. "What color did you say her head was going to be?"

"Daddy." Meri rolled her eyes dramatically, but she giggled and handed me a spray bottle. "Pink, of course. You do it, Dad."

"Wow. You're trusting me with the pink?" I clutched my chest dramatically. "I'm honored. Do you think I can handle it?"

Meri considered my question seriously and after a moment nodded. "Probably."

It was as good of an endorsement as I was going to get. I shrugged my jacket off and left it on the rail before getting to work.

The three of us worked together to finish the snow princess, and it didn't take long before she was completely colored with pink and purple. Meri ran inside for the finishing touches, and I boosted her up on my shoulders to drape the cape over our creation and place a crown atop her head.

"She's beautiful." Meri clapped her hands with delight when I set her down.

"I'm afraid she's going to melt soon." I frowned. "This isn't going to last but she looks great for now and the snow was perfect for it."

"That's what Kane said."

My head snapped toward Lucy, who was crouched down next to a pile of quickly melting snow.

"Kane?" I heard the jealousy I wasn't entitled to in my voice and swallowed hard before I spoke again. "Kane Nelson?"

Was that who she was dating? I didn't know Kane well, but we had mutual friends. He seemed like a nice guy, and he had that whole snow god, Viking look going for him that made him popular with the ladies.

And Lucy, too, apparently.

I inhaled through my nose as Lucy stood and nodded. "He said that this last minute spring snow was just wet enough for the perfect snowman." She pointed to their creation. "Or snow princess, in this case. It doesn't really snow much in Vancouver, so truthfully, this is my first time."

She tossed the snowball she created up in the air.

"Can you believe that, Dad? She's never made a snowman before."

"Or snow princess," Lucy corrected her with a wink.

I eyed her and glanced at Meri. "So," I said as I crouched to make a ball of my own. "Does that mean you've never had a snowball fight before?"

Lucy laughed. "Not since I was a—" The snow hit her in the leg. Stunned, she looked down and then back at me.

For a moment, I wondered whether I'd gone too far. Maybe I shouldn't have thrown a snowball at her, but I needed to do something to get the image of Lucy and Kane Nelson together out of my head. "Sorry, I couldn't help my—"

"Now you're going to get it." A wicked grin crossed her face, and she cocked her arm back.

Meri shrieked with joy as her new nanny hurled her snowball at her daddy and hit me directly in the chest.

"Impressive." I scooped up some more snow. "But now it's on!"

The snowball fight began in earnest, with Meri hiding behind the snow princess, taking turns to cheer for each of us. Lucy put up an impressive fight for a woman who didn't have a lot of experience with snow.

I was sure I had the upper hand as I crouched in the snow to build my final giant snowball that would end it all when Lucy surprised me by appearing over me with an armful of snow.

"Surrender now." She held her armful of wet snow over my head. "Before I bury you."

Her voice was laced with laughter as she tried to maintain her composure.

I looked up into her eyes, twinkling with mischief. She was right; she definitely had me cornered. But I wasn't going to give up that easily.

With a quick breath, I leapt up from my crouch and cried out,"Never surrender," as I wrapped my arms around her waist. Together, we tumbled backward into a large, wet pile of snow.

I used my arms to shelter and protect her as we fell so she wouldn't get hurt. Her eyes were wide with surprise as I looked down at her pretty face, flushed from the exertion of our fight. Her tongue darted out to wet her lips and her breath came fast.

I knew what those lips felt like. What she tasted like.

I had never wanted to kiss a woman more than I did at that moment.

Our faces were only inches apart, and lying that way in the snow with her in my arms, it was damn near impossible to remember that our relationship was strictly professional.

"I win."

"You…Craig…I…"

"Daddy wins!"

Meri's cheer jarred me from the moment and brought me back to stark reality. I leapt off Lucy, putting much-needed distance between us.

"You won, Daddy!"

I nodded at Meri before offering Lucy a hand up out of the snow. "Looks like I won."

"I give." She released my hand the moment she was on her feet. "You win." Lucy turned and brushed the snow from herself as best she could before turning to Meri. "You know what I think? I think some hot chocolate is in order."

"Hot chocolate!" Meri didn't need to be asked twice.

"Hold on." I stopped Meri before she could take off. "Before we go, let me get a picture of you two with your snow princess."

"Oh no." Lucy stepped toward me. "Let me take one of the two of you instead."

"I insist." I held my phone out of reach. "You two did this together."

She hesitated for a moment, and I was sure she was going to protest again, but a small smile crossed her face. "Okay."

"Hold on." I pulled my glove off and used my thumb to wipe snow from her cheek. Lucy stilled under my touch, and her eyes snapped up to meet mine. "You had a little snow... got it."

I let my touch linger before almost reluctantly tucking my hand back into my pocket.

"Thank you." Her smile faltered a little, but just as quickly, it was back in place before she turned to Meri. "Let's pose with our princess."

LUCY

Ten minutes later, I set two mugs of hot chocolate on the table. "Here you go." I turned to Meri. "Such hard construction work deserves a treat. Good work on the snow princess, kiddo."

Meri beamed and wrapped her little hands around her mug.

"Congratulations on winning the snowball fight," I said to Craig. "I'll be more prepared next time."

"If there is a next time. The snow will probably melt by tomorrow."

I shook my head. "I don't know if I'll ever get used to this weird snow in the spring thing."

"I think I take it for granted that I'm used to the crazy mountain weather." He laughed. "But I have seen it snow in almost every month up here. So there could be another chance to beat me."

"No offense to the snow, but I'm hopeful for some warm

weather and I'll have to accept that you're the snowball champ." I winked at him before retreating to the counter to clean up.

"I do like my prize." Craig took a sip of his drink. "Where's your hot chocolate, Lucy? You have to join us."

"Oh no." I waved away his request. As much as I'd love a cup to warm up, I was still figuring out my role in the house. I didn't want to impose. "It wouldn't be right."

"It wouldn't be right if you didn't." Craig stood from the table and moved past me in the kitchen to fetch another mug, along with the kettle that still had hot water in it. "You worked way harder than I did on that princess. In fact, I'd say that you were the chief engineer…wouldn't you, Meri?"

The little girl looked up from her mug and nodded seriously, making me laugh with her chocolate mustache. "Have some, Lucy. You have to."

I looked between the two of them, still uncertain. There were lines between a boss and an employee, and I had no intention of getting anywhere near them, let alone crossing them.

"Please." Meri pressed her hands together and batted her eyelashes.

I looked to Craig, who mimicked his daughter, dramatically dragging out each syllable of the word. I gave in with a laugh. "Okay, okay. I'll have some hot chocolate before I go." I accepted the mug from Craig and moved to the table. "You two sure know how to lay on the guilt trip, hey?"

"It's kind of Meri's specialty." Craig winked at his daughter as he took his seat. "And it's not something I encourage." He tried to look stern. "But in this situation, I think it's warranted."

His face grew serious as he looked at me, and I felt that same heat wash over me as earlier when he'd wiped the snow from my cheek.

I picked up my mug more as a means to hide behind it than to drink my hot cocoa. Whatever that had been outside, it had affected me more than I cared to admit. *Had we almost kissed again?* The way he'd looked at me…his breathing…it felt like…

I shook my head clear, unwilling to let my thoughts travel down that path. Professional distance was important. And given the fact that my stomach did a crazy flip every time he was near, that distance was going to be crucial.

"You really don't have to rush off when I get home, Lucy. I want you to feel comfortable here. I mean, you are spending a lot of time here and…well, I don't want you to feel like you *have* to linger either." Flustered, he waved his hand in the air. "I mean, I know you have things to do and dates and…anyway. I think I'm making a mess of this."

"It's okay." His awkwardness was endearing and oddly, it put me at ease with him. "I don't mean to rush out, it's just—"

"Dad, can I watch a show before dinner?"

I sat back and watched as Craig negotiated one thirty-minute show with his daughter before she helped set the table, who was happy enough to accept the offer. She gulped down the rest of her hot chocolate and jumped down from her chair. But before running from the room, Meri wrapped her arms around me. "Thank you for our snow princess," she said. "It was the best day."

I returned the hug, but before I could say anything in return, Meri had turned and skipped from the room. I pressed my hand to my chest and swallowed hard.

"I think she likes you."

I blinked and turned to Craig, who was beaming. "I really like her, too. She's a great kid," I answered honestly. "I think it's going really well."

"I'm really glad to hear it." Craig put his mug down and placed both hands on the table in front of him, his demeanor suddenly serious. "I don't think it's a secret that I wasn't sure about this whole thing, and I hate to admit that my little sister might have been right, but I think having you around is going to be really good for her."

And me, I thought. The longer I spent with Meri in the little town of Trickle Creek, the more I could feel myself starting to heal. Maybe everything really did happen for a reason, and everything I'd gone through with Ross back in Vancouver had led me to the mountains and this job.

"I know it's not ideal. And I'm really sorry about the short notice, but there's really nothing I can do about it."

I shook my head as I realized I'd completely missed what Craig was saying. "Sorry? I was…do about what?"

The look on his face worried me. He wouldn't meet my eyes. "Craig? What can't you do anything about?"

"I'm sorry, Lucy. This whole situation is a little crazy, and I know that living here probably wasn't what you were looking for when you took this job but—"

"Wait." I set my mug down a little too hard on the table and hot chocolate splashed out over the rim. "What are you talking about, living here?" My mind raced to keep up—or catch up—with the conversation. "I'm living above the Sugar Shack. You said I could stay there since you—"

"I know what I said." He cut me off gently. "And I know this is coming out of left field, but when I offered you the apartment, I didn't think it through, and Chase has offered it to our new chocolatier and…" He waved away the explanation he was muddling through. "I guess it doesn't really matter why it's happening, but it is happening, Lucy. I'm really sorry."

I shook my head and blew out a breath. "So you want me to live here? In this house? With you and Meri?"

"The short-term rental situation in Trickle Creek is crazy because of the tourism, so there's really not a lot of options. I have a spare room, and you'd still have all your time off to do whatever it is you want. I'd respect your boundaries and—"

I held up a hand to stop him. As hard as it was to wrap my head around everything he was telling me, I could see how difficult it was for Craig to bring it up. I placed my hand atop his.

Slowly, Craig looked up into my eyes. "I really am sorry to spring this on you, Lucy, and I really hope we can work it out because Meri…" He shook his head. "Well, because Meri's doing really great with you, and I'd hate to ruin all that because of this."

I had the distinct impression there was something more he wasn't telling me, but whatever it was, it wasn't going to make any difference to the situation at hand. I inhaled through my nose and closed my eyes as I quickly considered my options. Of which, I didn't have many. If I said no, I'd have to leave Trickle Creek and Meri, just when I was starting to feel like I was finding my footing.

I opened my eyes and looked down at my hand that was still covering Craig's. As I watched, he slowly turned his hand over and took mine in his. The warmth of his grip flowed through me.

"Please." His voice was soft. "Stay."

CRAIG

Her hand felt good in mine. Better than it should have. But when she didn't pull away, I squeezed it a little tighter, as if I could convey by touch how badly I wanted her to stay. How much I *needed* her to stay.

For a moment, I contemplated telling her about my father's will and the stupid stipulation that had put us in this position in the first place. But, ultimately, I decided it wasn't fair to burden her with that information.

It was bad enough that I'd backed us into this corner. It probably wouldn't have made the conversation any less awkward if I'd broached the subject earlier in the week when I'd first learned about the situation, but I wasn't stupid— leaving it till the last minute hadn't made it any better.

If she said no, I only had myself to blame.

I'd have to find a new nanny and start all over again. It wouldn't be the end of the world; I was only two weeks in on a six-month term. But it wasn't the thought of starting over that made my breath hitch in my throat when I thought about Lucy leaving us.

"Lucy?"

I watched while she took a deep breath and held it for a moment before exhaling slowly. "I don't know, Craig," she said after an excruciating long pause. "I mean, it changes things. Between us."

Us?

A million questions raced through my brain. Had I been too obvious with my feelings toward her? Was I too forward? I didn't even know what my feelings toward her were, but maybe I'd unintentionally given her the impression that I was interested in her. Not that I wasn't. I was. But she was Meri's nanny. But maybe she was interested in me? Maybe she was having feelings for me that would be complicated by closer proximity. Dare I let myself think that way even for a moment?

No.

Lucy was Meri's nanny. Meri loved her, and I needed her. At least for six months. Sure, I could start over, but my instinct told me that Meri would not take kindly to a change in nanny when she'd taken to Lucy so quickly. I needed to keep her. It was for Meri. I needed to protect her future. That was the only thing that mattered.

"It would only change where you live." The words felt forced, but I needed her to believe it. It was crucial that Lucy understand that as far as I was concerned, it wasn't a big deal that she'd be sleeping only a few feet away down the hall. "That's it. Nothing else would change."

She didn't look convinced.

"I promise you, Lucy, I'll respect your privacy and your personal space and time. You will still have time off. Just because you'll be living here doesn't mean you'll be working more. Those days off are still yours to do with as you like. Obviously we'll have to have some rules about who you can bring home and…" I was rambling and I didn't want to go down that particular line of thinking at the moment. "I'll give you a raise if you like. I know it's—"

"No. You already pay me too much, and if I'm not paying rent—"

"You won't pay rent," I added quickly. "I promise, living here will be—"

"Lucy's going to live here?"

Meri bounded into the room, and before I realized what was happening or could consider how much she'd heard, Lucy had pulled away from my hand that was still wrapped around hers and had turned to face Meri, who was now bouncing up and down next to the kitchen table.

"You're going to live with us?"

Lucy's eyes were wide. Her mouth opened and shut as she stared first at the little girl and then back at me.

"We're talking about a few options." I steered the conversation. "But we haven't made any decisions yet."

"Your room would be right across the hall from mine." Meri jumped higher. "We could see each other every day. I'd let you have one of my stuffies to help you sleep, too. But maybe not forever." Her face grew serious. "Just until you get used to the house. Then they could come back to my room. Maybe Hoot. Would you like Hoot, Lucy?"

Meri was so excited, I found myself holding my breath for Lucy's answer, but I didn't have to wait long before she grinned and nodded.

"I would like it very much if Hoot could visit."

"I'll go get him." Without another word, Meri turned and fled the room.

Once she was gone, I waited until she turned to face me again before I asked, "Does that mean you'll move in?"

Chapter Twelve

LUCY

"NO PEEKING!" Meri clutched tightly to my hand. The little girl insisted on showing me her new room despite the fact that I'd seen it many times before and knew exactly what it looked like. Still, I played along.

"I won't peek."

"Are you ready? You're going to love it."

"I'm ready."

"I think you're going to like it." Meri released my hand, and I heard the snick of a doorknob. "Okay," Meri said. "Open your eyes."

I had expected to see the spare room the way I'd seen it earlier: a glorified storage space. What I hadn't been expecting was to see that the space had been completely transformed.

The curtains were open, letting the late afternoon spill in, making the space look much larger and more inviting than the first time I'd seen it. The boxes and clutter were gone. The queen-sized bed was freshly made with a bright-blue comforter with white and red tulips splashed all over it. There was a large white dresser on the far end of the room, and a little desk tucked into the corner. A vase of tulips sat on the desk, completing the look.

"Oh."

"Does that mean you like it?"

I turned to see Craig behind me, watching me with an expectant look.

"I know it isn't much, but I wanted to make it a cozy, inviting space for you. I didn't have much time. But if there's anything you don't like or want to change, we can—"

"It's perfect."

"You like it? Dad let me pick out the bedspread. I told him you liked tulips."

"I especially like the bedspread." Earlier in the week, over some coloring pages, we'd talked about flowers, and I'd mentioned that tulips were one of my spring favorites and already blooming in Vancouver. "Thank you for remembering."

"I remembered 'cause they're my favorite, too."

I winked. "That's right."

I walked farther into the room and ran my fingers over the dresser top before turning around to face them together. "Thank you. Both of you. This is really nice."

Craig put his hand on Meri's shoulder. "We just want you to feel welcome, Lucy. I know this has all happened really… well, a little strangely."

That was an understatement. I'd hardly had a chance to wrap my head around the situation and it had been less than twenty-four hours since Craig had sprung the situation on me. "You must have been really busy making this happen so quickly."

He shrugged. "Let's just say that I'll have to spend some time organizing the garage soon."

"Daddy dumped everything in there." Meri offered the explanation with a nod of her head that made me laugh.

"Anyway," Craig pulled the conversation back, "I think I speak for both of us when I say that we're really glad you're here."

"And Garfield, too!"

Craig groaned.

Meri had been thrilled to learn that Garfield and I were a package deal, while Craig had been less than excited with the idea of having a cat in the house.

"Why don't we let Lucy and Garfield get settled." Craig steered Meri from the room and returned a moment later with the cat carrier I'd wrestled the large orange tabby into earlier, along with my duffel bag. "I'll bring the rest of your things in for you, too."

Our arms brushed as I reached for the bag. I froze, and Craig sucked in a breath. He looked at me, with an unreadable expression in his eyes, but then I blinked and it was gone. I grabbed the bag and quickly looked away. "Thank you. I'll start unpacking and let Garfield get used to his new home."

What was happening to me? I wasn't supposed to have any feelings for Craig. Sure, he was ridiculously handsome, amazing with his daughter, and quite possibly one of the kindest men I'd met in years, but none of those things mattered because, he was my boss. Period.

I'd gone there once before and it hadn't turned out well, to put it mildly. Mixing business with pleasure was the entire reason I was in my current situation. There was no way I was going to do it again.

I waited until I was sure Craig had left the room again before I bent to release Garfield from his carrier. The cat hated to be confined, but after his escape attempt in the plaza, it seemed like the safest way to transport him. "Welcome to your new home, buddy. At least for a little bit."

The cat didn't hesitate as he leapt from the carrier and bolted straight for the door and—Craig.

"Careful." Craig tried to sidestep the cat, but Garfield, no longer in a hurry, began to thread himself through Craig's legs, forcing him to remain frozen in place, a box of my things in his arms.

"He likes you." I laughed and took the box from him.

"I think cats have some sort of radar for people who don't like them, and they're either determined to change our minds, or drive us crazy."

I scooped up the cat, who immediately nuzzled my face. "Oh, he's definitely trying to make you crazy. But he'll win you over in the process."

"We'll see about that." Craig shook his head with a chuckle but when he reached out to pet Garfield, it wasn't the cat he was looking at.

CRAIG

She'd only been in the house a few hours, and already things felt different. I paced the living room floor, unsure what to do since I'd excused myself to let Lucy unpack. She only had a few bags—it couldn't have taken too long—but I didn't want to intrude. It was important that she have her own space and that she felt at home and comfortable in my house.

The problem was, *I* was uncomfortable in my house.

She made me uncomfortable.

But it wasn't her fault. It was mine. Or more specifically, it was the feelings I was starting to develop. Whenever she was around, the room felt warmer. The air smelled better, and I was just happier.

It was ridiculous.

And it had to all be in my head. But whether I was imagining it or not, I couldn't shake the feelings.

But I also couldn't spend the afternoon pacing my living room.

I grabbed my cell phone and pushed the button to call my best friend, Andy.

Thankfully, he answered on the first ring.

"It's been a minute, Craig." Andy's voice came through the line. "What's going on?"

"Quite a bit, actually." I ran a hand over my face. "Turns out Dad had a plan for me in his will, too."

"I heard."

That stopped me. I dropped my hand. "You heard?"

Andy hesitated. "I was talking to Kat, and she mentioned it."

"Kat? I didn't think you talked to her regularly."

I knew my little sister had gone over to Andy's place in Vancouver when she'd been there for a hair show a few months ago, but beyond that, I didn't think they kept in touch.

"Yeah. We chat sometimes."

I shook my head. It wasn't something I could worry about at the moment. I glanced toward the hall and Lucy's room. "Hey, do you have a second? I kind of need to talk to you about something."

"Of course, man. Anything."

"So you obviously know that I've hired a nanny."

"I sure do."

The humor in Andy's voice stopped me. "What did you hear?"

"I heard she was cute."

I thought about denying it but there was no point. "She is."

"And that Meri loves her."

"She does."

"And that you smile whenever she's around."

"I—"

"Craig."

"Okay," I admitted. "I do." I walked through the living room and looked out at the pink and purple snow princess that, despite being in the shade of the tree, was already half-melted.

"So what exactly is the problem?"

Andy had been my best friend for years. Even after he moved to Vancouver to go to school to be a physiotherapist, we stayed in touch and made a point to visit each other regularly. But despite our closeness, there were still a few things Andy didn't understand.

My lack of female companionship was on the top of that list.

"You do know there's nothing wrong with having a woman in your life, right, Craig?"

"I do have a woman in my life."

"You know what I mean."

I chuckled. "Even if I did want a woman in my life, and I don't, I don't have space. You know that. Meri is my world. My priority. My everything."

"I know it, man. We all do. But I don't think you appreciate that maybe your world could get a little bigger if you'd give it the chance."

I blew out a breath and shook my head. It was annoying that Andy was right. A month ago, I would have wholeheartedly agreed with him. But things were different now. Because the only woman I could even contemplate letting into my life in any way would be Lucy. And she was the very woman I couldn't go there with.

"It's complicated, Andy. She just moved in and—"

"She moved in?" His friend's laughter boomed through the phone. "Well, that does add a little bit of flavor to the situation, now, doesn't it?"

"That's not helpful."

"I don't know, I'd think that maybe——"

"She's dating someone," I interrupted him quickly. "So even if I was interested, which I'm not, it doesn't matter."

"Uh huh."

I could practically see my best friend's smug smile.

"So you're calling because…"

I ran a hand through my hair and tugged at the roots.

"Hey," Andy said before I could reply. "I'm just giving you a hard time. I know you have a lot on your plate, and you weren't expecting your dad's…well, the whole will thing."

"I sure wasn't."

"I was thinking of coming out for a visit for Meri's birthday in July. We can go out and have a proper guys night. Blow off some steam and get your mind off everything. Cool?"

I nodded. "Very cool. That would be great, actually." A noise down the hallway grabbed my attention. "But I don't have a spare room anymore. Where will you stay?"

"Don't worry about that. I can stay with Kat. I'll sort it and let you know the details. In the meantime, maybe it wouldn't hurt to go out on a few dates yourself? Especially now that you have some help with Meri. Seems to me, it could be the perfect chance to put yourself out there."

"Yeah, I'll think about it." I was only half listening as I listened for the evidence of movement coming from her room. "I've got to go. We'll talk later, okay?"

It was only after I'd hung up that I realized my best friend had very casually mentioned that he'd stay with my little sister when he came to town, and for the first time, I wondered how good of friends the two of them really were.

LUCY

"Thank you." I accepted the glass of wine from Craig and took the seat across the living room from where he'd been sitting on the sofa.

"I hope red is okay."

I nodded, a little uncertain about the entire situation. After I'd settled into my room, which hadn't taken long considering I didn't have a lot of things, I hadn't known what to do with myself. It felt strange to stay holed up in my bedroom, but also, I was off the clock, so I didn't want Craig to feel like I was stepping on his toes in any way.

It was all still very, very new and considering we hadn't discussed how to handle, well, anything, when he'd invited me to share a glass of wine with him after Meri went to bed so we could sort things out, I'd accepted the offer.

"Red is great." I took a small sip. It was a delicious and light pinot noir. "This is nice." I gestured to the glass in my hand. "But I have to admit, it feels a little strange to be drinking with my boss at my place of work." I flinched a little at my own choice of words, but pushed the intruding thoughts out of my mind.

"That's why I asked you to join me," Craig said. "Because technically, you're not at work right now. Well, you are at work. But I really don't want you to feel like you have to stay cooped up in your room when you're not on the clock, Lucy. I know this is all…well, I don't really know how to do this either."

He was so genuine and sweet, I felt immediately at ease. "That actually makes me feel better because at least I'm not the only one."

He chuckled. "You are definitely not." He took a slow sip of his own wine, and I followed suit. "I actually think this gives us a chance to get to know each other a little bit better. After all, the last few weeks have been kind of a whirlwind, haven't they? I feel like I don't know much about you at all."

"The feeling is mutual." I tried to keep my voice light and

airy. I didn't know how much I wanted Craig to know about my life back in Vancouver. He seemed to like this new Trickle Creek version of me, and I was doing a great job with Meri. That was really all he really *needed* to know.

"There's not much to know," I said after a moment. "I was a workaholic back in Vancouver." That was the truth. "I didn't have time for a lot of hobbies or interests outside of work." That was mostly true.

"Is that why you came to Trickle Creek?"

I nodded, but then added a shrug, too. "Mostly. But I really just needed a change and to get away from…well…from everything."

"A guy?"

My head shot up, and I stared at Craig, open-mouthed.

"It's okay," he said. "You don't have to tell me. I just…well, I kind of got the impression that maybe that's why you were here. I find that people who come to the mountains are usually running away from something or looking for something. Maybe both."

"Fair." I nodded. "Maybe for me, it's a bit of both." Maybe it was the wine that gave me courage, or maybe I just needed to get it out. Either way, I surprised myself when I said, "I wouldn't say I was running away from him, but I did recently end a relationship and I guess I just wanted a bit of space from that." That was all true.

"I'm sorry to hear that."

"It's fine." I shrugged. More and more, every day, it was fine. Ross was in my past. "It wasn't meant to be. But it did help me realize I needed a change. And it's been a change I've really been enjoying." My smile was honest and genuine. "What about you? Have you been in Trickle Creek your whole life?"

Craig laughed a little as he nodded. "When I was younger,

I thought for sure I was going to get out of here the first chance I had. Teenagers know everything, right?"

I laughed.

"But what I didn't know was that not only was I going to stay, but that I was going to love it. Trickle Creek is home, and it's a great town to raise a child. I can't see myself ever wanting to leave now."

I knew I was prying, but I couldn't stop myself from asking the next question. "And Meri's mom? Does she…well, is she…"

He shook his head. "She's not from here. And she's not here now."

Craig spoke the words without emotion, just as the facts they were.

"Maybe I shouldn't ask, but…does Meri know her mother?"

Again, Craig shook his head and sighed deeply. He glanced down the hall to Meri's closed bedroom door. "We don't talk about it," he began. "Not that we won't. But not yet. I don't feel that she's old enough yet to understand, and the last thing I ever want is for Meri to ever feel that she's missing anything."

Like a mother?

Despite the fact that I didn't understand at all, I nodded, and Craig continued.

"We were young when we met, and we were never in love or anything like that. It was…well, totally unplanned to say the least. Donna was here to work a ski season, have a good time and go home, back to school in Australia. She never wanted to be a mother, especially then."

I put my free hand to my chest as I realized what Craig was saying. I'd imagined a variety of scenarios as to why Craig was a single dad, but abandonment by Meri's mother hadn't been one of them.

"I don't have any ill will toward Donna at all," Craig said, as if he knew exactly what I was thinking. "In fact, I'm very grateful for her and her sacrifice. She didn't even have to tell me she was pregnant, but she cared enough to tell me because she knew I'd want to know. Later, she confessed that she knew I'd react the way I had, with one hundred percent certainty that I wanted to raise the baby." He smiled a little to himself. "She knew I'd feel that way, and she still told me. She didn't have to do that."

I shook my head. "No. I don't think a lot of young women would."

"It's hard to know how you'll react to such a situation until it happens to you."

"True."

"Donna agreed to go through with the pregnancy with the understanding that she did not want any parental involvement after the baby was born."

"Wow." It was such an insignificant word for the situation. I took another sip of wine to keep myself from saying anything more.

"Very wow. Honestly, Lucy, it was the greatest gift she could have given me. And truly the most selfless thing she could have done."

"But to walk away from—"

"Donna never wanted to be a mother. I think it's very brave for a woman to make that choice. And even more brave for her to recognize that the best thing she could have done for Meri was to not try to force herself into a situation where she would have been miserable and resent her child."

I nodded slowly and let Donna's choice sink in. "I never thought about it that way. But I guess you're right."

"And Meredith has so much love in her life."

My smile once more crept over my face. "That's easy to see." We sat in comfortable silence for a moment. "Thank you for telling me, Craig."

"Of course. I should have told you earlier. It's just that—"

"You didn't want Meri to know."

He shook his head. "Not yet. I'll tell her when the time is right and she can understand. I always had six in the back of my head, like that's when I'd talk to her about it. But her birthday is coming up and…"

"She'll be ready."

Craig looked up at me with an expression on his face that I couldn't quite read. "Thanks, Lucy. And thank you for staying. I know I'm not the best boss, or the most experienced, and I've obviously never hired a nanny before. This all kind of… well, it was thrown at me, and you've been absolutely wonderful. I don't usually believe in these things, but the more I think about it, the more I can't help but feel that Garfield escaping in the plaza and you slipping on the ice in front of my store was all…"

"Serendipitous?"

"Exactly." He raised his glass, and I followed suit. "Cheers to serendipity."

Chapter Thirteen

LUCY

I ARRIVED at the big house at five o'clock exactly. I stopped to pick up a nice bottle of wine, guessing that white would be the right choice.

My first reaction when Craig had invited me to the family dinner was to decline. I didn't want to set a precedent for getting too involved in his life, especially on my days off. But he'd insisted that his family wanted to properly meet me since I was spending so much time with Meri. Finally, I relented. After all, I'd already met Asher and Kat. It felt right that I officially met the others, too.

I had insisted on driving myself, though, which felt a little ridiculous considering we lived in the same house, but I was grasping to have at least a few boundaries.

It felt important, even if those boundaries were only in my own head.

It was easy to see how Craig's childhood home got its name. The house was massive. Definitely bigger than anything I'd seen in Trickle Creek, the home rivaled those in the upscale neighborhoods of Vancouver with its long, winding drive up the mountain, protected by a heavy wooden gate. The circular driveway was filled with vehicles I assumed belonged to the Carlson siblings.

I parked behind Craig's Jeep and sat for a moment, staring at the imposing house.

"Here goes nothing." I gave my head a little shake, put a friendly smile on my face, and, wine in hand, left the relative security of my car.

Before I could make it up the steps, the front door swung open, and Craig appeared. He was dressed casually in jeans and a T-shirt, his hair tousled as if he'd just woken up. The sight of him standing in the doorway, despite the fact that it had only been a few hours since we'd awkwardly made small talk in his kitchen, took my breath away. I swallowed my reaction quickly and grinned.

"Don't tell me you were waiting for me?"

He shrugged. "Truthfully, I was getting some air after an epic Nerf gun fight." He ran his hands through his hair in an effort to straighten it, but it was a lost cause.

I reached out and brushed a lock from his forehead before snatching my hand away. "Well, it's good timing then."

"It sure is."

His smile was so warm and welcoming, that any unease I was feeling about the dinner quickly slid away.

"Are you ready for this? My family is kind of a lot."

"I'm sure they're nothing I can't handle. I'm used to dealing with hundreds of restaurant patrons every night. Most of whom have had too much to drink."

Craig laughed. "Well, then I'm sure you'll do just fine." He offered me his arm. "Shall we?"

There were at least half a dozen reasons I shouldn't take his arm as we walked into the house, but I ignored all of them, and we headed in to meet the Carlson clan.

"Lucy!" Meri greeted me first, by running headfirst at full speed into my legs.

I quickly released Craig's arm to bend down and scoop up the little girl in a hug. "Hey, kiddo. How was your day?"

"So boring." She rolled her eyes dramatically and dropped her head back.

"Boring? What are you talking about?" Craig pretended to look offended. "We just had an epic Nerf gun fight and—"

"Just kidding!" She straightened up and her eyes gleamed with mischief. "It was awesome," Meri declared. "But I'm so glad you're here now."

"Me too." I gave the little girl a kiss on the cheek and set her on her feet before straightening to greet everyone else.

"I'm Charli."

A tall, blonde woman pulled me in for a hug before I had a chance to catch my breath. She smelled like a garden and her embrace was strong.

"It's so nice to finally meet you," she said as she released me. "Meri and Craig won't stop talking about you."

"Is that right?" I shot Craig a look, but he only shrugged.

"Apparently you've made quite an impact on their lives in such a short time." Charli raised her eyebrows and gave her brother a knowing look before winking at me. "Thank you for that."

I chuckled and took an immediate liking to the woman.

"I'm so glad you came, Lucy." Kat appeared next by my side and wrapped her arm around me. "Don't let my brothers and sister scare you off. We're all harmless, I swear."

"You all seem quite lovely."

"That's because you don't know us very well yet."

I turned at the voice to see a tall, dark-haired man who could only be the eldest brother, Chase. His introduction confirmed it.

"It's nice to meet you, Lucy. I'm Chase and this is Annie.

Grady is around here somewhere. I'm sure you'll meet him soon."

I accepted a hug from Annie, too. "It's really nice to meet you all." I met Asher's gaze from across the room and nodded. "And to see you again, Asher."

"The pleasure is very much mine," he said. "I assure you."

He moved toward me, but Craig deftly stepped in front of his older brother. "Don't even think about it, bro."

Asher pretended to look disappointed, but Craig wasn't smiling and the minute he looked away, Asher winked in my direction.

CRAIG

She fit in so easily, that it was easy for me to forget that Lucy had only been part of my life for such a short time. It felt like she'd always been there.

I leaned against the wall and watched as Lucy helped Charli and Annie in the kitchen. The three women worked together effortlessly, as if they'd made the family dinner together many times before, and hadn't just met. A smile crept over my face when Charli said something I couldn't quite hear that made Lucy laugh. She had the sweetest, most honest laugh I'd ever heard.

"It's about time you brought a woman home."

Asher jabbed me in the rib cage, startling me from my thoughts. I glared at my brother, who was only trying to stir things up. "Lucy's not a woman." I caught myself with a shake of my head and took three steps out of the room before the women could overhear our conversation.

"Oh, she's most definitely a woman." Asher didn't even

bother hiding the look of admiration he shot in Lucy's direction.

I worked hard to swallow down the sudden anger toward my brother. "That's not how I meant it."

Asher chuckled, but before I could get too worked up, he held up his hand. "I know what you meant."

"She's Meri's nanny."

Asher nodded. "Uh huh."

"She is."

"I know."

I looked incredulous, and I felt my fingers twitch into a fist at my side. My brother had a very special talent for making me crazy.

"And she's a very attractive nanny, don't you think?"

"I'm warning you. Back off, Asher."

As if our eldest brother could sense trouble brewing, Chase appeared in the living room, a bottle of wine in his hand. He took one look at us and stepped between us. "Whoa. What's the issue, guys?"

Asher shrugged innocently. "I was just commenting on how it was nice that Craig brought Lucy over for dinner."

Chase eyed him suspiciously while I took the opportunity to pull myself together. I couldn't let Asher get under my skin. He was only trying to stir things up, the way he always did. Asher had a special version of middle child syndrome where, in an effort to combat the tendency to be invisible, he made it his personal mission to drive the rest of us crazy. A classic any attention is good attention kind of situation that he never seemed to quite grow out of.

"Don't make me regret inviting her for dinner." I glared in Asher's direction. "And don't do anything to ruin this situation, Asher. I mean it."

"By situation, you mean having a sexy woman living under your roof for the first time in—"

I didn't think; I only reacted. I lunged at my brother. I grabbed a fistful of his sweater by his throat and shoved him up against the wall. "I mean it, Asher. Do not go anywhere near Lucy. Meri loves her, and I—"

"You have the hots for her."

I growled and tightened my grip. "I need her."

"I bet you do."

That was it. I could only take so much. I wasn't a violent man and hadn't been in a physical fight since the school yard when I was a kid. Come to think of it, that fight likely involved my brother, then, too.

My right hand tightened into a fist, my arm cocked when Chase grabbed my arm, stopping me.

"Whoa. Since when is there fighting at family dinner night?"

"Since Asher is determined to be an ass." I yanked myself free from Chase's grip and stepped away. My breath came quickly. I gritted my teeth and looked down, forcing myself to calm down.

"Asher, can you go find the kids and tell them to wash up? Dinner is almost ready."

I didn't look up until I was sure I'd heard Asher leave the room.

"Are you going to tell me what that was all about?" Chase watched me carefully. "Because I can't remember ever seeing you lose your temper like that."

It was true. I was known as the calmest of all the siblings, with the exception of Charli, who was the most patient of all of us. I never got riled up. I never lost my patience or yelled and only very rarely even raised my voice. I swallowed hard, unable to answer my brother.

"Can I offer my opinion?"

"Do I have a choice?"

"No." Chase grinned and gestured for me to follow him

into the dining room. "I think you let Asher get to you because there might be a little bit of truth to what he's implying."

"Excuse me?"

Chase held up his hands. "Hey. Don't get mad at me. I'm just calling it like I see it and...well, I see it."

I pulled out a chair and sat down hard. "And what exactly do you see?"

"I see a very attractive young woman who is amazing with your daughter."

I saw that too, of course.

"And I see the way you look at her."

My head snapped up. "Excuse me? How exactly do I look at her?"

My brother took his time answering me as he opened the bottle of wine and poured out two glasses before handing me one. He pulled out the chair next to me and sat so we faced each other. "You look at her like you never want her to leave. And it has to do with a whole lot more than Dad's stipulation."

I opened my mouth to object but closed it again. I took a gulp of my wine and rolled it around my mouth. Of course I didn't want her to leave. Meri loved her and already she'd made my life so much easier and relieved so much stress. But that wasn't what Chase meant, and I knew it. Worse, I agreed.

"Be honest with me, Craig. Is there anything going on between the two of you?"

"What?" I set my glass down with a bit too much force. "No. Of course not. Why would you even ask?"

Chase didn't bother to hide his disbelief. "Nothing?"

"Well, we kissed once, but it doesn't count because it was before I hired her, or even knew her name. It wasn't even a real kiss." It may not have been real, but it hadn't stopped me from wishing it was, or replaying that moment in my mind when I closed my eyes. "But no. Nothing is going on. Why does it even matter?"

Chase shook his head. "The fact that you're even asking that is a problem, brother. I know you're not that stupid. Getting involved with an employee, especially one who lives with you now, is setting you up for a world of problems. And you can't afford any disruptions with this situation, Craig. None."

I swallowed hard. Of course, Chase was right. And I wasn't an idiot. "Don't worry about it, Chase. Like I said. Nothing is going on. It's purely professional."

My brother gave me the side eye, but didn't say anything more for a moment. Finally, he picked up his glass and took another sip. "Keep it that way, Craig. I mean it. If this blows up…for any reason…it's done."

I forced what I hoped was a reassuring smile to my face. "It won't blow up, man. There's nothing to worry about here. Lucy is the nanny. It's totally professional."

Chase still didn't look convinced, but thankfully, he didn't push it. "Good." He gave me a nod. "Keep it that way. For all our sakes."

LUCY

The Carlson family dinner turned out to be just as loud and boisterous of an affair as I had expected. And I loved every minute of it. Everyone had been so welcoming and friendly that I didn't feel like an outsider at all, but part of the family.

Even Asher had obviously gotten the message that I wasn't interested in him as more than a friend, and had dropped his overt flirting. The only thing that seemed a little off about the whole evening was Craig.

From the moment that I'd carried in the bowl of salad and

taken my seat across from him at the table, he'd avoided making eye contact with me completely.

I didn't let myself dwell on it or how quickly his attitude toward me had changed since I'd arrived. I didn't have a lot of experience with big families, but I did know that there were dynamics at play with that many siblings, and there was a good chance Craig's change in demeanor had nothing to do with me.

After talking to Charli and Annie in the kitchen, I'd learned more about the pressure Craig was under with his business and how he'd been a single father trying to run a business and be both a father and a mother to little Meri for far too long. I'd also learned that the entire family had been under some extra stress since their father had passed away and that Craig was currently under some additional pressure due to something regarding their father's will.

I'd left the conversation with about as many new questions than answers to the ones I already had. But regardless, it sounded like Craig was dealing with a lot.

"So, Lucy." Kat spoke up from the far end of the table. "What do you think of Trickle Creek so far? Is it everything you thought it would be?"

I smiled and speared a cucumber with my fork. Considering that the only thing I'd ever heard about Trickle Creek came from my ex who couldn't stop talking about how romantic the town was, *no*, it was definitely nothing I thought it would be.

"It's so cute," I said with a smile in my voice. "I especially love the plaza with all the shops. Living right in the middle of things is…was really fun."

"Oh, that's right, you were living in the plaza." Kat grinned at me. "I do love the energy there. I live above my shop, too. People say that a small town has nothing on the energy of the downtown in a big city, and maybe that's true, but there's still a special vibe there."

"The plaza is nothing like a big city." Chase laughed and shook his head.

"Wait a minute." Charli grabbed the conversation. "What do you mean, you were living in the plaza? Where are you now?"

"You didn't hear?" Asher's voice was laced with glee that I didn't care for.

"Hear what?" Annie asked the question widely, but looked to me for the answer.

"Lucy lives with us now." It was Meri who answered the question, practically jumping out of her chair with excitement. "Isn't it awesome? She moved in yesterday."

Charli blinked slowly. She and Annie looked at each other, eyebrows raised.

"Chase found a chocolatier who agreed to move to Trickle Creek, but part of the deal was accommodation." Craig spoke quickly, not making eye contact with anyone in particular. "It was kind of a rushed situation, but Lucy was super gracious about it and agreed to stay in our spare room. She moved in yesterday."

I could see that the conversation was only adding to whatever discomfort Craig was already feeling, so I tried to take over. "It's actually going to work out really well," I said agreeably. "And it means I don't have to get up extra early to get over to the house to wake up Meri."

"I like it when Lucy wakes me up."

I smiled at the little girl and gave her a wink.

"I'm glad it all worked out." Charli reached for the salad dressing. "It would have been such a shame if—"

"But it did work out, Charli," Chase interrupted her smoothly. "So no one needs to talk about the what-if."

I looked slowly between the siblings. As an only child

myself, I couldn't be sure about the dynamics of a large family, or whether this type of back and forth was normal or not. Regardless, it was kind of exhausting.

"And you just moved yesterday?" Chase tilted his head in question. "That doesn't give the cleaners much time to do the turnover for the chocolatier. She arrives tomorrow."

"Well, I only found out on Friday, so I'd say we made the move pretty quickly." I took a bite of my bun.

"Friday?" Chase choked on his wine. "Craig, I talked to you about this ages—"

"Things have been kind of busy, Chase."

I didn't miss the look Craig shot him across the table.

"We made the move as fast as we could."

I didn't have a chance to explore whatever it was that Chase was talking about, because Meri jumped into the conversation. "I think Garfield likes it at our house." Meri looked at Annie's nephew when she spoke. "You have to come meet him. He's so cute. He's like Auntie Charli's kitty, but twice the size."

I laughed but still wasn't completely distracted by what Chase had just said. Ages ago? What did that mean?

"You have a cat?" Grady's interest was piqued. "You're so lucky. I want a cat, but Auntie Annie won't let me."

"I thought you wanted a dog?"

"I can have a dog?" Grady almost jumped out of his seat.

"I didn't say that." Annie held up her hand. "We are not talking about a dog right now."

"But, you—"

"Did not say anything about a dog. Maybe you can go over and visit Garfield sometime?" She glanced at me for help.

"You come anytime you like. I'm sure Garfield would love the attention."

The kids immediately got swept up in conversation about the cat and what games they could play with him. I chuckled a

little; Garfield was a cranky old boy and wasn't likely to partici-
pate in any of their games, but I decided against telling them.
They'd figure it out soon enough.

The rest of the dinner passed quickly and soon the women
were settled in the living room with cups of tea for some, and
refills on their wine for others, while the men cleaned up.

"So, Lucy. How was your first family dinner?" Kat asked
the question as she fell into an overstuffed chair and crossed
her legs.

"My first?"

"We do this every week," Charli chimed in. "So I guess
we'll see you every Sunday." She winked but I shook my head.

"I'm not family."

"Oh, yes you are." It was Annie who spoke up. "You're
living with Craig and Meri and—"

"That's only because I don't have anywhere else to live."
Again, I made a note to talk to Craig about how exactly that
went down. "I work for Craig. I'm hardly family."

Charli waved her hand, dismissing my protests. "I don't
think that's how any of us see it."

I had no idea what to say to that. Instead, I lifted my mug
of peppermint tea and took a sip. "I think it's great that you
guys do family dinner every week. I never had a big family. It
was just me and Mom most of the time, growing up. It's nice
that you all are so close."

"Most of the time we are." Kat shrugged. "Trust me, there
have been moments. Like earlier tonight, you guys missed it,
but I was sure Craig and Asher were going to come to blows."

"What? Craig?" Charli set her tea down on the table.
"Asher, I believe. But Craig?" She shook her head in disbelief,
but Kat nodded, her lips pressed together.

"It's true. Chase told me he had to get between the two of
them before Craig punched him."

I hadn't known him very long, but from what I'd seen of

Craig, there was no way I could imagine him getting into a fist-fight with his brother. It just didn't fit. Maybe that was why Craig had been so withdrawn during dinner?

Charli sighed. "What did Asher do?"

"Because you know it was Asher who instigated it," Annie agreed.

"I'm not one hundred percent sure, but..." She looked straight at me and held my gaze.

"What?" I pressed a hand to my chest. "Me? They were fighting because of me? I've only met Asher once and..." I looked around at the women. "I'm just the nanny. There's no reason to fight about that."

Kat raised her eyebrows and took a sip of her wine, but didn't say anything more.

"There isn't," I said again. "Trust me."

"Are you dating anyone, Lucy?"

It was a bold question, and I shouldn't have been surprised that it had come from Kat.

Her sister smacked her arm, but I laughed. "No. And I don't see that changing anytime soon."

The last thing I wanted to do was get into the nitty-gritty of my love life, or lack thereof, with these ladies. "I'm just really enjoying how simple things are right now."

I smiled and tried my best to actually believe the words I'd just spoken aloud, because my current situation felt like a lot of things at the moment, but none of them were simple.

Chapter Fourteen

CRAIG

IT WAS late by the time I carried Meri in from the car and tucked her already fast asleep into her bed, taking the time to position all her stuffed animals around her so she wouldn't be upset if she woke in the middle of the night.

I knew I shouldn't have stayed at the big house so late, especially on a school night, but it felt easier to deal with an overtired little girl the next morning than it would be to face Lucy alone in the house we now shared.

I'd seen the look on her face when Chase made a comment about how long I'd waited to tell her about the move. I owed her an apology. I knew that. I also owed her an explanation, and that would be the harder thing to handle.

Because for the life of me, I did not know how to explain to Lucy that my lack of attention to the entire situation wasn't because I didn't care. It was exactly the opposite. I cared too much.

When I was done tucking Meri in, I returned to the kitchen

to grab a beer out of the fridge. Lucy's bedroom door was still closed. She'd excused herself from the big house hours earlier.

I was tempted to knock on her door to see whether she was still awake. Maybe it would be best to have the conversation right away. That way, she could just get on with being upset with me.

The idea of upsetting Lucy in any way didn't sit right with me. Maybe I was a chicken shit. No, I definitely was. Wasn't that the entire reason we were in this situation in the first place? Because I hadn't faced things head-on?

I cracked the can of beer and took a long sip. The clock on the microwave said it was already after nine. I didn't know anything about Lucy's habits. It was likely that she was already asleep. Waking her up would just make things worse.

Or was I being a chicken shit again?

A loud mewl at my feet, followed by a head butt against my leg, startled me. "Holy shit." The curse word slipped out. Fortunately, Meri was fast asleep and couldn't hit me up for the swear jar. I looked down to see Lucy's giant tabby cat threading his fluffy body through my legs. "You scared me," I said to the cat.

I had never been a cat guy. I'd had a friend in grade school with a crazy Siamese cat who used to lunge out at our ankles every time we'd walked past. It hadn't left me with a good impression of felines in general, but...

"You're not so bad, are you?" I bent and scratched the cat's head. He meowed in response. "Nah. You're pretty cute."

I took my beer and pulled out a chair at the table. Immediately, Garfield jumped up onto my lap. "Oh. I don't know about this." I tensed, but the cat was not to be deterred. Garfield nudged his head against my chest and nuzzled into me. He circled a few times until finally settling with a heavy thud onto my lap. "Okay, I give in."

I had to admit, his fur was soft and as far as cats went,

Garfield wasn't too bad. The more I patted him, the louder the purring got, until finally, I chuckled at the small engine vibrating in my lap. "You're not afraid of getting comfortable here, are you?"

"He sure isn't."

My head shot up to see Lucy leaning against the wall. "Hi. I thought maybe you were asleep."

"I heard you come in."

"Sorry."

She moved past me to get a glass from the cabinet. "Don't be. It's your house."

Unsure of what to say, I continued petting the cat and took another sip of my beer while Lucy filled the glass at the sink. It wasn't until she'd hopped up onto the counter across from me that I spoke again. "I'm sorry."

"I told you, it's not a big deal. It's your house and—"

"No." I stopped her. "I'm sorry about not telling you sooner about the apartment and having to move. Chase was right. He talked to me about it ages ago, and I should have said something sooner. I was just…"

"You were just what?"

"Afraid." It was an honest answer, in more ways than one.

"That I would say no?"

I nodded and took a breath, looking down at the cat in my lap for courage. "And also…that you'd say yes."

The silence in the kitchen was broken only by Garfield's loud purring.

"I don't understand," she said after a moment. "You were afraid I'd say yes?"

No doubt I'd already said too much. I inhaled through my nose and looked up. "It's just been Meri and me for…well, forever." I shrugged. "I've never lived with a woman before. I wasn't sure, well…" There was so much more I wanted to say to her, but I had no idea how to even begin.

It wasn't like I could tell my daughter's nanny that I was starting to develop feelings for her, or that the idea of her sleeping just down the hall from me made me feel a whole lot of things I hadn't felt in a very long time.

No. There was no way I could say that. She'd turn and run out of there so fast that I wouldn't be able to stop her. And I wouldn't blame her, either.

And regardless of how I felt about Lucy, I couldn't have her leaving. Everything depended on her staying. It was crucial she felt comfortable there.

Chase's voice was in the back of my head: keep it that way. I hated that Chase was right, but at the same time, it had been years since I'd had feelings like this for a woman and it was getting harder and harder to hold them back.

"I don't think any of this is coming out right." I shook my head. Garfield let out a loud mewl and jumped from my lap. "I guess I said something to offend him." I chuckled and watched the cat run from the room before looking back at Lucy, who still sat on the counter. Only she was no longer grinning and swinging her legs.

Was she...dammit, she was.

Lucy was crying.

"Hey." I jumped up from the chair and grabbed the only thing I could find at hand. "Don't cry." I thrust the towel at her, dabbing awkwardly at her face with the towel. I knew I was handling the situation completely wrong. I usually did when it came to women and tears, but I couldn't seem to stop myself.

LUCY

The tears had come out of nowhere. But the moment I'd started to cry, I couldn't seem to stop. I probably should have jumped down from the counter and run back to my room before Craig could see me, but it was too late.

He'd noticed me.

"Don't cry." He swiped awkwardly at my face with a tea towel. "Lucy, I'm sorry."

"No." I managed to say after a moment. "It's not…" Mortifyingly, sobs swallowed the rest of what I was trying to say.

What was wrong with me? I hadn't cried in months. Not since I'd discovered the truth about Ross…oh shit.

I should have known better. I'd been doing my best to suppress my feelings and ignore the fact that my life had been falling apart that I hadn't even seen the emotional breakdown coming.

The realization only made my sobs come harder and faster, which only made me feel worse. I was in a vicious cycle and the only way to end it was going to involve chocolate and a hot bath.

"I'm sorry." I tried to speak, the words coming out in a garbled mess. "I should go." I tried to jump off the counter and flee, but Craig stopped me.

He stood directly in front of me with a tea towel in his hand, and he didn't look as if he'd be moving anytime soon.

I shook my head, unable to speak again.

Undeterred, Craig used the corner of the towel to wipe my tears, more gently this time, from my cheek. "It's okay, Lucy. You don't have to run away. Whatever it is I said, I'm so sorry. It's not that I don't want you here. That's not what I was trying to say, and I'm sorry if it sounded like that."

He looked genuinely concerned that I was upset. Maybe I should have been concerned about crossing a line with my boss so soon after moving into his house, but his proximity didn't feel wrong. Exactly the opposite.

Craig wiped my other cheek, and when I tried to take the towel from him, he gently shook his head. "Let me. Please."

I didn't have the energy to fight him on it, and more importantly, I didn't want to. Having Craig wipe my tears and speak gently to me was calming in a way I didn't even realize. Soon, my sobs quieted, and I felt more like myself.

"Thank you," I said softly, suddenly embarrassed. "I'm not a crier. Honestly. I don't know what…no." I shook my head. "I do know what happened. And, it had nothing to do with you. It was just bad timing."

He didn't look convinced.

"Really."

"Do you want to talk about it?"

I shook my head.

"You're sure?"

I wasn't sure. And now that I'd just sobbed and snotted all over the place, it wasn't as if I could be any more embarrassed than I already was. I took a breath. "It's just that I left a lot when I came here, and I don't think I ever really dealt with any of it."

"The guy?"

I nodded.

"Ross." For the first time when I said his name out loud, I didn't feel anything except disappointment. "It was…well, it was a bit messy and I…well, I'm over it all now, but I…"

"Sometimes you just need to let it out or it stays inside and builds up until—"

"This happens?"

He chuckled. "Exactly."

"How do you know the right thing to say?"

"I certainly don't." Craig shook his head. "But I do have two sisters, and I've seen my share of situations like this."

I sniffed and tried to stop the tears, but they weren't done falling.

"I'm so sorry. This job is…well, I absolutely adore Meri. I'm really grateful you gave me the opportunity. To be honest, I never could have imagined that I'd be doing this and spending my days with a little girl, but I think it's exactly what I needed and—"

He stopped me with a hand on my cheek. "You're exactly what we needed, too."

I blinked and looked at him through a blurry veil of tears.

"I'm sorry if I'm overstepping, Lucy. And I can see that you've had a lot going on before you moved here, I feel really awful because I would hate to think that I added to that stress with this whole mess of making you move in…well, the last thing I want to do is scare you away. Meri adores you, too."

I swallowed hard and my stomach flipped as I stared into Craig's eyes. He watched me with an intensity that should have scared me, but it only pulled me closer to him.

He leaned closer at the same time I leaned in.

Every part of me knew it was wrong, but it also felt perfectly right.

"Would it be okay if I kissed you?"

His breath hit my lips in warm, gentle puffs of air. I swallowed hard and answered him with a slight nod.

The kiss was gentle. His lips were soft and almost soothing to my frayed nerves. A sigh escaped my lips, and I leaned in as we deepened our connection together.

It was over too soon. Craig sucked my lower lip gently as he pulled back.

He wiped away one last tear and cupped my cheek gently.

"I'm really glad you're here, too, Lucy."

Chapter Fifteen

CRAIG

I FELT like I hadn't slept more than a few hours a night in the last month. Between the new chocolatier taking over my kitchen at the Sugar Shack, the uptick in business as winter was finally left behind, and of course the not-so-simple matter of trying to avoid my growing feelings for Lucy, I was exhausted.

After our shared moment in the kitchen the night of the family dinner, and the kiss I could not stop obsessing about, my feelings for her had only become more intense. We hadn't kissed again, but the lingering touches, the hugs good night in the kitchen that lasted a bit longer every evening, and the stolen glances across the room only increased my need to get her alone again.

But my brother's comments were still very much in the forefront of my mind. I couldn't screw things up with Lucy. There was more at stake here, and I needed to remember that, even if it was getting increasingly harder.

If Lucy was watching TV in the living room in the evenings, I made excuses to go to bed early, or putter in the garage until she'd gone to bed. As much as I wanted to spend time with her, I no longer trusted myself to keep things professional.

Instead of driving to work, I'd opted to leave my car at home and walk the short distance to the plaza in the warm June sun. There hadn't been any more late late-season snow storms, so the grass had a chance to green up, and the leaves were popping on the trees in vibrant shades of green while the gardens of the little houses lining the streets were starting to fill with colorful blooms, too.

It was my favorite time in the mountains, when the weather was warm, but before the summertime crowds once more descended on our little town.

Not that I'd ever admit how much I enjoyed the shoulder seasons in town, not when my own business relied on the influx of tourists for its survival. Still, I enjoyed the slower pace while I could.

Including the opportunity to get a cup of coffee at the Bean Bag, my favorite coffee shop, without waiting in long lines.

The fresh aroma of roasting coffee drew me into the little shop on the corner of the plaza. Another shot of caffeine would definitely not be a bad idea.

No sooner had I ordered my dark roast with milk and turned to lean against the counter than I was recognized.

"Hey there, Craig."

I scanned the room to find the source of the voice, nodding a greeting to a handful of others I knew before my gaze landed on Krysta. "Hi." I accepted my coffee from the barista and made my way across the room toward her. "It's been awhile," I said when I approached.

There was a selection of product catalogs, dusted in muffin crumbs, spread out on the table in front of her.

"I'm just finalizing some orders for the season." She waved

her arm over the mess. "How are things at your end of the plaza? I heard you have a new addition?"

"A new…" I stumbled over my response. "You mean Lucy?"

Krysta laughed. "I didn't mean Lucy. But yes. I have heard a lot about her as well. Kane talks about Lucy all the time."

Of course he does.

Jealousy flared through me. Lucy had mentioned Kane more than once. I tried to put the other man out of my head, especially when it came to thinking about the two of them together. I'd never considered myself a jealous man before, but maybe it was because I'd never had something or someone to be jealous about.

Not that Lucy was mine or that I had any right to feel jealous. One kiss between us didn't give me any claim. Well, one real kiss.

Still.

"Is that right?" I tried my best to sound casual. "They've been spending some time together, then?"

Judging by the look on Krysta's face, I was failing miserably at the whole casual thing.

"I think they've seen each other a few times, yes. It's good to see that Lucy's settling into town so easily."

"It is." I took a sip of coffee and swallowed the still way-too-hot liquid hard.

"But I wasn't talking about that addition." Krysta gave me a wink. "I'm talking about the delicious smell of chocolate coming from your place every day. When are we going to get to sample your new chocolates, Craig? I think you're holding out on us."

Happy to have the conversation change tracks, I chuckled. "It does smell pretty damn good, doesn't it?"

Mya hadn't wasted any time taking over the small kitchen in the back of my shop, whipping up different concoctions, all of which smelled more delectable than the last. But she'd yet to deem any of them worthy enough for taste testing.

"Trust me, Krysta, you're not the only one who'd like a taste."

I never would have expected that a chocolatier would be a perfectionist akin to an artist working on her masterpiece, but in only a few short weeks, I was getting a crash course in all things chocolate. Except, of course, how they tasted.

"It's literally all any of us can talk about around here." Krysta shrugged. "As soon as you're ready, you let us know. Maybe you can set some aside for locals before the tourists snap up all the good stuff?"

"That's not a bad idea." I nodded to myself, another idea starting to take shape. "In fact, I'll talk to Mya about it today. She should be getting close with some of the first confections. Maybe we can do a tasting for some of the other businesses in the community?"

Krysta exaggerated a swoon. "Count me in."

LUCY

"Lucy! Watch this!"

I turned my head to see Meri on the swing next to me, pumping her little legs as hard as she could to launch herself farther into the air.

"Look how high I can go!" Meri tipped her head back and let her hair stream out behind her as she sailed through the air.

"You're so high!"

"I'm so high!"

I knew when I was beat. I hopped off my swing to properly watch as Meri all but took flight.

After a moment, she slowed and came back to earth. "That was so fun."

I laughed. "You were as high as a bird, kiddo. I couldn't keep up."

"I went higher than you." Meri hopped off the swing and grabbed my hand. "Didn't I?"

"You sure did." Together, we walked through the playground.

"Did you ever go that high before?"

I pretended to think about it for a moment. "You know what? I don't think so. I was never a very high swinger when I was a kid. But you know what I was good at?"

Meri stopped and stared up at me. "What?"

"Monkey bars," I said as seriously as I could manage.

"Whoa. I've never been good at the monkey bars." Together, we looked at the bars attached to the play structure. "Can you still do it?"

I shrugged. "Only one way to find out."

I truly had no idea whether I could still manage the monkey bars. It had been at least twenty years since the last time I'd even attempted it. I rubbed my hands together and hoped that the few months I'd actually belonged to the CrossFit gym next to my apartment building had paid off. While Meri looked on, I wrapped one hand around the bar and stepped off the platform. I swung for only a moment before I remembered the rule: go fast.

One hand over another, I swung my body with each movement until, a moment later, I stood on the far platform. I thrust my arms in the air and let out a whoop.

"You did it." Meri ran over and gave me a high five.

No one was more surprised than me. I squeezed my hands together and was about to ask Meri whether she wanted to try when a friend from school ran over and asked her to play.

"Is that okay, Lucy?"

"Of course. I'll be right over there." I retreated to the sidelines to watch Meri play as my pocket vibrated with an incoming text.

You busy?

I felt a flash of guilt at the disappointment that washed through me when I saw Mandi's name and not Craig's. Even though our texts were mostly focused on Meri, I still looked forward to hearing from him. Every time I saw his name on the screen, my stomach did a flip.

It was ridiculous and completely inappropriate, and I knew it. Which was exactly why I'd done my best to maintain the professional distance between us that I'd let slip that night in the kitchen.

I'd been absolutely mortified about the way I'd lost control of my emotions that night, but it was the kiss I couldn't stop thinking about.

It kept me up at night, fantasizing about the feel of his mouth on mine and the way every single part of me had lit up with his touch.

It had been so fleeting, so soft. But at the same time, it had been so much more.

More than anything, I'd wanted a replay, but I'd forced myself to keep a distance and I could tell, Craig was too. That helped. I didn't know whether I'd have the strength to have professional boundaries if he didn't.

I tapped out a quick reply to Mandi and a moment later, my phone rang.

"I only have a few minutes, Mandi. We're at the park and—"

"I had to call. I couldn't text this."

Something in my friend's voice stopped me. "What's wrong?"

"Have you seen his social media lately?"

I didn't have to ask who Mandi was referring to. "You know I deleted it. Why?"

"He's there."

"Where?"

"There, Lucy. He's *there*. In Trickle Creek."

I froze, my blood running cold. It had been easy to forget about Ross and our mess of a relationship for the last few weeks. After deleting his social media accounts, I'd found it easier and easier to put him out of my head. Probably the space he'd occupied had been taken up by Craig. I pushed that thought out of my head and focused on what Mandi was saying.

"What do you mean, he's here? Why?"

"You said yourself he used to talk about Trickle Creek all the time. Well, I guess he decided to go for a visit for the last few months of the pregnancy."

Pregnancy.

I'd managed to forget that Ross's wife was pregnant.

"It's a babymoon or something." Mandi was still talking. "One of the hostesses mentioned that she's been under stress, so the doctor recommended rest and relaxation. It wasn't until she said Trickle Creek that I even paid any attention, Lucy. I just needed to give you a heads-up."

"I appreciate it." I looked over in time to see Meri racing down the slide. She landed on her feet and thrust her arms up in the air. "It's not that small of a town, I'm sure I won't run into him." Even as I said it, I didn't believe my own words. Trickle Creek was that small of a town. But it didn't make it an impossible task. All I had to do was avoid the touristy, busy spots for a few days. No problem.

"I'm sorry, Lucy. I know it shouldn't matter anymore because you're doing so well there, and I know you're over him and everything."

Was I?

To my surprise, the feelings of hurt and sadness that had always lingered when it came to Ross were gone.

I was over him. But that didn't mean I wanted to run into him. Then he'd know that I'd fled to the one place he'd always talked about taking me.

And there was no way I was going to subject myself to that kind of mortification.

"I am over him." I said the words aloud more for myself than Mandi. "But I really do appreciate you letting me know." Meri had waved goodbye to her friend and was heading my way. "I gotta run. But thanks for calling. I'll lay low for a few days so I don't have to deal with him."

I ended the call as Meri joined me, breathless and exhausted from her time at the park.

"So. Fun."

I laughed. "You look like you could use a break." I handed Meri her bottle of water, which she quickly downed.

"Well, I guess we should probably go in search of some more water, huh?" I dusted off my pants and gathered up our water bottles, stuffing everything into my backpack. "And maybe a snack."

"Can we say hi to Dad on the way home?"

The plaza wasn't really on the way home, but in a town the size of Trickle Creek, it wasn't far out of the way. Besides, it was a beautiful day and because it was a professional development day off school, we had all the time in the world.

"Why not?" I held my hand out for Meri. "Come on. You can tell him all about how high you went on the swings."

Chapter Sixteen

CRAIG

I SAID my goodbye and began to make my way toward the mouthwatering scent of sugar and cocoa when my eyes caught on the sight of my older sister struggling to maneuver a large urn out the door of her flower shop, Alpenglow.

"Let me help you with that." I rushed over and handed her my cup of coffee to hold.

Charli groaned and leaned back against the brick wall of her shop. "I can't decide if this coffee smells amazing, or awful. No shade to the Bean Bag, but pregnancy hormones have me messed up. I miss coffee."

I glanced over to see her, eyes closed, inhaling the coffee.

I shook my head. "What are you doing trying to move this?" I easily maneuvered the large clay urn out the door into place. "You shouldn't be doing this type of thing in your—"

"Careful." She shot me a warning look that made me laugh.

"Okay, but seriously. You have to ask for help."

"You know I hate doing that." Charli handed the coffee

back. "It's such a beautiful day, I wanted to get started on some spring flower arrangements."

Charli had a booming flower business that included providing unique seasonal arrangements for most of the shops in the plaza, as well as everlasting bouquets created from her dried flowers and, of course, the fresh blooms she grew in her own local fields in the summer months. It was a lot for one woman to do. Especially a woman who was going to be having a baby in a few months. But I knew better than to point that out to my sister.

"It smells amazing out here." Charli pushed up from the wall and tipped her head back. She inhaled deeply. "Damn. How have you not gained a thousand pounds by now?"

"Easy. She won't let me taste it."

"I can appreciate that." Charli laughed. "She keeps to herself, doesn't she?"

"Who? Mya?"

Charli nodded.

"She does." I shrugged. "I think it's because she's so focused on her work. I tried to introduce her to a few locals, but she didn't seem interested."

"Maybe she's just shy?"

I shrugged. "She's definitely a perfectionist. She's been working on things for weeks now without anything to put in those shiny new display cases. I'm afraid I may have to push the issue soon."

It was the last thing I wanted to do, but at the same time, busy season was only a few weeks away and I wanted the new chocolate products to be well established before then. "Hey, I know you're not drinking coffee, but maybe an ice cream on this beautiful spring day? On the house?"

"It's a little early for ice cream, don't you think?"

"Hey." I pretended to be offended. "That's my business you're talking about. It's never too early for ice cream."

Charli laughed and started toward the Sugar Shack with me. "I don't think this baby likes sugar." She rubbed her tummy. "Do you have any sugar-free options?"

"You're kidding, right? It's ice cream, Charli. Of course I don't have any sugar-free options."

Judging by the look on her face, she most certainly wasn't kidding. "I assume that means you don't have any lactose-free choices?"

I held the door of the shop open for her. "Like I said, it's ice cream. Sugar and lactose are kind of part of it."

She shook her head but offered me a smile to soften what was certainly going to be criticism. "I agree with you."

"You do?"

Charli laughed. "Of course. Ice cream is a sweet, sugary treat. That's what makes it so delicious."

"Exactly."

"But…"

"There are no buts. It's ice cream."

"There are people who can't have sugar or lactose." She pointed to her swollen stomach. "At least not without a few repercussions."

"Then maybe ice cream isn't for them."

Charli's head snapped up. "Why shouldn't it be?"

"For the very reasons you just said. If you can't have extra sugar or lactose, then you can't have ice cream."

"No." She tapped a fingernail on the cooler. "You can't have *this* ice cream."

"What are you saying?" I crossed my arms and leaned back against the counter behind me. "You're saying I should bring in non-ice cream-ice cream just for my pregnant sister?"

"I don't think it's a bad idea." She winked at me. "But I prefer the term specialty ice cream. And yes, that's exactly what I'm saying. I think you're missing out on a growing segment of customers who would love the opportunity to enjoy a sweet treat without sacrificing their dietary requirements. And I don't mean just pregnant women."

Before I could open my mouth to object, Charli fired off a question. "Have you noticed times when a parent will buy ice cream for his or her children, but not one for themselves?"

I dropped my arm and reluctantly nodded. "I have."

"Maybe that person doesn't like ice cream. But maybe they do and just don't have a choice."

"I see what you're saying."

"I thought you might."

She grinned, and I couldn't help but shake my head and laugh. I knew when I'd been beat.

"Honestly, it's not something I ever had to think about before. But this baby is making me think of a lot of things in a different way. Maybe just a small scoop of that raspberry sherbet?" She winked. "Baby better like it."

Ten minutes later, we were settled at the table by the window, each with a scoop of sherbet in front of us.

"I don't want to overstep, Charli, but how are you going to manage…" I gestured toward her stomach. "When the baby comes? I mean, you're busier than ever and I know you have Symon to help, but he'll be right in the swing of things coaching ski season when the baby comes and trust me when I say, a baby is a lot of work."

Thankfully, my sister laughed and didn't take offense to the question. "I can imagine the baby will be a lot of work. But you're right, I'll have Symon to help when he's not on the road. You did it all on your own, Craig, and I can't even begin to think about how much work that was. But you have Lucy now. That seems to be working out pretty well, isn't it? After the six months are up, do you think you'll—"

"I don't know what's going to happen at the end of October, Charli."

"That's when the time's up? End of October?"

"You know it is."

"Will she stay?"

I swallowed hard. I didn't know what she would do. But I did know what I wanted her to do, and I was too afraid to ask whether they were the same thing.

When I didn't answer, Charli pointed her spoon in my direction. "You should ask her."

She wasn't wrong. "I'll think about—" A pair of familiar faces, holding hands and skipping through the plaza, caught my attention.

Charli followed my gaze through the window to where I was looking. "They're pretty cute together."

"Aren't they?" I shook my head, aware I'd spoken aloud, and pushed up from the table. "I'll be right back."

I ignored my sister's laughter as I made my way outside. "Hey, you two."

Meri turned at the sound of my voice and ran into my arms. "Daddy!"

I'd never grow tired of the enthusiasm from my little girl every time I saw her, even if it was only a few hours ago.

"What are you two up to today?" It was a professional development day at Meri's school and over breakfast that morning, we'd been very seriously discussing our options, but we hadn't settled on a plan by the time I left.

"We've already been to the park," Lucy said. "And it's clear that Meri can swing higher than me."

"I can go so high. Higher than anyone else."

"Is that right?" I lifted my eyebrows and glanced at Lucy, who nodded seriously.

"It's like she's flying."

"Well, I don't know if I love the idea of you flying away, but that is pretty cool."

"Silly, Daddy. I'm not going to fly away." Meri rolled her

eyes, and I chuckled. "But Lucy can do the monkey bars better than anyone I've ever seen."

"Is that right?"

Lucy shrugged. "What can I say? I'm part monkey." She tucked her hands under her arm and started to make monkey noises.

"Me too, me too." Meri joined in and the two of them circled me, and I couldn't help but laugh.

"You, too, Daddy."

How could I resist?

I followed suit, adding in some big monkey jumps until we were all laughing.

"Maybe the monkeys would like a scoop of ice cream?"

"Yes!"

"It's not even lunch yet."

"Please, Lucy!"

I took a step back and assessed the situation. It felt odd that my little girl deferred so easily to Lucy after such a short time, but at the same time, it felt kind of okay, too. Maybe even better than okay. But it was easy to see that Lucy cared about Meri, and she did have a point. Still, when Meri looked at me and batted her big lashes, I folded like origami.

"One scoop won't hurt."

"Thank you, Daddy!"

I ruffled her hair as Meri hugged my legs. When I looked up, Lucy was watching me with an expression on her pretty face that I couldn't quite read…and I had the distinct impression I'd just screwed up.

LUCY

I sent Meri ahead into the Sugar Shack to wash her hands before letting her choose the one scoop of ice cream her father had decided was a good idea. At least I could enforce good hygiene, if not good nutritional habits.

It bothered me that he'd overridden my authority on the ice cream because now I was going to have to deal with Meri not wanting to eat her lunch and crashing early from a sugar high while he was at work.

It was true that he was her father. But shouldn't I have some authority if I was the nanny? At the very least, he shouldn't undermine my decisions. It wasn't a good habit to get into unless we wanted total anarchy.

"I'm sorry," he said as soon as Meri was inside. "I shouldn't have agreed to the ice cream." He shook his head. "Not after you said no."

"No. You shouldn't have." I crossed my arms over my chest.

His self-awareness took me off guard. Still, I didn't want to let him off the hook so easily. We'd never discussed these types of situations, and it seemed like a good time to cross such a discussion off the list.

"I don't want you to think that I'm unreasonable."

"I don't."

"But ice cream before lunch is almost never a good idea."

"I agree."

"If she doesn't eat a good lunch, she's going to hit a wall mid-afternoon and then I'm going to have to deal with the crash."

"I know." He nodded. "And I really am sorry."

"Okay." I exhaled sharply. "That was…well, I guess that was a lot easier of a conversation than I thought it would be."

He laughed and touched my forearm. "I really am sorry, Lucy. And I swear, I do know better. I mean, I've dealt with it all. It wasn't fair of me to override you. I think sometimes I forget that you're allowed to make some rules, too. I've been numero uno her whole life. Up till now." He shrugged, and I shook my head.

"I'm not number one."

His smile was kind, if not a bit sad. "Maybe not, but you're sure getting up there. She loves you and she listens to you and…"

A familiar figure at the far end of the plaza caught my eye and stole all my attention. Craig was still talking and apologizing for his misstep, but I wasn't listening. The only thing I could focus on was the dark hair, the broad shoulders, the slight dip of his head as he looked down at—

"Lucy?" Craig squeezed my arm, forcing me back into the moment. "Are you okay? I know I shouldn't have done that, but please don't be upset with me."

"I'm not." I glanced over his shoulder. Ross hadn't seen me, but he wasn't far away. Walking hand in hand with the blonde I'd never met but would recognize anywhere from her caller ID picture. Wifey. How had I been so stupid? It hadn't even been forty minutes since Mandi had called to warn me, and what did I do? I went directly to the busiest part of Trickle Creek. The one place where I'd be sure to run into him.

The couple paused in front of the kitchen store. The woman disappeared into the store while he waited out front.

"Sorry," I said to Craig. "I'm not upset, I just…"

He was only a few shops away and looking around.

"Is everything okay?"

No. Nothing was okay. Not with Ross right there. I hadn't seen him since I kicked him out of my apartment that final time, and I did not want to see him now. Not with Craig there. I couldn't tell Ross that I'd walked away from my career to be a small-town nanny. Wasn't there some sort of rule that when you ran into an ex, you were supposed to show off how much better you were doing without them?

I hated to admit it, but Ross looked good. Way better than was fair, really. And I already knew from Mandi that his restaurant was doing well. Of course it was with Mandi in charge. He hadn't suffered from our breakup at all. Hell, his wife didn't even know about me. It was like nothing happened.

"Everything's fine." I pasted on a smile that probably looked a lot faker than it felt, but I hoped Craig wouldn't notice. "I just need a minute, okay?"

If he didn't believe my less-than-convincing act, he didn't say so.

"As long as you're not upset with me."

Craig flashed me a grin that in any other moment would have flipped my stomach and had me thinking all kinds of things. He really was a charming man.

"I'm not," I said honestly. "Promise."

"Can we hug on it?"

And there it was, the little stomach flip that Craig always seemed to incite in me. I really didn't have time to entertain any such thoughts about him right then, but I stepped into his waiting arms and returned his gentle squeeze.

Damn. He smells good.

I knew now the slightly sweet smell that clung to Craig wasn't from the ice cream shop, but because he used his daughter's cotton candy-scented shampoo in the mornings.

Any other time, I would have lingered in Craig's embrace, but there was no time. I gave him a quick pat on the back and stepped deftly away. "I'll be right in, okay? And maybe I will have a scoop after all. Something sugar-free."

Craig laughed. "What is it with you women and your disdain for sugar?" He shook his head and turned for the door. "Don't be long, okay?" He gave me a wink and disappeared inside, with no time to spare.

"Lucy?"

I turned slowly at the familiar voice, taking a quick second to put a smile on my face before I faced him. "Ross?"

I didn't miss the way Ross glanced toward the door Craig had just gone through. Was that a frown?

"What are you doing here?"

"I think I should be asking you that question." His hand-some, a little too self-assured smile was back in place. "I didn't think you'd ever been to Trickle Creek."

"I hadn't. Until recently." I didn't owe him any further explanation. Or really, any explanation at all.

"You look..." He waved his hand before dropping it to his side. "You look really great, Lucy. I've never seen you so... casual."

I glanced down at my outfit of jeans and a flannel. It was true that I'd never owned an outfit like this before and Ross had only ever seen me in dresses or the business casual—with a side of sexy—outfits I wore as manager.

"Well, mountain living requires a bit of a different dress code." I tried to keep my voice light.

"You're living here now?"

I panicked for a moment, unsure how to answer that question without telling him about my job. "Well, my boyfriend lives here and—"

"Your boyfriend?"

I hadn't meant to lie; it had just slipped out.

"Is that who I..." He gestured toward the ice cream shop. "I thought I saw you with someone...but it doesn't..."

"Yes." I doubled down on the lie. "That's my boyfriend. I should actually get—"

"Rossy? Where did you go? I saw the cutest placemats in the store there and—who's this?"

Rossy? I tried not to roll my eyes and instead forced myself to keep my expression neutral as Ross's wife joined us. She threaded her arm through Ross's and leaned against him.

"Sorry, honey. I saw Lucy and came to say hi."

I waited to see how he was going to handle the introduction of his former girlfriend to his current wife.

"Lucy used to work at the restaurant."

"Is that right?" She turned her perfect and completely ignorant face toward me and smiled. "It's nice to meet you, Lucy. I'm Maria. Ross's wife."

I know. I bit my tongue to stay quiet and smiled instead.

"I don't bother myself with the restaurant," Maria continued. "It's just too busy and stressful. I prefer to stay far away and let Rossy handle all that."

Which was why I never knew about you. Again, I struggled to stay quiet. But I didn't win a prize in destroying their marriage. Especially with a baby on the way.

"Rossy practically lives there." Maria put her free hand on her swollen, perfect beach ball of a belly. "Which is why it took the doctor telling him I needed to have some peace and quiet for a few weeks to get him to bring me on this babymoon."

I swallowed hard. "A few weeks?"

"Isn't it great?" Maria grinned. "Rossy rented us the most beautiful house up on the ski hill for the next few weeks. And I get him all to myself."

Few weeks?

I was going to have to deal with him in town for weeks.

"That does sound great." My jaw was getting sore from forcing the smile. "I hope you enjoy your time here. But I really do need to get going."

"Of course. It's so nice to meet you, Lucy."

"It was really nice to see you." Ross reached for me.

Was he really going to try to hug me? In front of his wife? What an ass. I sidestepped him. "Enjoy your stay." I breathed in through my nose and escaped into the relative safety of the ice cream shop before exhaling.

Chapter Seventeen

CRAIG

THERE WAS some sort of documentary playing on the TV, but I had no idea what it was about. It had taken a bit for Meri to settle down and get to sleep. I knew it was my own fault with the ice cream, so I did my best to be patient and read book after book, until finally her eyes closed, and she succumbed to sleep.

By the time I slipped from my little girl's room, Lucy's bedroom door had been closed.

I'd toyed with the idea of knocking to see whether she'd come out and talk to me, but what was I supposed to say? "*Who was that man you were talking to earlier?*"

Or maybe I should just tell her that I was incredibly jealous to see the way she smiled at him.

No. Both ideas were bad. Very bad.

For the hundredth time that day, I wished I hadn't looked out the window of the shop and seen Lucy talking to the man. I blamed my sister for pointing it out. And worse, for insinuating that they knew each other *really* well.

"I can tell," Charli said. "They have a past."

"You can't possibly know that from watching through a window." I tried to sound casual, but I narrowed my eyes and looked harder to see what my sister had noticed. "They're just talking." Even as I said it, I wondered, Was this the man Lucy had cried over earlier? Was this Ross? If it was, should I go out there? Should I—

"Uh huh. They clearly have a past."

"You can't know that."

But she did. *I* did.

I knew instinctively that this guy was the ex. I didn't know how, but I knew that he was the man who'd hurt Lucy and made her cry. A combination of rage, jealousy, and protectiveness rushed through me. I put my hands flat on the table, ready to—

"Daddy! Can I please have two scoops?" Meri called from the other side of the shop, where Kristie was dishing out her treat.

I took a breath and forced myself to calm down.

"One." I held up a finger. "A small one." I gave them both a look. "I mean it. Just a small one, and you better eat all your lunch."

Meri groaned dramatically.

"You're jealous," Charli said as soon as I turned back to my sister and the clear view we had of Lucy and the man outside, who'd been joined by a woman.

"I am not." Jealousy didn't begin to explain what I was feeling.

"You are." She put a spoonful of her treat in her mouth. "But I think the real question is, why?"

"There is no question at all." I shook my head. "And I'm not jealous."

But I was jealous. And worried and angry at the man who would dare to hurt Lucy. It was an unfamiliar feeling, and it was unsettling. And those feelings had sat with me all day, growing and morphing into something bigger. It didn't help that when Lucy joined us inside, Charli immediately asked her about the man.

"Who was that?"

Lucy immediately looked uncomfortable and shifted in her seat a little. She wouldn't meet my eyes, which only confirmed what I knew. "Just somebody I knew from back home."

Her response only fueled the strange feelings simmering inside me, but it wasn't the time or place to push any further.

Long after Lucy and Meri left the shop to continue their day, the feeling remained. It simmered beneath the surface while I sorted through résumés and conducted phone interviews. And then later, when I got home and saw Lucy in the kitchen with Meri preparing dinner, I still couldn't help but think about it.

I'd run about a hundred different scenarios in my head and was on the verge of making myself completely crazy.

I had almost talked myself into knocking on her door to see whether she'd join me for a drink when I heard the snick of the doorknob down the hall.

I jumped up from the couch as Lucy appeared in the living room.

"Hi."

"Hi." I lifted my hand awkwardly. "I thought you might be asleep already."

She shook her head a little. She'd changed out of her jeans and sweater into a pair of leggings and an oversized T-shirt. Her hair was pulled away from her face in a messy bun and as far as I was concerned, she'd never looked sexier.

Oh yes. I was in trouble.

"I couldn't sleep." She gestured to the couch. "Can I sit for a minute?"

"Of course." I grabbed the throw cushion on the far side

of the couch and tossed it to the floor. I waited until she sat before I took my own seat on the far end. "I'm not really watching this…" I picked up the remote. "If there's something else you—"

"This is fine."

I watched her for a moment as she stared, unblinking at the television.

"So that was him, huh?"

Her head spun around, and she stared at me, her mouth open.

"Ross," I clarified. "The man who made you cry."

Her shoulders sagged, and she dropped her head as she nodded. "I forgot I told you about him."

I hadn't.

I'd spent far too many hours thinking about the man who was stupid enough to walk away from her.

"I had no idea he was in town." She tucked a leg underneath her and turned so she faced me.

I shrugged, trying hard to look casual and unaffected. "Does it matter? I mean, do you still—"

"No." She spoke so quickly and with such vehemence that I wanted to believe her, yet she'd clearly been affected by him.

I turned so I, too, faced her. Our knees were close enough to touch.

"It's not what you're thinking, Craig. Really. I'm not…well, it's just…"

The corner of my lip twitched. "And what am I thinking?"

"That I'm acting crazy."

"I don't think you're crazy." I reached for her and let my fingers rest gently on her knee. "Not at all."

"I don't really know why I did it, but I lied to him and told him you were my boyfriend."

Boyfriend.

"Now you probably really think I'm crazy."

I shook my head. "Not even a little bit."

"Then you probably think I'm still in love with him and I was just trying to make him jealous."

I pressed my lips together and took a breath. "Are you?"

"In love with him? No." She inhaled slowly before exhaling with a wry grin. "Trying to make him jealous? Maybe a little."

I laughed and leaned forward so I could take her hand in mine. "Can I tell you something?"

She nodded.

"When I saw you with him, I…" I dropped my head and took a breath, unsure how much to say. Ultimately, I decided on the truth. All of it. "I was jealous. And then I realized who it was you were talking to, and I was angry because he made you cry."

Lucy opened her mouth to say something, but I stopped her gently.

"Let me finish." When she nodded, I continued. "And then I felt this overwhelming urge to swoop you up in my arms and keep you safe from assholes like him because no one should ever make you feel that way. Not even for a second. I'm glad you told him that I was your boyfriend, and I hope it made him think about anything he'd ever done to hurt you and, for even a second, he realized what a damn fool he'd been to let you walk away."

"Craig. I…I don't know what to say. No one has ever said anything like that to me."

"That's a damn shame." I reached out and cupped her cheek. "I have spent the last few weeks trying not to think about kissing you again. And I've failed miserably."

She bit her bottom lip and sucked it between her teeth.

I swallowed back a groan. "I know I probably shouldn't be doing this. But there is no way I can stop myself."

There was no probably about it. I knew I shouldn't do what I was about to do. But I couldn't stop thinking about the taste of her on my lips and the perfect way she fit into my arms.

It had been torture to be so close to her and not touch her. Not press her up against the wall and kiss her the way she deserved to be kissed.

And seeing her asshole ex had only magnified things. She'd told him that I was her boyfriend—well, dammit, maybe I could try to act like one. Even in the slightest way.

I twined my fingers through hers and tugged her toward me until she slid onto my lap. The warm weight of her felt right.

"Craig."

"Lucy."

She leaned in. "We shouldn't."

"No." I shook my head slightly. With one arm holding her against me, I traced the index finger of my free hand gently down her cheek. "We shouldn't." My finger landed on her mouth, and I used it to part her lips. "But I can't stop thinking about you, Lucy." I closed the distance between us so we were only inches apart. "You did say I was your boyfriend, right?"

She nodded.

"Then, I can't think of any reason why we shouldn't."

She sighed, her breath warm on my lips as she closed the distance between us and pressed her lips onto mine.

She tasted just as I'd remembered and fantasized about. Only better. The rest of the world melted away, and we sank into the kiss and each other.

I held her face in place as we took our time exploring each other, easily falling into a rhythm. Lucy shifted on my lap and pressed me back into the cushions, taking charge as my hands came up to her back in gentle encouragement.

At some point, the kissing grew more urgent. As much as I wanted to continue to explore this new part of our relationship, I was all too aware that we were in the living room and if Meri happened to wake up, there would be questions I was completely unprepared to answer.

LUCY

Kissing Craig slowed down time. Nothing else existed when his lips were on mine, and as far as I was concerned, that was perfect.

I'd been fighting my attraction for so long, it hardly felt real that I was finally in his arms with his mouth on mine.

I could kiss Craig forever, and I was fully prepared to do that when he pulled back. I opened my eyes slowly, confused and disoriented until he spoke.

"Meri could—"

"Oh my goodness. Meri!" Mortified, I realized what we'd been doing and what we could have easily gone on to do. What I *wanted* to do. Right there in the living room, where Meri could walk in and find us.

I tried to pull away and put distance between us, but Craig held me in place on his lap. "I'm so sorry I didn't even—"

"Lucy." He put a finger to my lips, stilling me. "You have nothing to be sorry for." He kissed me again. Slow and soft. "And trust me, I want nothing more than to continue this." He groaned a little and bit his bottom lip. "But I don't think either of us are prepared for the questions she'd have if she found us."

"No." I reluctantly slid off his lap and scooted to the far end of the couch, out of reach. I snagged the throw cushion from the floor and held it in my lap like a shield. "You're right. I'm—"

"Please, Lucy. Do not apologize. I kissed *you*. And dammit, I wanted to." His handsome features looked pained, and he wouldn't meet my eyes for a moment. "Did I ever want to. I've wanted to kiss you again since that night in the kitchen. Every time I see you, which is all the time, I think about your lips and how soft they are and how you make me feel things and..." He took a deep breath and exhaled slowly. "I'm the one who should be sorry. I'm your boss and I know this is a unique situation."

Boss.

I flinched at the word and the reminder of exactly what I was doing. And who I was doing it with. I'd gone down that road before.

Look how that had turned out, Lucy.

I wanted to sink into the couch and disappear.

There had to be something fundamentally wrong with me that I continued to get involved with unavailable men. Disgust for my choices—and, more specifically, my mistakes—flooded through me, and suddenly it was impossible to be so close to him. I shook my head and blinked back the hot tears that threatened to spill down my cheeks to make what was already a mortifying situation completely unbearable.

"No. I *am* sorry. You're right. You're my boss, and I was coming in here tonight to...well, I shouldn't have told Ross anything about you. And I definitely shouldn't have told him you were my boyfriend, because that's just the thing." I blew out a breath. "You're not. You're my boss and that was totally unprofessional." I squeezed the pillow tight against my chest and blinked hard. "I'm sorry, Craig." I jumped to my feet. "I understand if you want to fire me."

I turned to go, unwilling to wait around for his response, but Craig's hand on my arm stopped me.

"Lucy. Stop." He tugged my arm gently, and I whirled around into his embrace.

This can't be happening.

I kept my eyes squeezed shut, unwilling to look into his

kind eyes. I'd been beyond stupid to let this happen again. I'd fallen for my boss and now I was going to walk away from the best thing that had happened to me in a very long time.

He held me close and cupped my cheek so tenderly, it was almost impossible to hold the tears at bay. I swallowed hard and shook my head.

"Open your eyes, Lucy. Please."

Reluctantly, I did as he asked and, just as I knew he would be, Craig was watching me with nothing but care and concern in his gaze.

"I'm not going to fire you."

"Then I'll quit."

"You're not going to quit." I started to shake my head again, but he stopped me. "Lucy, you have to know that I wanted to kiss you just as much as you wanted to kiss me." He chuckled. "Hell, probably more. And I'm not going to fire you because I acted on those feelings. And I'm sure as hell not going to let you quit."

There were too many emotions rushing through me. Seeing Ross earlier had thrown me in a big way. Maybe more than I'd realized. On one hand, it had been good to see him and realize that I no longer felt anything for him, except maybe disdain. But it had shaken me to meet his wife, knowing that the poor woman who thought her husband was so amazing had been betrayed. And that I had played a part, even unknowingly, had shaken me.

But none of what I was feeling in that exact moment had anything to do with anyone but the man in front of me.

It was Craig.

"I think I'm falling for you." I blurted out the words before I could change my mind. "No, that's not true. I have fallen for you, Craig. And that's why I have to quit." It was the last thing I wanted to do, but it was the right thing to do. For all of us.

"Quit? No. You can't quit."

"You don't understand, Craig. I have to." I wouldn't meet his gaze as I explained. "You see, Ross wasn't just my ex-boyfriend, he was my boss. I knew I shouldn't have gotten involved with him, but I did it anyway and then when I found out—well, when it didn't work out, my whole life imploded." I sucked in a breath, determined to be strong this time. "And I can't let that happen again. I won't. I can't be that person again."

"You won't be."

"I already am, Craig."

"But this is different."

I chuckled a little, but nothing was funny. "How is this any different?"

"It's different, Lucy, because I'm falling for you, too."

"What?" I tried to pull away, but he held me fast.

"I said that I think I'm falling for you, too." He lifted my chin so I was looking up at him. "The thing is, I don't know what this feeling is, or what to do about it. This is all new to me. All I know is that I like you. A lot. And…I'm pretty sure you like me." He winked, and I laughed.

"I do."

"Let that be enough."

I stared at him incredulously. How could he possibly think it could be that easy?

"We like each other and it's still so new, why do we have to make it more than it is?"

"Remember the whole boss thing?" I tilted my head. "I've been there, done that, and it didn't work out."

"I'm not Ross."

Thank God for that.

"So, you don't have a wife?" I hadn't planned to tell him that detail, but suddenly it became especially important to tell him everything.

Craig's mouth fell open, and he shook his head. "You mean…that woman…"

"His wife." I nodded. "And to be perfectly clear, I had no idea he was married. And the moment I found out, I ended it."

"Wow." Craig took a step away and shook his head. "He was married? And you…"

"I didn't know," I repeated. If Craig thought less of me because of this, it was better I knew right away. There was a part of me that almost hoped he did, because it would be the out I needed in what was only going to be a very complicated situation.

Craig had his back to me, but I didn't rush him while he processed the information I'd just shared.

Finally, he turned around and stepped toward me again. "What an asshole." He took my hands in his and squeezed. "He really did a number on you, didn't he?"

I swallowed hard.

"It wasn't your fault, Lucy. I believe you that you didn't know."

"You do?"

"Of course I do." He was incredulous. "You would never do anything like that to hurt another person, Lucy. And I would never do anything to hurt you." He pulled me close. "Ever. I'm not him. That's in the past."

I nodded. It was in the past. And of course Craig was nothing like Ross. Not even a little bit.

"This is about us now. Can that be enough?"

"Yes." It was more than enough. "But that doesn't change the fact that you're still my boss. I can—"

He pressed a finger to my lips. "Do not say you're going to quit. You can't. It would kill Meri. She would be so upset."

"Even if we were dating?"

Craig nodded. "You have to understand. I've never dated

anyone since Meri came along. It will be very new and…we need to go slowly."

"Okay. So I won't quit."

"No one is quitting." He kissed me softly on the lips. "But I do think we should keep it quiet for a little bit. Just until we figure out what we are."

I opened my mouth to object. I'd been a secret once before. Of course, that was very different, and the situation was clearly not the same. Still, it didn't feel right.

"For Meri," Craig added. "We have to think about her first."

Meri.

He was right. If we told Meri and then things didn't work out between us, Meri would be devastated. That was a different type of heartbreak. One I wasn't completely prepared to deal with.

"For Meri." I nodded. "That makes sense."

"You know what else makes sense?" Craig's lips curled up into a wicked grin. "Us." He pressed me up against the wall and kissed me until my knees grew weak.

CRAIG

Having Lucy in my arms after all this time of only dreaming and fantasizing about it was better than anything I could have imagined. Even if we were still fully clothed and cuddled on the couch instead of naked in bed, twisted up in sheets. The reality was so much better.

I couldn't remember ever feeling so strongly about a woman as I did about Lucy. It had been overwhelming and all-consuming, but now that I'd finally told her how I felt and stopped the ridiculous dance we'd been doing around each other for the last few weeks, everything already felt so much better.

We should have gone to bed hours ago, but neither of us wanted to be the one to end our evening, so after making out like teenagers with one ear listening for the creak of Meri's door opening, we'd finally settled into the couch to watch a movie.

There really wasn't a very big chance that Meri would wake up, but even a minimal risk was too much. And for that reason, I'd worked hard to keep things very PG with Lucy, despite every cell in my body wanting to carry her down the hall into my bed, where I could show her exactly how I was feeling about her.

But I was patient.

And having her gentle weight pressed up against me, her head in my lap, was pretty much the best thing in the world. She'd fallen asleep about halfway through the movie, but self-ishly, I still didn't want the evening to end.

Now that the credits were rolling, there was no more putting it off.

I stroked her hair back from her face. "Time for bed, Lucy," I whispered.

In response, she snuggled further into my lap.

I dropped my head back and stifled a groan before forcing myself to do the right thing.

I wiggled out from under her and stood for a moment, watching Lucy sleep.

She was absolutely gorgeous. I did not want to wake her up. How could I? She looked so peaceful.

I was no stranger to carrying sleeping females to bed, but I was, however, very out of practice for anyone over the age of five.

Somehow, I didn't think it would be a hardship.

I knelt and gently scooped my arms underneath Lucy. I

stood slowly, and she naturally fell toward me, wrapping her arms around my neck.

Unable to resist, I paused to kiss her softly on the cheek before moving carefully down the hall to her room.

Garfield was curled up in the center of her bed, and the cat did not look impressed to see me. Especially considering it meant moving. I nudged the cat over, and Garfield mewled in protest but jumped off the bed long enough for me to pull the comforter back before carefully lowering Lucy to the mattress.

I stifled a yawn and pulled the blankets up over her still-sleeping body. "Good night, Lucy." I bent to give her one final kiss.

"Don't go." Her eyes weren't open, and I almost thought she was talking in her sleep, except she said it again before adding, "Please?"

It was already after one in the morning. I was exhausted. Still…

"Only for a second."

Before I could talk myself out of it, I moved to the other side of the bed so I could spoon Lucy from behind. Cognizant that I couldn't stay, I didn't get under the blankets. Which was probably a good choice, because when Lucy wiggled backward into me, my body forgot my exhaustion and reacted with intensity.

I groaned a little and nuzzled into her neck, inhaling the sweet scent of her.

The last thought in my head before I drifted off to sleep was that I was going to need a miracle to drag myself away from her.

Fortunately for me, that miracle came in the form of a large, very heavy cat with no sense of personal boundaries who walked over my face a few hours later, startling me awake an hour before my alarm was set to go off.

Chapter Eighteen

LUCY

I STIFLED a yawn and poured the hot water over my teabag. I was exhausted from the late nights spent with Craig, talking, cuddling, and sneaking kisses over movies that neither of us actually watched.

Despite the lack of sleep and the fact that we still hadn't been together physically, for the first time in my life, I felt like I was building something solid with a man.

It was definitely worth the lack of sleep.

After the first night when Craig had carried me to bed and I'd convinced him to stay with me—something I did not remember doing—we made an agreement to be more careful. If it hadn't been for Garfield's lack of personal space, Meri could have found us that way in the morning, and the last thing either of us wanted to do was scare or confuse her in any way.

Craig was right; we needed to move slowly and cautiously where Meri was concerned. Initially, I hadn't loved the idea of keeping our blooming relationship a secret, but I could see that it was the right choice. At least for the time being.

I swallowed back another yawn and eyed the coffeepot I'd just set to brew. It was mornings like this one where I was tempted to shift my caffeine source. Or maybe double up. I was up extra early this morning for a very special reason.

"Good morning."

Craig, somehow looking much more rested than I was, walked into the kitchen, fresh out of the shower. I poured him a cup of coffee, but he ignored it in favor of giving me a kiss.

"Good morning to you," I said as he pulled away. I was suddenly much more awake, my senses filled with the sexy scent of him.

He moved in for another kiss, but I put the mug of hot coffee between us. "The birthday girl is going to be awake any minute. Did you see what I did to her door?"

Craig laughed. "I did. It's amazing. What's the idea again?"

It was my turn to laugh. "It's something my mom used to do for me. She'd string crepe paper back and forth across the door and then when I woke up, I would burst through the doorway and into a new year. I thought it might be fun for Meri."

"She's going to love it." For the first time, Craig looked around and took in my early morning efforts. "And she's going to love this."

I smiled. Birthdays were important, especially to six-year-olds, and I wanted Meri to feel extra special when she woke up, which was why I'd sacrificed sleep in favor of blowing up dozens of balloons that now hung from ribbons attached to the ceiling. There was also a banner taped to the wall over Meri's spot at the kitchen table and a tiara at her place setting.

"You're amazing."

"I know." I winked in his direction and laughed as he shook his head.

"I mean it, Lucy." Craig reached for me and pulled me quickly into his arms. "You're absolutely incredible." He kissed me at the same moment we heard the crack of Meri's bedroom door.

"She's awake!" I pulled away from his arms and sprinted down the hall right as Meri came face-to-face with the crepe paper streamers.

The little girl rubbed her eyes in confusion.

"Remember when I told you I had a surprise for you if you got up on your own to your alarm?"

Meri nodded, and Craig looked at me in surprise.

I hadn't told him that I'd convinced Meri to try her alarm clock in the mornings.

"Here it is, kiddo." I waved my arms toward the decorated doorway. "It's a big day, remember? You get to burst your way into a brand-new year."

Through the streamers, I saw the recognition dawn in Meri's eyes.

"Did you forget it was your birthday?" Craig asked.

"Of course I didn't! Can I do it now?"

Craig grabbed his phone and started to record. "Go for it, kiddo!"

Meri didn't have to be told twice. She took a small running start and with a whoop, burst her way into a new year.

CRAIG

Lucy had done an amazing job making the morning special for Meri, but it wouldn't be complete without my annual contribution.

I worked meticulously at the stovetop, pouring batter into a perfect 6. It only took me three tries before I had a pancake that I deemed acceptable.

"What is it?" Lucy peered over my shoulder.

"It's the number six." I stared incredulously at her. "See?" I gestured wildly to the pancake bubbling in the pan. It was almost the perfect shade of golden. "How can you not—"

The words died on my lips as Lucy started to giggle. "I'm kidding. It looks great."

It did look pretty good. "It was a whole lot easier than last year."

"Easier than a five? I bet." She gave me a quick kiss on the cheek.

I spun around, but Meri hadn't been there to witness the kiss.

"Don't worry. The birthday girl is still getting dressed." Lucy winked.

Of course she was. We'd gotten really good at sneaking in little moments while Meri was in the other room, or getting dressed, or even a few times, looking in the opposite direction. I knew we were taking too many chances, but it was getting harder and harder to keep my hands off Lucy.

We still had almost four months to go before we could reevaluate the situation but I already knew exactly how I wanted things to look going forward, and it had nothing to do with hiding our growing feelings. For now, however, it was so much easier to keep it to ourselves rather than deal with the criticism and concern from my siblings and the questions from Meri.

There was something kind of fun about having a secret that was ours and ours alone.

I moved the pan off the heat and moved quickly to press Lucy up against the counter.

"What are you—"

"Ssh." I kissed her and let a hand travel down her body. My body responded at once to the taste and touch of her.

We still hadn't been alone together, and although the anticipation of finally having her naked in my bed had given me more than enough material to fuel some very hot fantasies while I sought relief alone, I knew even my sexiest fantasy wouldn't come close to the real thing.

Soon.

She groaned and pressed her body against mine for a moment before pulling away. "The birthday girl is going to be here any second. And I don't think this would be her idea of a present today."

She was right. And sure enough, only seconds after I stepped away from her, Meri flounced into the kitchen.

"It smells like pancakes!"

"You know it does." I returned to the stove, grabbed a plate, and slid my masterpiece onto it. "What do you think?"

Meri clapped her hands. "I'm six!"

"You sure are, kiddo." Lucy led her to the table and settled the tiara onto her head. "Now, would the birthday princess like syrup or whipped cream and strawberries?"

Meri's eyes grew wide, and I laughed when she declared that she had to have both.

I leaned back against the counter as Lucy drizzled syrup on Meri's huge number six pancake before spraying whipped cream on it and dropping strawberries on the top.

I shook my head, but I couldn't keep the smile off my face. In all the years I'd been making my daughter's birthday pancakes, six was proving to be the best one yet.

"What do you think your dad's smiling at?" Lucy had a wicked grin on her face. She pointed the whipped cream can at me. "Do you think he wishes he had some whipped cream?"

Meri picked up on her meaning right away. "Oh yeah."

"I think so, too." Lucy held the whipped cream can out and stalked toward me.

It took a valiant effort to keep my thoughts G-rated, because I could think of about a million things I'd like to do with that whipped cream and the woman who wielded it.

"You want some, don't you?"

I swallowed hard.

"Behave." She mouthed the word at me before aiming the can directly at me and pressing the nozzle.

Meri squealed with delight as my face was covered in whipped cream.

"I can't believe you did that." I reached up and wiped whipped cream from my cheek before putting the finger in my mouth to lick the sweetness off.

Lucy's eyes widened, and she licked her own lips.

If only we were alone.

I swallowed back my growing desire and before she could react, I wrapped an arm around Lucy and pressed her back up against my chest. With my free hand, I snatched the can of cream from her and with Meri cheering and screaming in delight, I covered Lucy's face in the sweet stickiness.

A full-fledged whipped cream fight ensued, with Meri standing on her chair, breakfast forgotten as she took turns cheering for both of us until finally Lucy declared it a tie because we needed to get cleaned up and get organized for Meri's birthday party.

Lucy tossed me a towel to clean up.

I made sure Meri's attention was back on her breakfast before following Lucy to the sink. "I think we both know who won that one," I whispered in her ear.

She spun around, so there was only inches between us. "I never lose." She winked. "And not to worry, I'll claim my prize later."

"Promises, promises." I forced myself to walk away and headed straight into a cold shower.

LUCY

Saturday was technically my day off, but I didn't care. More and more, I chose to spend my time off with Craig and Meri because it was so much better than the alternative. There truly was nothing else I would rather be doing with my free time than spending it with them.

I knew exactly what Mandi would say about it if I told her. Which was why I'd kept that particular piece of information from my best friend. Not that I'd been able to keep everything from Mandi, though. She had some kind of specially honed radar for the juicy details and had somehow sensed from a simple video chat that Craig and I were involved.

Involved.

It didn't seem like an adequate word for what Craig and I were. But at the same time, I had no idea what we were.

What I did know was that I would like very much for us to be more. Meaning, it had been a very long few weeks and if we didn't find ourselves with some time alone soon, I was afraid we might break down and take a risk in order to finally be together.

I was trying very hard to respect the fact that Craig wanted to keep our relationship quiet, but it was becoming harder and harder. And for the life of me, I was having trouble remembering why exactly he'd wanted to in the first place.

My phone vibrated in my pocket, pulling my attention as I left the car in the parking lot behind the plaza.

> Did the birthday girl like her surprise this morning?

I grinned and tapped out a response to my mom.

> She loved it. And Craig made her a pancake in
> the shape of a six. He does it every year.

I smiled to myself at the image of Craig working hard over the stovetop to create the perfect pancake. It was one of the sweetest things I'd ever seen.

> That's so sweet. Tell Meri happy birthday for
> me. I hope to meet her one day.

I hoped that, too. Only maybe by the time my mom met Meri and Craig, I'd officially be more than just the nanny.

I ended the text exchange with my mother and tapped the buttons to pull up my to-do list for the morning. I was in charge of the last-minute supplies for Meri's party up at the big house while Craig took his daughter out for their traditional day together.

Every time I heard about another little tradition the two of them had together, the more I fell for him. He was absolutely the best dad I'd ever met. And that was exactly why I trusted him when it came to the right time to talk to Meri about our relationship. Besides, now that Meri was six, he'd committed to talking to her about her mother. And that was probably enough for a little girl to handle all at once.

Ten minutes later, I was questioning my judgment as I wrestled two huge bouquets of helium-filled pink and purple balloons through the door of the Sugar Shack. I probably should have picked up the ice cream for the party first, but I didn't want to risk it melting while I waited for the balloons.

"It looks like you have your hands full there."

I jumped at the voice behind me. Caught off guard, I didn't have a chance to put a smile on my face before I turned around to face Ross.

It had been weeks since I'd run into him, and I'd been so caught up in my life—and Craig—I'd hardly given him, or the fact that he was still in town, a second thought.

"What are you…"

"Ice cream." Ross shrugged. "Maria has a craving and once she discovered how good the ice cream is here, she wants it all the time."

Right.

Pregnant wife.

"I guess pregnancy cravings are a real thing." I raised my eyebrows and tried to move past him, unwilling to have any further conversation with him when he stopped me.

"Lucy, I'm actually really glad I ran into you."

I shook my head and tucked the balloons into the corner behind a table, using the weights of the bouquets to keep them from flying away. "I don't really have time to—"

"I wanted a chance to say…"

Was he going to apologize to me? I hesitated. I might just have time in my day for that. I straightened my shoulders and waited as he continued.

"Well, I appreciate it that you didn't say anything to Maria the other day about…well…"

"*Us?*" The word came out with a lot more venom than I'd intended. "You appreciate that I didn't tell your pregnant wife that we *dated?* Is that what you appreciate?" I didn't wait for an answer. "Did you really think I would, Ross? That I would take some kind of perverse pleasure in destroying another woman's happiness?" I narrowed my eyes, unable to reconcile the man I'd once cared about with the piece of shit in front of me. "I'm not that woman," I said with a final shake of my head. "That's exactly why I broke up with you, remember? Because I refused to be *that* woman."

I crossed my arms over my chest to keep from vibrating. "Do I think it's pretty shitty that she doesn't know what an asshole her husband is? Yes. Do I think she deserves better? Absolutely. No woman deserves to be with a man who doesn't put her first. But it's not my job to tell her that, Ross. And don't think for a second that I stayed quiet to protect you."

I scoffed. "That's the last thing you deserve. But I'm not worried about that either, because life has a way of working out. You'll get what you deserve. But as for me, I'm done with you. Now if you'll excuse me, my boyfriend's little girl is turning six today and I have a party to get to."

I didn't wait for a response before I walked away, but as I disappeared into the relative safety of the back room, I did hear him mutter something that sounded a lot like crazy bitch —and that was just fine with me.

Chapter Nineteen

CRAIG

THE BIG HOUSE had been completely overrun by children, and already I was exhausted, even if the kids showed no signs of slowing down.

It was good that Meri was having so much fun with her friends; she wouldn't even notice that her uncle Andy had to cancel his trip to town. My best friend had called an hour earlier to let me know he'd been held up in Vancouver and wasn't going to make it to Meri's birthday after all.

Andy had always made it a point to make Meri feel special, and she looked forward to his visits. Even last year, she would have been devastated to learn that Andy couldn't make it. Now, though, it seemed she'd moved into the stage of life where her friends were more important. I wasn't ready.

I couldn't help but smile, although it made me a little sad to see how fast my little girl was growing up.

There was a giant unicorn piñata hung from the ceiling of the great room. A little boy I vaguely recognized from Meri's class swung a stick around while the unicorn spun wildly on the string, just out of his grasp.

"This is going to end badly." Chase appeared at my side while I watched from a safe distance. "I will never understand who thought it was a good idea to give children bowlfuls of candy before blindfolding them and handing them a stick."

I laughed at my older brother, but I couldn't disagree. "Meri insisted on a piñata." I shook my head. "A purple and pink unicorn, to be specific. I have no idea how Lucy managed it, but she found one."

Lucy stood in the center of the throng of children. She was calm and composed as she put a hand out to prevent the whacking stick from smacking a child in the head. I watched her single-handedly manage the children while keeping a smile on her face throughout.

"She's pretty incredible."

I nodded. She was fantastic.

"She's going to deserve some kind of bonus after today." Chase chuckled. "Isn't Saturday her day off?"

I blinked hard before turning to face my brother. More and more frequently, I forgot that Lucy was still the nanny and not my girlfriend. *Not yet.* Leave it to one of my siblings to bring me back to reality.

"It is her day off." I nodded. "But she offered to help out. She loves Meri."

And maybe me, too?

The L word was one that popped up in my head more and more lately, which was crazy, because I'd only known Lucy for a few months and we'd only been *together* officially—whatever that meant—for even less time. Hell, we hadn't even slept together. But I couldn't fight my feelings. I was falling for her harder and harder every single day.

"I'm glad it's working out, Craig. I was worried."

I turned away from the chaos in front of me and focused on Chase. "You were worried?"

"Of course I was." He laughed. "We all were. Or I should say, are. This dad shit isn't easy."

I didn't know about that. Sure, I'd been pissed at first, and if I really thought about it, I was still annoyed that my father had thought I needed help with Meri. After all those years of doing it all on my own, I'd more than proved to everyone that I was an excellent father and I didn't need—okay, maybe I was still pissed. But I wouldn't have thought it hard.

"It's not hard, Chase." I shrugged. "I was told to hire a nanny, so I did."

"And that's that?"

I nodded. "That's that. We're a few months in already. Meri's doing great, Lucy's…well, Lucy's awesome. It's fine."

Chase shook his head and whistled under his breath. "Yeah, I'm glad you think that now."

"What? It *is* fine. Dad's getting what he wanted and I'm…" I swallowed hard. Apparently, I was still upset about it all. "I'm fine. Compared to Charli, I think I'm getting off easy."

"What about me?"

It was my turn to laugh. "All you had to do was stay in town for six months. I would hardly call that a hardship." I elbowed him in the ribs. "Besides, you got to spend those six months with Annie." I raised an eyebrow. "You can't tell me that was awful."

"It was definitely not awful." Chase winked. "What about you?"

"Annie's great, but I haven't spent much—"

"You know I'm not talking about Annie." He looked at me pointedly. "What's going on with you and Lucy?"

For a split second, I contemplated telling my brother the truth. That I was falling a little bit more in love with my nanny every day that passed. I swallowed hard and did a quick scan of the room. Besides the gaggle of children, all my siblings were in attendance for their favorite niece's party. I took a moment, looking at each of them. Would they understand if I was involved with Lucy? Or would they freak out? It was hard to tell how each of them would react. I returned my focus to Chase, who watched me intently. If anyone would understand, it would be my eldest brother.

Before I had the chance to confide in him, I noticed Asher walking in our direction with a handful of beer bottles.

"Every good children's party needs some adult beverages, am I right?" He handed us each a bottle.

"It's definitely not a bad idea." We tapped the necks of the bottles together in a cheers and took a drink before Asher spoke again.

"It looked as if the two of you were having a pretty serious conversation. I didn't mean to interrupt."

I shot him a look, and he laughed.

"Okay, I did mean to interrupt. But only because it's a party. No serious conversations allowed."

Both Chase and I cast our brother a suspicious glance, and he laughed again. "I am capable of being sensitive to a situation, you know?"

"Is that what this is?" Chase shook his head. "You being sensitive?"

"Hey, take what you can get."

"Don't worry," I added. "We will."

There'd been a time when I wasn't sure I'd ever again be standing with both my brothers, sharing a beer without arguing. Begrudgingly, I had to admit that our late father was responsible for all of us coming back together by forcing Chase to stay in town for a period of six months after he'd died.

But just because there'd been a happy outcome from Chase's particular stipulation didn't mean I expected the same kind of outcome. I just needed to get through it.

"So, what are we talking about?"

"Well, we're not talking about anything going on between Craig and Lucy, that's for sure."

I almost spat out my beer. "Dude."

"Good. There better not be anything going on." The smile on Asher's face had been replaced with a frown. "You can't risk it, Craig. This isn't just your life you're screwing with here."

"I know." I shook my head. "And there's not anything going on."

I didn't miss the look my brothers exchanged.

"There's not." I hated lying to them, but it was clear there was no way I could tell them the truth. They would lose their minds, and they would definitely not believe that what Lucy and I had between us was real and that it would absolutely not blow up.

No. It was easier if I kept that to myself for now.

"Seriously, Craig," Asher continued. "I see the way you look at her. We all do."

I looked between my brothers. Chase didn't deny or confirm what Asher was saying. "I look at her like she's an excellent nanny and a good friend."

Asher opened his mouth again but opted for a sip of his beer instead of another objection.

A choice I was just fine with.

"Lucy's just a friend," I said again. To convince them? Or myself? "Don't worry, Asher. Everything is still on schedule, just the way it's supposed to be. It'll be your turn to go through Dad's bullshit soon enough."

Only four more months.

I'd already waited my entire life for a woman like Lucy. I could wait a few more months.

LUCY

I was exhausted. But the party had been a success. All the kids had enjoyed themselves with the activities I'd organized after an extensive online search of party games. And most importantly, the piñata had been a smashing success. Literally.

Most of the kids had been picked up, with only a few of Meri's best friends from school and Grady having stayed later to have some pool time.

Craig had vetoed an entire pool party at the indoor pool when Meri first came up with the idea, a decision I was thankful for because I could not imagine what it would have been like trying to monitor twelve kids in the water at the same time.

The compromise was that Meri could pick two of her closest friends to stay late and have a swim before they, too, were picked up. Despite the fact that they'd been partying for close to two hours already, the kids didn't show any signs of slowing down, but fortunately they were all playing well together and for the first time in hours, I had a chance to get off my feet.

I collapsed in a nearby chaise next to Annie and Charli.

"Great party, Lucy." Annie offered me a beer, but I shook my head.

"I'll have a drink when all the children have been safely delivered back to their parents."

"Fair enough."

"I'll have yours." Kat joined us and grabbed the beer from Annie's hand. She popped the cap off and tipped back the bottle, drinking down half of it while the rest of us watched in wonder.

"Something on your mind, sis?" Charli grimaced. "Or are you just really thirsty?"

"I was just…" She sighed dramatically. "You know when

you're expecting something to happen and you've really been looking forward to it, but then it doesn't happen and you're just…"

"Disappointed?" Annie offered.

"Yes." Kat pointed the bottle in her direction. "Disappointed. I am disappointed." She tipped the bottle back and drank deeply again. "Very, very disappointed."

"Anything you want to talk about?" Annie asked.

"Nope." Kat finished her drink. "Sure don't. But I do need something to do tonight now. What's everyone up to? We should have a girl's night out."

I didn't mean to do it out loud, but I groaned at the idea.

"If you don't want to hang out with us, Lucy, just say so." Charli pretended to look offended.

"Oh no! It's not you guys, honestly." Truthfully, I would have loved to hang out with all of them, and a ladies' night would probably be a lot of fun. Under different circumstances. "I'm straight up exhausted. The only thing I want to do is crawl into bed and sleep for nine hours." I couldn't tell them that besides the party, the reason I was so tired was because I'd been up until well past midnight cuddling with Craig and sneaking kisses the night before. And the night before that. And the night before that.

"Fair enough." Kat nodded. "Another time?"

"Absolutely."

"I'm out, too." Charli stretched backward in her chair and pushed her belly up and out. "Baby says no to late nights."

"Baby doesn't know what she's missing." Kat blew a kiss in the direction of Charli's baby bump. "Annie?"

"I don't know, Kat. I was actually going to offer to keep Meri overnight tonight to give Lucy the night off."

I perked up. A night off?

"Technically, I'm not on the clock this weekend," I admitted. I tried not to look excited about the prospect of Craig and me having the house to ourselves with no chance that Meri could walk in on us at any moment. The last few weeks had been so busy with the school year winding down, and then Meri's birthday, despite the fact that we were in the same house, I felt like I'd barely seen Craig. My body vibrated at the thought of finally being alone with him.

"Lucy?"

I blinked and swiveled in my chair to look at Annie, who stared at me, waiting for a response to a question I hadn't heard. "Sorry. I…what were you saying?"

"You must be tired." Annie laughed. "I was just saying that Craig mentioned how even when you're not officially working, you're always kind of helping out with Meri."

"He did?"

Annie nodded. "He was going on and on about how great you are with her and how hiring you as her nanny was the best decision he'd ever made."

A strange sensation flowed through me. On one hand, I was happy that Craig said such glowing things about me, but on the other, it stung a little to hear that he'd called me the nanny. Which was stupid, because that's exactly what I was. Still.

"I'm glad he thinks it's working out so well."

"Oh, I think it's working out very well." Kat wiggled her eyebrows.

Of all his siblings, I was the most concerned about Kat discovering that there was something going on between us.

I opted to play dumb. "It is. Meri's great."

"And Craig?"

"He's a really great dad."

"He is." Charli looked between us in question. "Is there something—"

"No."

"Nothing."

Kat and I spoke at the same time.

Oh yeah. She definitely knew there was something going on between us. At least, if she did suspect something, she wasn't saying anything.

"Right." Annie drew out the word and shook her head. "I'm too tired for this."

"Me too," Charli agreed. "And honestly, as long as nothing is going on between the two of you, that's a good thing."

Charli's choice of words struck me. Fortunately, Annie asked the question I didn't have to. "Why is that a good thing?"

The smile slipped from Charli's pretty face and was replaced with a serious frown. "Look, I'm not saying that under any other circumstances it wouldn't be awesome if Lucy and Craig…you know…." Her finger danced back and forth.

We all knew what she meant.

"But not in this situation," Charli continued. "Not with everything on the line the way—"

"I don't think we need to go into details." Kat jumped up and put a hand on her sister's shoulder. "And it doesn't matter anyway, because Lucy said there's nothing going on."

"There's not." I hated lying to them, especially now that we were all becoming friends. But it would only be for a little bit longer. Things were going so well between Craig and me, and now that Meri was six, and Craig had committed to talking to her about her birth mother, it was only a matter of time before we would tell her, and the rest of the family, about our relationship.

But what had Charli meant about everything being on the line? I wanted to ask, but the conversation quickly turned, and the women were soon talking about Charli's latest OB appointment. I half listened while I continually scanned the pool and the kids who were thankfully still playing really well together. The other girls' parents would be by in about thirty minutes to pick them up, so we still had a few more minutes before I had to start the process of getting them dried off and changed.

I let my gaze drift around to the edge of the pool room where Craig was in conversation with a man I'd never met, but knew to be a family friend, Steven Larson. The man handed Craig an envelope, but he didn't even look at it before he folded it in half and stuffed it in his back pocket.

"What do you think, Lucy?"

I spun my attention back to the women. "About what?"

"Baby shower before or after the baby is born?" Annie asked. "I say, before."

"Nope." Kat shook her head. "It's bad luck."

"It is not bad luck. It's practical."

"Just because it's practical doesn't mean you should risk it."

Charli's head swung back and forth between them as they debated the issue. "Lucy? Please help."

"Well…" I bit my bottom lip. "I don't think it's bad luck to have the shower before the baby is born. But—" I added quickly before Kat could protest. "I do know a lady who had two baby showers before her little girl was born. She got heaps of dresses, and pink blankets, for baby Samantha. And then she had a boy." I shrugged to make my point. "So, there's that."

"No way? That did not happen."

"It sure did," I told Annie.

"Well, that won't matter to me anyway." Charli rested her hand on her belly. "Because I'm not finding out either way. We want to be surprised."

"I still don't think it's a good idea." Kat shook her head. "But I guess it's not my choice." She crossed her arms over her chest, and Charli laughed.

"What is the problem with you today? Seriously."

"You are acting…off." Annie shrugged.

I didn't know her well enough to make that determination, but my new friend didn't seem herself.

"I'm fine. Just disappointed in…well, it doesn't matter. Maybe it's best if we don't have a ladies' night after all. I'm probably not good company." She left her empty beer bottle on the table. "I'm going to take off, girls. I'll catch up with you all later."

"What do you think's going on with her?" Charli mused as soon as she was out of earshot.

"It's a guy," Annie, who had been close friends with Kat for years, said casually. "It's gotta be. She only acts crazy like that when it's a man."

Charli's eyes widened, but she nodded in agreement. "Makes sense."

It did. At least to me, who was currently feeling a certain level of crazy over a man herself.

Chapter Twenty

CRAIG

IT TOOK a herculean effort for me not to rush out of the big house and race straight back to the house, where I knew Lucy was home. Alone. For the first time since…well, in what felt like forever.

After Annie and Chase told me they'd asked Meri to stay for a sleepover with Grady and a movie night in the theater room, Lucy offered to pack up the presents and take them home.

The poor woman looked exhausted. She'd worked so hard to make Meri's party perfect. My brothers were right—she definitely deserved a bonus of some kind—and I planned to show her exactly how much I appreciated her as soon as I got home.

As soon as it was reasonable, I gave the birthday girl a big hug and kiss, and told her good night. "I'll pick you up in the morning, okay, kiddo?"

"Can you wait until after lunch? I want to go swimming with Grady again."

"Only if it's okay with Uncle Chase and Annie."

"It's more than fine with us," Annie said. "I know Lucy can use the break. So make sure she sleeps in and takes tomorrow off."

I examined Annie closely, looking for any indication that she knew more about the situation than she'd let on. I was fairly sure that Lucy wouldn't have said anything, but Annie was perceptive. Maybe she'd figured it out.

"Sunday is Lucy's day off."

"So was Saturday," Annie said pointedly. "I know she loves Meri, but if she doesn't take a real day off, I'm going to kidnap her and take her camping or something."

I laughed. Lucy was a proper city girl. I couldn't imagine that her idea of relaxing would be sleeping in a tent or cooking over a fire. Although, I personally did like the idea of having her all to myself in the great outdoors.

I forced the thought from my head and focused on the moment. "I'll make sure she doesn't work in any way."

Annie appeared satisfied with my response and didn't give any further indication that she thought something more was going on.

Twenty minutes later, I was home. The house was quiet, but Lucy's car was parked out front and the pile of presents had been deposited on the coffee table in the living room.

"Lucy?"

For a moment, I thought she might be asleep, but then I heard the sound of the shower and my body lit up with increased anticipation of a wet, naked Lucy. I stripped my clothes off and knocked on the bathroom door as I twisted the handle.

I stepped into the steam-filled room and fisted my already hard cock. "You have room for one more in there?"

I hesitated when nothing but silence greeted me. It was

Lucy in the shower, wasn't it? Andy hadn't decided to come to town after all, had he?

Shit.

I didn't have time to overthink it any further because the shower curtain slid over, and Lucy poked her head out. "It took you long enough." Her eyes traveled the length of me, widening as they lowered to the evidence of my arousal. "Get in here."

"I thought you'd never ask."

She took a step backward as I entered the stall, crowding us in the small space. I hardly registered the hot water as I moved. "I've been waiting all day for this." My mouth crashed onto hers and as soon as my lips were on hers, nothing else mattered.

"I've been waiting a lot longer than a day." She groaned and pressed her slick, curvy, absolutely fucking perfect body against mine.

The water pelted my back. I pushed her up against the tile wall and let my hands move down Lucy's curves. My hands explored her perfect, lush tits. I pressed them together and lowered my mouth to worship their perfection. My tongue lapped up the water that ran off her in rivulets before I sucked one nipple between my lips.

She groaned and arched her back, pressing forward, which only encouraged me to suck more before releasing the nipple and turning my attention to the other one. After all, fair was fair.

Her fingers laced through my hair, and she squirmed beneath me.

"I need you so bad, Craig."

The need was entirely mutual, but before I had her, I needed to worship her. I pulled my head away from her delicious tits and looked up. "You are so fucking sexy, Lucy."

"Take me to bed, Craig."

I shook my head and my cock throbbed in protest. "Not yet." I sank to my knees on the shower floor, the hot water hitting me in the back of the head. "There's something I need to do first."

She tried to move, but I held her in place, pressing her gently up against the tiles with one hand, while my other hand pushed her legs apart.

"Craig, I—"

Her words were lost as I ran my tongue along the seam of her sex. She shivered and vibrated under my attentions, and it didn't take long before she stopped trying to speak at all. She tasted sweeter than I'd expected, and in seconds, I knew I'd never be able to get enough of her.

I lost myself in her, exploring every inch of her deliciousness as her body slowly came undone around me. Again, her hands twisted in my hair, only this time she braced herself against me as her first orgasm crashed through her.

She cried out her pleasure, and I groaned in appreciation of her release. I didn't move right away, soaking in the moment.

"Holy shit, Craig." Lucy was still shaking her head with her eyes closed as I got to my feet. When she opened her eyes and saw me, her lips curled up into a wicked grin, and her hands were once more on my body.

It was my turn to groan as her hands traveled between my legs. When she wrapped her hand around my cock and squeezed, I was sure I was going to lose control right then and there. "Fuck, Lucy. I need you."

Her eyes sparkled, and she squeezed again before letting her hand slide up and down the length of me.

I groaned. "I will not be able to be held responsible for my actions if you keep doing that."

"Good."

LUCY

My body was still vibrating from the incredible orgasm he'd just given me, but I needed more. I needed so much more.

Still dripping wet, I managed to snag a towel from the shelf as we kissed and groped our way out of the bathroom and into the hallway.

"Hold on." I gasped for breath and attempted to wrap the towel around my dripping mass of hair.

"Don't you dare cover up." Craig tried to snatch the towel away. "I like you naked." A low growl vibrated from him. "I like you naked very, *very* much."

"It's my hair." I giggled and once more tried to wrap my hair.

This time, Craig was successful in snatching the towel.

"Leave it." He tossed it behind him, back into the bathroom. "Please."

"But I'm dripping—"

"I like you dripping." He wiggled his eyebrows, and I laughed.

"Not like that."

"Oh yes." He stalked toward me and pressed my naked body against the wall. "I think it's very much like that."

He once more devoured me in a kiss, and I forgot all about the towel.

"I need you, Lucy."

I could feel exactly how much he needed me. The hard length of him pressed against my belly. I reached down between us and wrapped my hand around him. When he groaned and tipped his head back, I grinned and stroked him slowly.

"Woman…"

"Yes?" I bit my bottom lip and did it again, enjoying the way he moaned and every muscle in his body tensed because of my touch. "You don't want me to stop that, do you?"

"I don't want you to ever stop." He closed his eyes and tilted his head back for a moment before regaining his senses. "But if you don't, I'm afraid this will be over before it begins because, dammit." He growled again and then, before I could react, he grabbed both my hands and pinned them against the wall over my head.

I swallowed hard and grinned. "You do know we have all night, right?"

"Oh I know. And I plan on using every single minute of it." He kissed me, and sucked on my bottom lip as he drew back. "And those plans start with being inside you."

I had no problem at all with that plan, and there were no objections when he led me across the hall to his bedroom and laid me back on the pillows.

He took a moment to retrieve a condom from the night-stand and sheath himself before joining me on the bed again. Hovering over me, Craig caged me with his arms.

He bent down to kiss me as he lowered his entire body between my legs and pressed himself inside me. A groan slipped from my lips as he filled me completely.

"Lucy." My name was barely a whisper on his lips as he gave me a moment to let me adjust to him. "You feel amazing."

My body tightened, already seeking release.

I exhaled a ragged breath, and we began moving together in unison as if we'd always been together. Our bodies knew what to do and responded perfectly to each other.

Never before had I experienced a connection with a man that came close to what I was feeling with Craig. I stared deeply in his eyes as we moved together, completely in tune with each other.

"I've been dreaming of this moment for what feels like forever."

"You're not the only one." I clutched the muscles on his back and arched up into him as another orgasm began to build deep inside me.

"Oh, yeah, baby. Come for me."

I did not have to be asked twice, not with Craig.

I squeezed my eyes against the storm of sensations that spiraled up within me and finally burst in a crescendo of color and pleasure that sent me spinning. I cried out as he, too, took his release along with me.

It wasn't until I came back down to myself that I opened my eyes again to see Craig watching me with a small smile.

"That was... I can't even..."

"I feel exactly the same." He kissed me tenderly and brushed a strand of wet hair from my cheek. "Damn, Lucy. Where have you been my whole life?"

I laughed as he rolled off me and pulled me up onto his chest for a cuddle. "I'd say that was worth the wait." I kissed his bare chest and snuggled closer to him. "Very much worth the wait."

"Just so you know..." He chuckled, and I shook with the vibration. "Now that I know how fucking amazing that is...I definitely won't be waiting that long again."

I moaned my agreement and twisted a leg up over his. My hand drew lazy patterns on his chest before my fingers slipped a little farther south.

Craig caught my hand in his, and I protested, "Hey. You're not the only one who doesn't want to wait again." I looked up and smiled mischievously when our eyes met.

"You're trouble, Lucy."

"You know it." I wiggled my naked body against his. "And you love it."

"I do."

I froze.

Did he just say that?

Surely he didn't mean it. Not like that.

"Lucy?"

I nodded and blinked but didn't speak.

He reached down and brushed my cheek gently. "I do, you know? I love it. And I love this, too." His mouth once more found a nipple.

And soon his sucking and nibbling made me forget everything but sensations he easily pulled from me. Over and over again.

Chapter Twenty-One

CRAIG

"FRIDAY," I repeated for the third time. I hadn't wanted to put pressure on Mya and the chocolates she'd been producing, but it was long past time to have the official launch and now that the busy summer season was officially upon us, we were out of time. "You're ready, Mya."

"I'm not ready."

I sympathized with her perfectionism, but she was wrong. She was ready. The chocolates were ready, and the town was more than ready. I'd been fielding questions from the other business owners in the plaza about when they could reliably send their customers for the delicious confections they'd had the opportunity to taste periodically over the last few weeks.

"Mya. Everything you've made is delicious." I knew it didn't matter what I said to her; the woman was a strict perfectionist and she'd found issues with every single product she'd put out so far.

"They're okay." She shook her head. "But I need consistency. I don't know if it's the altitude here, but I'm really struggling to make every batch consistent."

I put my hand on her arm and looked her in the eyes. "Mya, every single thing you've made has been amazing. We need to start selling them."

That was an understatement. Chase had tried to explain that there'd be a period of loss while Mya got settled in the shop and we figured out our offerings for the Sugar Shack, but it had been too long. It was time to start selling the chocolates and building up the brand recognition, and there was no better time than the already busy summer season.

"I already have interest from a few of the vacation rental properties in town to offer welcome packages to their guests, at least two restaurants would like to offer the chocolates, and I'm hoping for even more interest in the form of walk-in traffic." The potential for the chocolates was huge. But we needed to move forward. "We're going to have an open house on Friday. Lots of samples and some takeaway gift boxes to purchase. I'll extend the invite to all the business owners in the—"

"Friday?"

I could see the panic in her eyes, but in the short time I'd known her, I'd already figured out that although Mya seemed to be confident and self-assured in almost every other aspect of her life, when it came to her work, she definitely had a few hangups. Maybe it was like that with all artists? I certainly considered Mya an artist at what she did.

I smiled kindly and despite the fact that I desperately wanted to get out of there and leave work behind, I slowed down and gave her a moment. "Mya, please believe me when I tell you that your chocolates are amazing, and the community is going to love them. There's a reason Chase brought you here. You're incredible. I wish you could see that."

A flicker of something I couldn't quite read crossed her face, and I was sure she was going to object again.

Instead, she swallowed hard and pulled her shoulders back. "You're right. I'm ready for this."

"You are ready for this." I grinned. "Friday, okay?"

"Friday." She nodded and wiped her hands down the sides of her white chef's coat. "I'll be ready."

"I like that attitude." I patted her on the back and gathered up my things. "Let me know if you need anything, okay? I'm going to leave you alone to work your magic and I'll be back tomorrow morning."

I left her standing over the stove in the kitchen, checked in with Kristie and the summer staff we'd hired, who all seemed young and energetic. Confident I was leaving the shop in good hands, I slipped away before I could be called back for anything else, jumped in the car, and headed straight out of town.

It had been about a week since I'd finally been alone with Lucy, and it had been one of the best nights of my life. And it wasn't just the sex. Although that had been very memorable indeed. It had been so much more. We'd talked and cuddled, and she'd fallen asleep on my chest before waking up to make love again. We'd cooked grilled cheese sandwiches in the middle of the night and eaten them naked at the kitchen table.

Neither of us could keep our hands off each other, and it wasn't until long after the sun came up that we'd finally fallen asleep, tangled in each other's embrace.

Now that I'd had a taste of her, I couldn't stay away. Every night since, I'd disregarded my own rules and snuck into Lucy's room. Most nights, we made love quickly and quietly, but some nights it was just about being together. She fit in my arms perfectly, and it became harder and harder to slip out of her bed and return to my own, very empty one.

Being with her was easy, and when all three of us were together, we were really a little family, which was problematic only because it was getting harder for me to remember why I couldn't tell anyone about us. Especially when the only thing I wanted to do was scream it from the rooftops.

I just needed to get through the summer. The end of October would mark our six months and I'd be done with my part of the whole stupid stipulation of my father's will thing and I could move on with my life. With Lucy.

The prospect of being with Lucy for real made me giddy like a teenage boy with his first girlfriend. It had been a very long time since I'd even let myself imagine a life that included a woman. In many ways, I'd convinced myself that it wasn't something I wanted or needed. Meri and I had done just fine without anyone else. Despite what my father had clearly thought, I hadn't actually needed a nanny for my daughter. But I did have to admit, I was sure glad I had one. More for me than for Meri. Although, I couldn't deny that Meri had benefited from Lucy's presence as well.

Get through the summer.

I pulled my car into the parking lot at the lake, next to Lucy's car.

I hadn't been sure when I'd be able to sneak away from the shop, so Lucy had insisted on bringing all of the picnic supplies herself for our first summer picnic together.

A smattering of other small groups were scattered around the grassy area just above the beach, but I found my girls right away. I watched for a moment and took in the scene of Lucy and my daughter working together to pile the sand in one big heap. My heart swelled and a smile took over my face.

"Daddy! You're here!" Meri abandoned the sand pile and ran full speed toward me.

I caught her sandy body and lifted her into a quick spin before holding her against me and walking through the sand toward Lucy. She'd stood up, but was also still covered in sand. She wore a white tank top over a bright-pink bikini top. The matching bottoms showed off her long, lean legs.

"Hey. You made it."

More than anything, I wanted to pull her into my arms, sand and all, and give her the greeting she deserved.

"I'm glad you're here, Daddy." Meri twisted around in my arms. "You can help us with our sand tower."

"I'm glad I'm here, too." I kissed her on the top of her head. "It's officially summer once we get to the beach."

"Silly, Daddy. It's been summer for weeks." Meri giggled. "Come build the sand tower." She wiggled until I put her down. Without waiting for a response, she took off across the beach and back to work on the tower.

Lucy laughed and turned to follow her. "She's pretty—"

I grabbed her hand to stop her, but as soon as she turned around, I realized my mistake. The problem with touching her was once I started, I didn't want to stop.

Lucy smiled as if she knew exactly what I was thinking and squeezed my hand. "Come on. I have your bag with your swim shorts. You better get changed and start helping out with this sand tower."

LUCY

The combination of the fresh air and sun on my face was making me very sleepy. Meri had been going nonstop since getting to the beach earlier that afternoon after a half day of school.

It was impressive how much energy a six-year-old had. It was going to be a very busy summer. But for the first time in years, I was looking forward to the long days in the sun. Instead of juggling schedules and shifts for all my summer student employees who all wanted to avoid working on the busy patio in the heat, I'd be playing outside in the sun with the sweetest little girl I'd ever met.

And then, of course, there was Craig.

I pulled my sunglasses down over my nose and gazed out over the beach from where I lounged under the umbrella to watch him in the lake with Meri.

Of course I'd seen him without a shirt on before, but the sexy sight of him bursting out of the water, droplets glistening off his hard chest as the afternoon sun hit him, sent all kinds of sensations between my legs.

Damn. Aquaman had nothing on my man.

My man.

It sounded nice to me. *Very* nice.

The only part of it all that wasn't nice was the fact that we were still keeping our relationship under wraps. I'd secretly hoped that after our absolutely perfect night together, we'd both be ready to go public with things, but Craig insisted we wait until the fall before telling Meri and the family about us.

I'd never dated a man with a child before, and not having one of my own, I had absolutely no experience with things like this. It only made sense to defer to Craig on issues that directly affected his daughter. If he wanted to wait, I trusted him to know what was best.

I watched as Craig scooped Meri up and tossed her in a gentle arch through the air and into the water. She squealed and instantly clamored for more. Soon, Craig was surrounded by other children, all wanting to be tossed in the air. Dutifully, he gave them each a turn until finally he begged off, needing a break.

A moment later, he hovered over me, dripping cold droplets of water on my sun-baked skin. "Come for a swim."

"It's freezing!"

"I'll keep you warm." The look in his eyes promised all

kinds of heat I knew he couldn't deliver on, given the circumstances.

When I didn't answer right away, he leaned closer. My entire body lit up with a need to touch him. I reached up to wipe water from his chest when Meri burst between us.

"Savi wants to know if I can go in her boat! Can I?"

Craig jerked backward and reached for a towel. "Boat?"

I looked down the beach. Savi and her mom, Dina—whom I'd met at the school on a few occasions—were walking hand in hand toward us.

"What kind of boat?" Craig asked as they approached.

"It's just our canoe," Dina answered as she joined us. "We were going to take the girls for a little paddle if it's okay with you both." She looked at Craig and then at me. "Hi, Lucy. It's nice to see you again."

"It's nice to see you, too." I got to my feet. "I wanted to thank you for sharing your recipe for cupcakes in the ice cream cones. They turned out really well."

Dina beamed. "Savi said Meri brought them in for her birthday at the end of the year. I'm glad they worked out for you."

"Can I go in the boat, Lucy?" Meri grabbed my hand and tugged.

"I think you should probably ask your dad." I gave Craig a quick look before turning my attention back to Dina. "Do you have an extra life jacket?"

"Of course. And I promise we're just going to go along the shoreline there." She pointed to the south side of the lake. "There's a loons' nest on the point there, and if we get lucky, we'll be able to see the new hatchlings out for a swim."

"That sounds pretty incredible." Craig nodded. "I don't see why you can't go check it out," he told Meri, who whooped with joy and immediately took off running down the beach, hand in hand with her friend.

"We won't be gone long." Dina laughed. "It'll give you two a chance to have a bit of alone time."

"What?" I shook my head. "Oh no. It's not like—"

"Thank you, Dina," Craig interjected smoothly. "Have fun."

I waited until Dina walked away before I turned to Craig. "She knows."

"She doesn't know."

"Oh yes she does. She winked at me."

Craig's response was to laugh and drop onto the beach blanket next to me. He reached up for my hand. "Let her think whatever she wants to."

"Really?" I turned in my chair so I peered down at him. He reached up and pulled me down onto him. "What about keeping things quiet?"

We were blocked from view by the beach chairs and the umbrella; still, it felt risky to be in such a compromising position with him in public. Then again, if he didn't mind if anyone knew about us, neither did I. I inched closer to his lips but stilled when he spoke.

"There's a big difference between thinking something and knowing it. Just a bit longer, sweetheart."

His words reminded me of his sister's comment at Meri's party. I wiggled until I sat next to him on the blanket. "I know you said you wanted to wait until the timing was right to talk to Meri about us, and I totally understand that. Meri comes first."

He nodded and propped himself up on his elbows, giving me his full attention.

"But your family…" I bit my bottom lip and sucked it between my teeth, unsure how to properly express myself. "Your sister said something the other day that's been bothering me."

"Who, Charli?"

I nodded, and Craig sat up straight.

"What did she say?"

"All the ladies were teasing me a little bit about how they thought maybe there was something going on between us, and when I assured them there wasn't..." I pressed my lips together, remembering how I'd lied to my new friends. "Charli commented about how that was a good thing. It was just a strange comment. Do you know why she would say that?"

A shadow passed over Craig's face, and then, in an instant, it was gone. "I have no idea. Probably because she thinks you're so great for Meri, which you are, and she doesn't want me to screw it up. Which I won't," he added with a wink.

I tilted my head and gave him a look. I believed him. He wasn't going to screw things up with me. But the sneaking around was starting to get old. I wasn't a teenager anymore.

"I can't remember why you don't want to tell them about us." To be honest, I couldn't ever remember discussing it specifically; I'd just gone along with it.

"You know I want to tell the whole world about us, don't you?" He slid a hand up my leg and squeezed my thigh.

I shrugged.

"I do." Craig looked me straight in the eyes, and I could see the honesty there. "I really do, Lucy. Every moment I spend with you is amazing. But it's not enough. I want to spend all my time with you, without hiding from anyone. And I really want to make sure you know how I feel about you."

I swallowed hard. "How?"

Craig scooted closer to me on the blanket until I sat between the V of his legs. He cupped my cheek and rubbed his thumb gently over my soft skin. "I'm falling for you a little bit more every day."

My stomach somersaulted.

I leaned toward him. "I feel the same way."

"You do?"

I nodded. "You make me feel things I've never felt before. With you, it feels…" I exhaled slowly. "Real."

"Very real." He nodded. "Lucy, I can honestly say I've never felt this way about a woman before. Not even close."

We kissed, and for the first time, I didn't worry about who might see us. I wrapped my arms around his neck and pulled him closer, unwilling to ever break our connection.

It was Craig who pulled back first. "I can't wait to tell the world about you. About *us*."

My heart soared with the idea that we could finally be open about our relationship. "Really? So we're going to talk to Meri about—"

"I will talk to her." He cupped my cheek tenderly and kissed me softly. "Soon. I promise. But I can't rush it, Lucy. She's never had to share me with anyone before. I need to make sure it's right, and I still haven't had a chance to talk to her about her birth mother. It's going to be a lot."

It *was* going to be a lot. The last thing I wanted was for Meri to be upset.

"And I think it's important for Meri to be the first to know."

I swallowed hard and nodded. I didn't disagree with that. Meri and Craig were a team. And over the last few months, the three of us had also become a team of sorts, too. It was important to make sure Meri felt included.

I blew out a deep breath, and Craig captured my lips with his again.

"Thank you for being patient," he whispered, his breath hot on my lips. "Just a little bit longer, I promise, and then the world will know how I feel about you."

After Ross, I'd vowed to never again be someone's secret, but this was different. It felt different. And it wasn't forever. Just for a little longer.

I just needed to keep reminding myself of that.

Chapter Twenty-Two

CRAIG

I BEAMED with pride as I scanned the crowd that had packed into the Sugar Shack for the official launch of the chocolates. If I was being honest, I had to admit that I'd been a little nervous about putting pressure on Mya to be ready for the open house.

But my little pep talk must have worked because not only were the display cases packed, but dozens of purple—Meri's choice—little boxes stuffed with each of the five new chocolates Mya had decided on were stacked in perfect pyramids.

Tasting trays were being passed around by the summer employees, who were all more than happy to work a little overtime for the party, and everyone seemed to be enjoying the samples.

"What did I tell you about this?" Chase handed me a glass of champagne as he joined me. "The chocolates are going to be a huge success."

"I have to agree, brother." We clinked our glasses in a toast.

"Thank you for your help on this one and finding Mya and… well, all of it. You were right."

"I like to hear that." Chase laughed. "It turns out I do know a few things about business after all. Diversification is key. And the orders that have come in already look very promising."

I couldn't disagree with that. Based on early projections, the Sugar Shack was set to have the best year we'd ever had. By a lot. I definitely had my brother to thank for that.

And Lucy.

I searched the room quickly before my gaze landed on Lucy, who was chatting with Krysta and Kane. The jealousy I once would have felt was gone, replaced only with love.

"So I take it you're not mad at Dad anymore." Chase wiggled his eyebrows and winked when he saw where I was looking.

"What are you talking about?"

"Hiring a nanny? It wasn't such a bad idea after all, was it?"

Lucy had been a great idea, but that didn't change the fact that I still didn't agree with the stipulation my father had placed on me. I scowled. "I never needed a nanny."

"But look at all you've accomplished with all your extra time."

I shook my head sharply. "None of this is happening because of Dad's stupid will, brother."

"Are you sure about that?" Chase raised an eyebrow. "What did your letter say?"

I stared at him. "What letter?"

"You must have gotten a letter. Didn't Steven give you a letter? Charli and I each got one."

I got one. Steven Larson had given me an envelope with my name written in my father's familiar handwriting the day of Meri's party. I'd stuffed it into my back pocket, and later I'd slid it under the stack of books I meant to get around to reading on my nightstand.

"I got one." I shrugged. "I'm not interested in what it says. I'm only doing this for the family and for Meri's future. That's it." I wouldn't make eye contact with my brother. "I know you and Charli both felt like you learned something from Dad's final test or whatever this is, but I don't need to learn anything."

"Craig, I don't—"

"He wanted me to hire a nanny for six months. That's what I did. There's exactly fourteen weeks and two days left until we can move on to whomever will be subjected to Dad's torture next."

"Not that you're counting or anything." Chase smirked. "What happens then?"

"I told you." I tossed back the rest of the champagne and set the glass on a nearby table. "It's someone else's turn."

"And Lucy?"

I froze. I forced myself to exhale slowly before I turned to face my big brother. "You would have to ask Lucy. Now, if you'll excuse me, I need to mingle."

It was a bullshit, copout answer, and I hated myself for it. Lucy deserved so much better than this stupid game I had to play with her. But it was only for a bit longer. I had to keep reminding myself of that. It wouldn't be long, and then we could be together for real. I just needed to get through this for my daughter's sake. As much as I cared about Lucy, there was no way I was going to risk Meri's future.

LUCY

I took a bite of the coconut cluster one of Craig's summer employees had handed me and almost moaned out loud. "This is amazing, Mya."

The woman, who was clearly uncomfortable being the center of attention, blushed and ducked her head.

"Seriously," I said. "Your chocolates are truly the most delicious things I've ever put in my mouth. You are amazing."

"Thank you." Mya shook her head. "This has all been so—"

"Lucy?"

I spun toward the voice that had interrupted us and immediately wished I hadn't. A very pregnant Maria—whom I had completely forgotten even existed, let alone in my new hometown—stood in front of me. Her hands rested on her swollen belly, a radiant smile on her face, and a somewhat shocked and uncomfortable-looking husband at her side.

"Hi." I excused myself from Mya, who quickly scuttled away, no doubt to the refuge of the back room, and turned to face my ex-boyfriend and his wife for the second time. "I didn't realize you two were still in town."

"My blood pressure is still a little high." Maria's face grew serious. "So the doctor recommended we stay away from the stress of the big city as long as we can."

If only the poor woman knew the potentially stressful situation she was currently in. Not that I would ever do or say anything that would put her health—or that of her unborn baby—at risk.

"This is pretty incredible, isn't it?" Maria gushed. "I know I probably shouldn't be eating so much sugar, but these chocolates are so delicious I had Rossy buy a bunch to take back home with us."

Ross lifted a carrier bag full of the purple boxes I'd helped tie earlier.

"They are delicious." I held up the half-eaten coconut chocolate. "I think this might be my new favorite."

"Mine, too," Maria said. "If you'll excuse me, I need to go find the little girl's room. Wait here?" She waited until Ross nodded and then disappeared into the crowd.

The last thing I wanted to do was make conversation with my ex, and I was about to excuse myself when Meri ran through the crowd and slammed into my legs.

"Hey, kiddo." I bent and took her hand. "What's going on?"

"Auntie Kat said I couldn't have any more chocolates." Meri—who looked like she'd already had more than her share—was teetering on the edge of an epic emotional meltdown. The sugar crash.

I ignored Ross and knelt so I was eye to eye with her. "I'm sure if Auntie Kat said that, there's a good reason. And we need to listen to her. But," I added quickly when her lower lip started to quiver, "the best part of this being your dad's shop is that any leftovers are coming home, so we can have them tomorrow."

Meri considered that, then sniffed hard and nodded. "Promise?"

"I promise we'll have at least one chocolate tomorrow."

Satisfied, she gave me a quick squeeze. "I'm gonna find Grady."

She took off before I could respond. It wasn't until I stood that I realized Ross was still there.

"She's super cute," he said. "Your boyfriend's daughter?"

I swallowed hard and nodded curtly. I'd forgotten that I'd let that slip the last time I ran into him. Not that it mattered. He'd be leaving town soon and—

"Lucy, I'm so sorry." Kat appeared, looking slightly flustered. "Did Meri come and tell you how awful her auntie was?"

I tried not to look at Ross. "She did, but it's okay. I sorted it out."

"I really am sorry, Lucy. But she was eating so many chocolates, I didn't want to make your job any harder tonight than it needed to be. I know Meri is a total bear after too much sugar."

"Job?"

Kat turned, noticing Ross for the first time. "Sorry, I don't think we've met."

"Ross." He held out his hand.

"I'm Kat. This is my brother's shop. And that little sugar fiend is my niece. Nice to meet you."

They shook hands while I silently wished for the floor to open up and swallow me whole.

"I used to be Lucy's…" Ross glanced at me. "She used to work for me at my restaurant."

"Really?"

"It feels like a lifetime ago now." I swallowed hard and searched for a way to end the conversation.

"I always forget you used to work at a restaurant." Kat laughed. "I just assume you've been a nanny forever. You're so good at it."

"Nanny?"

My face burned. But there was no way out now.

"Oh yeah," Kat continued completely unaware of my impending meltdown. "Lucy is Meri's nanny. She's been working for my brother for what— a few months now?"

I nodded.

"So you're the *nanny*?" Ross's lips twisted into a smirk. "I wish I could say I'm surprised."

Heat flooded my face as I searched desperately for an escape.

"Anyway," Kat said quickly, "it was nice to meet someone

from Lucy's other life, but I've got to run. See you soon, Lucy —and sorry again about the sugar."

I lifted my hand in a weak wave. Before I could escape, Ross leaned closer.

"I guess old habits die hard, huh, Lucy? Fucking the boss again?"

My stomach dropped. Shame burned through me. "It's not like that." I stepped back. Away from Ross and his cruel words.

"It sure looks that way to me." His laugh was harsh. "Never would've guessed the nanny angle, though. That was a surprise. And here you were, trying to make me feel like I was in the wrong."

I glanced around for Maria. She was nowhere in sight. "You were wrong," I said, raising my voice before catching myself. We were surrounded by Craig's family. The room felt both crowded and empty.

Then a solid presence appeared at my side. Craig didn't touch me, but his presence steadied me.

"Ross, is it?" Craig said coolly before looking to me. "Is he bothering you?"

Relief washed through me. He remembered. He cared.

"You must be the *boss*," Ross said. "Lucy has a thing for men in authority."

Craig's hand curled into a fist. Asher and Chase appeared instantly.

"Everything okay?" Asher asked as he stared directly at Ross. "I would hate for there to be a scene tonight."

"No scene." Ross held up his hands and the carrier bag full of chocolate. "I was just buying some treats for my wife when I ran into an old *friend*. It's nice to see that Lucy has a boyfriend."

"Boyfriend?" Chase shook his head. "Lucy is Meri's nanny."

Why wouldn't the floor just open up already?

"I was under the impression she was both."

More than anything, I hated the smug tone of Ross's voice.

"The *nanny* and also involved with her boss."

Next to me, I felt Craig tense.

"Oh shit," Asher mumbled under his breath.

"I...um..." I shook my head and looked to Craig for help. True, this wasn't the way we wanted people to find out, but surely he wasn't going to humiliate me in front of Ross and his brothers. Not like this. He wouldn't do that to me. "It's just—"

"I'm not sure what you heard, or what you think you know," Craig interrupted me.

He took a step toward Ross, and I exhaled. He was going to stand up for me. It would be okay. This humiliation would soon be a distant memory.

"Hell," Craig continued. "I'm not even really sure who exactly you are or what you're doing here. But what I do know is that Lucy is my daughter's nanny, and she's a damn good one. And you being here, in my shop, insinuating that there is anything inappropriate going on in any way, is just an insult."

"I was just—"

"I don't care." Craig held his hand out and gestured toward the door. "I think it's time you left."

Once more, I thought I was going to collapse—but this time for a very different reason. I stared, open-mouthed, as Ross turned and left, and then I turned to Craig, but he wouldn't meet my gaze.

My knees buckled a little.

Asher reached out and put an arm around my shoulder. "Do you want to tell us what that was all about?"

I exhaled a breath I didn't know I'd been holding. "That was my ex-boyfriend. He's...well, it turns out he's not the nicest person."

"Yeah, I got that much." Asher raised an eyebrow and looked at Chase, who picked up the line of questioning.

"Is there anything you two want to tell us about—"

"We've been—"

"There's nothing to tell," Craig snapped, cutting me off before I could say more. He looked at me then.

I tried desperately to read the expression in his eyes and communicate silently with him. It would be okay. He could tell his brothers. He didn't need to keep our relationship—*me*—a secret. Not anymore.

"Craig?" I reached for his arm, but he pulled away, and a little piece of my heart broke. He wasn't going to tell them. Not today. Maybe not ever. "Please." I hated myself for pleading with him when it was already so clear he wasn't going to stand up for me. But as long as there was still a shred of hope, I had to cling to it.

But the second he tore his eyes away from mine, the hope vanished, and I knew the truth. I was just another dirty little secret. I wasn't worth fighting for. Not to Craig.

A point that was confirmed when Craig finally answered his brothers. "You have to be kidding, guys. I would never jeopardize our family by getting involved with the *nanny*."

Chapter Twenty-Three

CRAIG

IT DIDN'T MATTER ANYMORE that the new chocolates were a success. It didn't matter that they had so many orders already that my biggest problem at the Sugar Shack was going to be hiring help for Mya just to keep up.

None of it mattered.

The moment I saw the light in Lucy's eyes dim and her face crumple because of the words that came out of my mouth, nothing else mattered.

Nothing.

The noise of the room faded away, and the only thing I could hear was the thumping of my heart. Just like a scene in a movie, everything else disappeared as I stared at Lucy and tried to make her understand why I'd said what I did.

But it was too late.

I saw it in her eyes. She looked at me like I'd betrayed her —because I had. And then she blinked, and somehow that was worse, because when she looked at me again, it was like I was a complete stranger.

People and noise swirled around us, leaving the two of us alone in a bubble, but I didn't speak. I didn't say the words that might have made it better. I didn't reach for her or offer any reassurance.

I froze.

Tears filled her eyes, and a second later, she was gone.

As if she'd broken a spell, the sounds of the room rushed back in, the freeze-frame lifted, and suddenly I was being pulled away by my brothers. The whole interaction couldn't have lasted more than seconds, yet it felt like a lifetime.

Chase wrapped an arm around my shoulder. I tried to turn, to see where Lucy had gone, but he held me back.

"Leave her."

"I can't—"

"You need to give her a minute," he said firmly.

They flanked me and led me straight into the kitchen before finally stepping back.

"What the fuck was that?" Asher demanded before I could even catch my breath. "What have you done?"

"Asher," Chase said sharply, stepping between us. "Back off."

"Back off?" Asher spun on him. "Was I the only one who just witnessed that? Holy shit, Craig." He turned back to me, right in my face.

I still couldn't find the words. I'd done what I had to do. I was protecting my family. I was protecting my daughter.

I'd done it for *them*. For all of them.

And Asher was yelling at *me*?

Fuck that.

I shook my head and turned away before I did something I wouldn't regret. And right then, I was pretty sure I wouldn't regret punching Asher. Not even a little.

"What's going on?" Charli asked as she and Symon joined us. "We just saw Lucy run out of here, crying."

The knife in my chest twisted deeper.

"Craig basically just told her she's *just* the nanny," Asher said.

"Not basically," Chase added. "He did say that."

"Why would you say that?" Charli turned on me. "Craig? Why would you—"

"Because she *is*," I snapped, surprising even myself. I never yelled. Ever. "Isn't that what you all wanted? I needed to hire a nanny, so I did. And that's what Lucy is. The *nanny*. I hired her and lived with her and—"

Held her at arm's length. Fought my feelings. Sacrificed hers.

"I did it for all of you. Because that's what we do, right? We follow Dad's orders from beyond the grave, no matter how fucked up they are, no matter how much they hurt the people we love in the process."

"Love?" Chase asked quietly. "You love her?"

I looked at him and inhaled through my nose. "It doesn't matter now. I've fucked it up anyway. She's going to leave before the six months are up, and it's all because I failed."

"How?" Charli asked softly, putting a hand on my shoulder. "How did you fail?"

"I chased her away. I tried so hard not to have feelings, and then when I did, I convinced myself it would be okay because I love her so much that there was no way it couldn't be okay. I just needed to make it through the six months and then we—" I shook my head. "Now it's too late. I fucked it up. I failed at keeping it all together. I thought I could have it all."

"Why can't you?"

I looked up to see Kat standing in the doorway.

"I assume we're talking about Lucy," she said carefully, "and how you love her."

"You know?"

Behind me, Asher burst out laughing, followed by the rest of them trying—and failing—to hide it.

"What is so funny?" I snapped, scanning their faces until my gaze landed on Symon.

"We knew," he said simply. "I mean, I've hardly been around lately, and even I could see how much you care about Lucy."

"Love," Charli corrected.

"Sorry," Symon said, nodding. "How much you *love* her."

"The question isn't whether you love her," Kat said as she stepped closer. "It's why you tried so hard to hide it."

My blood pressure spiked. This couldn't be happening. Everything I'd done had been to protect them—and now they were giving me shit for it?

No.

I shook my head and turned away.

"You had to know we'd understand," Chase said gently. "Why didn't you talk to us?"

That was it.

"You're kidding me, right?" I snapped, turning back on him. "You're all seriously kidding me." I looked around the room. "There is no way you can stand here and tell me—with a straight face—that you would've understood me falling in love with the nanny I was forced to hire to save our fucking family." No one spoke. "Because all any of you ever said was that I needed to stay away from her. Keep it professional."

I made air quotes.

"You even told Lucy it was a good thing we weren't involved," I said, glaring at Charli. "What kind of shitty thing was that to say?" She opened her mouth, but I held up a hand. "I don't want to hear it. If you all saw this coming a mile away, then why didn't one of you step in? Why didn't any of you help me figure out how I could be with the woman I love *and* fulfill Dad's will?"

Silence.

"You're all a bunch of hypocrites." I dragged my hands through my hair.

"What happened tonight—that's on me. I was an asshole. I hurt the woman I love. The only woman I've ever loved." Emotion threatened to take over, but I forced it down. "It's my fault and I'm going to fix it. I don't know how yet, but I'm going to try."

I straightened my shoulders.

"But you all need to recognize the part you played, too." I looked at Charli and Chase. "You both know how hard this is. Carrying the future of the family on your shoulders."

"You're right," Chase said softly.

"We should've been there for you," Charli said, tears streaking her cheeks.

"I don't want to hear it." I shook my head and turned toward the door. "I need to get out of here."

"I'll bring Meri home," Kat said quickly. "Go find Lucy."

I nodded. It was all I could manage.

Chapter Twenty-Four

LUCY

I HAD NOWHERE TO GO.

I didn't have a home. Not in Trickle Creek.

It hurt to admit it to myself, but it was the truth, and sometimes the truth stung.

I was *just* the nanny.

He didn't love me. He didn't care about me.

I would never jeopardize our family by getting involved with the nanny.

The nanny.

His words echoed in my head.

Humiliated, I fled from the Sugar Shack and the man I'd allowed myself to fall for. I'd been so stupid to let my guard down and think that Craig was any different from anyone else.

I knew better.

I drove straight to the house—*Craig's* house—and moved quickly. I packed a small bag. Most of my clothes were in the washer, but they weren't important. I'd get them later. The important thing was getting far away from him before he came home. I needed space to think about my next move, and I would never get that if I stayed.

With my bag packed, the only thing left was Garfield. I found my cat curled up among the pile of stuffed animals on Meri's bed.

"Come on, buddy. We need to go."

He lifted his large head and mewled at me before readjusting himself and snuggling deeper into the bed.

"Traitor." I scratched his head quickly and found a pad of paper on Meri's desk that she'd been using to draw. I scratched out a note and left it on the bed next to the sleeping cat, and then I was gone.

The drive to Vancouver would take almost ten hours, but with nowhere else to go, and nothing but time, I didn't have any other options.

I knew Craig would probably have to help Meri read the note, but it didn't matter.

CRAIG

I jumped up from the couch the moment I heard the click of the door handle. "Lucy?"

"It's just me." Kat walked through the door, a very sleepy-looking Meri holding her hand. "I think someone might have hit a wall."

Grateful for the distraction, at least for a moment, I opened my arms, and Meri climbed up into my embrace. "Time for bed, kiddo."

She nodded against my shoulder, already half asleep.

"Is she…?"

I shook my head. Lucy wasn't there. She'd been gone when I got home. I'd spent hours driving around town, but I didn't have any idea where to look, so it had been a useless search.

"She's not answering her phone either."

Kat exhaled deeply and shook her head. "Go," she said. "Put her to bed. I'll make some tea. Then we can talk."

It was the last thing I wanted to do after my explosion at the party, but I knew my little sister well enough to know she wasn't about to go anywhere until we talked.

"Where's Lucy?" Meri lifted her head sleepily. "Can she read me a story?"

I swallowed hard against the lump in my throat as I walked toward Meri's room, carefully averting my gaze from where Lucy's bedroom door stood ajar.

"I'll read you a story tonight, kiddo. Let's get you tucked in."

It felt like a miracle that Meri didn't protest while I helped her into her pajamas and then did a quick brush of her teeth. She was so tired, she almost didn't notice the note left on her bed next to Garfield, who had recently claimed Meri's bed as his own.

"What's this?"

Meri peered at the paper, her little lips forming around the letters as she sounded out the words.

> Meri,
> I needed to go on a trip.
> Please take care of Garfield for me.
> He loves to cuddle with you.
> Lucy

"She went on a trip?" Meri gazed up at me, suddenly more awake than she had been a moment before. "Where?"

I wished I knew.

Gently, I took the note from her and pulled the covers back, careful not to disturb the cat, who was eyeing me as if he knew what an asshole I'd been to Lucy. Maybe he did.

"Don't worry about it for tonight, okay, kiddo? Get some sleep, and I'll make sure Garfield's water bowl is topped up."

"But she asked me to do it," Meri protested as she slipped under the blankets and dropped her head to the pillow next to the cat.

"I know she did, kiddo, and you're going to do a great job, but first you have to sleep."

She must have been exhausted, because she didn't protest the way I was sure she would. I sat next to her and stroked her hair while her eyelids fluttered closed and she finally drifted off to sleep.

I took Lucy's note with me as I backed out of Meri's room and closed the door softly behind me. No doubt Garfield would scratch to be let out later.

I found Kat in the kitchen, not with tea, but two glasses of wine. She handed me one as I walked in.

"I thought something a bit stronger would be appropriate."

I eyed the cupboard where I kept a bottle of whiskey, but shook my head and took a sip of the wine instead. Whiskey in my state would be a bad idea. I didn't need to lose control of myself any more than I already had.

"I'm sorry, Kat."

"For what?" She jumped up on the counter and swung her legs.

Instantly, the memory of Lucy sitting on the counter filled my head and I looked away. "For blowing up the way I did earlier. That wasn't okay."

"No," she said simply. "It wasn't okay. But I get it, and you were right. We should have been there for you. We're the ones who should be sorry."

I sank into a chair at the table and drank my wine.

We sat in silence until Kat spoke again. "You didn't have to do that with her, you know?"

I looked up in question.

"You didn't have to hide your feelings for Lucy," Kat clarified. "I know why you did it," she added quickly before I could interrupt her. "But you didn't have to. We would have understood. In fact, I think we all would have been really supportive about it."

I shook my head. "Maybe you would have been, but not the others. At least, not all of them. In fact, I know that. They told me. They were worried that if I got involved with Lucy, I'd screw it up and she'd leave."

"They were wrong." Kat jumped off the counter and moved into the chair across from me. "And I'm not trying to defend them." She shrugged. "Okay, maybe a little bit. But if they said that, it was only because they were scared. We're all scared, Craig. These stipulations Dad gave us…they're crazy. It's a lot to take in."

"You honestly don't think I know that?"

I wasn't in the mood to listen to my sister, but I didn't have the energy to make her leave. Besides, the alternative to having Kat there was to sit alone in the kitchen and drive myself crazy with all the ways I'd screwed up the best thing that had ever happened to me.

"It doesn't matter anyway." I tossed the rest of my drink back and reached for the bottle. "She's gone. It's over. All of it. I failed to hold up my end of the bargain, and I lost the best woman who's ever walked into my life. I screwed up, Kat."

"What do you mean, she's gone?"

I pulled out the note Lucy had left for Meri and handed it to Kat, who read it quickly.

"She's not gone." Kat's lips curled up into a smile. "I mean, she might be right now. But not forever."

"What are you talking about? That's exactly what's happened."

"Nope." Kat laughed, but there was nothing about the situation I found remotely funny. "She's hurt and she's definitely upset, but she's not gone, Craig. She wouldn't leave her cat behind if she really wasn't coming back. But I think, more importantly, Lucy loves Meri. She wouldn't leave her without saying goodbye."

I looked up into my sister's eyes.

"She's not Donna, Craig. She won't just leave."

Her words hit me in the gut.

"Don't write her off. Not yet."

Was that what I was doing? Was I comparing Lucy to Donna?

Shit.

I really wasn't good at this. I took a breath and dropped my head into my hands.

"And if you're right?" I looked up to see Kat watching and waiting. "Then what? Can I fix it? What about Dad's will?"

"Oh, big brother." Kat shook her head. "First off, I am right. She'll be back." She winked. "As far as the will is concerned, I think that's a good question for Steven Larson, but I feel like it's probably okay for your nanny to have a little vacation. I don't remember hearing anything contrary to that." She got up from the table and pushed the chair in. "As for fixing things with Lucy…" She shrugged. "I'd say that part is totally up to you."

Chapter Twenty-Five

LUCY

I HAD SPENT the better part of the last forty-eight hours on the threadbare couch in Mandi's downtown Vancouver apartment. My back ached and there was a crick in my neck, but my physical aches and pains were nothing compared to the hurt in my heart.

"Did you sleep last night?"

My best friend pulled open the blinds on a bright summer day outside, but I pulled the blanket up over my head, unwilling to face another day.

"You have to get up." Mandi ripped the blanket off, exposing me to the light.

"Hey!"

"Hey, nothing. I'm not going to let you fade into the fabric of this couch."

"It would be an improvement." I pulled myself up to a sitting position and ran my hands through my wild hair. I tugged it back into a ponytail.

"Don't insult my furniture." Mandi pretended to be insulted. "This is my favorite couch. The things it's seen…"

I groaned. "Please don't tell me that."

"Will it help you get up if I fill you in on all the details?" She wiggled her eyebrows, and I couldn't help but laugh a little.

"No." I stood and headed into the tiny, attached kitchen to make coffee. "But I'm up. Happy?"

Mandi twisted around, so she faced me. "No. I'm not happy. And I won't be until you are. Has he called?"

I shrugged. I'd turned off my phone before driving away from Trickle Creek and hadn't turned it on yet.

"What's that mean?"

"That means I don't know." I put the kettle on and scooped grounds into the French press. "I haven't looked, and it doesn't matter. I don't want to know."

Mandi groaned. "Heterosexual relationships are so ridiculous." She threw her arms up and headed over to the pile of clothes and things I'd created on the other side of the room.

"It's not ridiculous," I said. "It's called self-preservation. And you can't tell me that's a heterosexual thing."

Mandi straightened up, a sweater of mine in her hand. "It's not self-preservation, Luce. It's…well, it's stupid."

"That's the best you've got?" I poured the hot water over the coffee grounds and put the lid on the press. "It's stupid?"

"It is." Mandi resumed rifling through my things. "You can't just stick your head in the sand when something goes wrong and ignore it."

"I'm not ignoring it."

I was running away. There was a difference. Not that I felt like pointing that out to my best friend.

"Sure looks that way to me." Mandi pulled my cell phone from the bottom of her purse and held it up triumphantly. "Why don't we see all that you've been ignoring."

"No!" I launched myself across the room at her, and she quickly sidestepped me. "Don't do it, Mandi."

With her back to me, Mandi twisted and turned while I made a few futile attempts to grab my phone. When I heard the tell-tale chime of the phone powering on, I sagged onto the couch in defeat.

"Don't you want to see if he called?" Mandi asked without looking up from the screen.

"No. And yes. And—"

"Ohhh."

"What?"

"I thought you didn't want to know."

I shot her a look. "What if he didn't call, Mandi? What if everything I thought we had wasn't real?" I dropped my head in my hands and willed myself not to cry again. I'd already done enough of that over the last few days. "I thought he was the one, Mandi. Really. I thought he was different."

The phone abandoned for the time being, Mandi joined me on the couch and wrapped an arm around my shoulders. She pulled me into her, and that's when the tears started to fall in earnest.

"It's okay, Luce. I'm sorry I tried to make a joke out of it. I know how much you liked him."

"No." I sniffed and swiped at my nose with the back of my arm. "I love him, Mandi. I really thought…it felt so real."

"It doesn't mean it wasn't real."

I pulled away enough to look at my friend. "You weren't there, Mandi." My heart squeezed as I remembered the way I'd stood there and let first Ross make me feel small, and then worse, Craig. The memory of how he didn't claim our relationship to his brothers stung. "He acted like we were nothing. It was almost worse than what Ross did because…"

"Because you didn't love Ross," she finished for me.

"No," I agreed. "I didn't love him. Not the way I love

Craig. And Meri." Again, the tears came. "Oh, Meri. Do you think she understands that I'm not there? That I just left? I shouldn't have done that. It's not fair to just leave her like that. I just didn't know what else to do. I—"

"You're just taking a little holiday."

Mandi sounded so confident, I calmed down a little bit.

"Let's just take it one thing at a time, okay?"

I nodded. "A holiday."

"A holiday." Mandi held up the phone. "Now go make yourself a tea, because you're going to need to deal with this."

CRAIG

"I think Garfield is sad, Daddy."

I looked up to see Meri carrying the giant orange cat in her arms as she joined me on the deck, where I was watering the potted geraniums Meri and Lucy had planted a few weeks earlier.

"I don't think the cat should be outside." The last thing I needed was for Lucy's cat to run away while we were looking after him. How would I explain that when she came back?

If she came back.

"I can't leave him alone," Meri said. "He's sad. He misses Lucy."

You and me both, kitty.

I put the watering can down and scratched Garfield's head. "You miss Lucy?"

"Yes," Meri answered. "We do. When is she coming home?"

Home.

More than anything, I wished I had an answer for my little girl. And for myself.

It had been almost three days since she'd left, and I still hadn't heard from her.

"Honestly?"

Meri looked up at me with wide eyes. I wouldn't lie to my little girl. But she was too young to understand the truth. Especially when I didn't even understand how to explain that by trying to do what I thought was right, I'd screwed everything up.

No. I wasn't ready for that particular talk yet.

"She'll be back soon." Damn, I hoped I was telling the truth. "Now please go put Garfield back inside before he decides to go for a walk on his own. It's time to go to Savi's. You don't want to be late, do you?"

Just as I guessed, Meri quickly returned Garfield to the safety of the house, put her shoes on, and was ready to go in no time flat for her day of play at Savi's.

Ten minutes later, I'd dropped Meri off, thanked Dina profusely for bailing me out, and was headed to the plaza and the piles of work that were waiting for me at the shop. Despite the way the chocolate launch had ended, it had been a wildly successful evening. Dozens of orders were waiting for me, as well as a few contracts for providing the confections for corporate events, and even one wedding that was scheduled to be held at the ski hill in the fall.

But I couldn't concentrate, and I only had one person to blame. I turned away from the plaza and drove my car up behind Main Street and toward the outskirts of town. I parked in the empty lot and made my way into the cemetery.

I hadn't been to visit either of my parents' graves since the day they buried Dad, and I felt a flicker of guilt as I stopped first at my mother's headstone.

"Hi, Mom." It had never come naturally for me to talk to her out loud, but she was never far from my heart. "Sorry it's been awhile." I crouched and pulled at some grass around her marble headstone. "Things have been busy with Meri and... well, you should see her. She's so big, and she reminds me so much of you." I smiled a sad smile and let my head drop. "I met a woman. She's amazing. But she..."

My words drifted away, but I didn't try to pick up my train of thought.

"I love you, Mom."

I dusted off my legs as I stood and turned slowly to look at my father's headstone for the first time.

Emotions flooded through me. With everything that had happened since Dad had died, with his ridiculous stipulations to his will, I hadn't had time to really process what it meant now that my father was gone.

Michael had been a great father. Firm and fair. But there was never a doubt that he loved his children and would do anything for them. He'd been an excellent grandfather, doting on Meri every chance he got.

When I announced I'd decided to be a single father, my own dad had been nothing but supportive. Of course, he was concerned for me and the baby's future, but he'd only ever made me feel like I could do it. Like I could do anything.

It was because of the type of father I'd had that I knew I wanted more than anything to be an amazing dad, too. I'd had such an excellent role model.

Until lately.

"Dammit, Dad." I shook my head. "This is all your fault." I kicked at the turf and inhaled sharply. "Why couldn't you just believe in me? Did you really think I was such a terrible father that I needed help?"

The anger I'd been suppressing bubbled up and threatened to spill out.

"And if you really thought I couldn't do it on my own, why wouldn't you just tell me? Why wait until after you're gone to throw this at me? Do you know what that's like? To know that the one man you thought had your back unconditionally didn't actually believe in you at all? It's like a dagger to the heart, Dad. And now I've gone and fucked it all up anyway. So everything you thought you were doing, I hope it was worth it. Because now it's all gone. Your legacy. The inheritance you left us. The house. The business. Meri's future. It's gone. Because you didn't believe in me."

Hot tears streamed down my cheeks, but I swiped them away.

"Worse…she's gone, Dad."

I sank to my knees and dropped my head into my hands.

"She's gone." I whispered the words and let myself feel the loss for the first time. "And that's not your fault. It's mine. Maybe you were right not to believe in me after all."

"You're wrong, you know."

I lifted my head at my little sister's voice but didn't bother turning around.

"He did believe in you." She knelt on the ground next to me. "Probably more than any of us. And he thought you were an amazing father."

"No." I shook my head. "He didn't, Kat. That's why we're here."

She sighed and sat back on the ground.

"Why are you here?" I finally turned to face her. I hadn't told anyone I was going to the cemetery. Hell, I hadn't even known myself until I got here.

"It's the last Wednesday of the month," she said, as if that cleared it up.

"And?"

"Dad and I had a date on the last Wednesday of the month." She shrugged. "We usually just went for coffee or a walk to talk and catch up. I guess I'm having a hard time letting it go."

"So you come here once a month?"

She nodded, a sad smile on her face. "It makes me feel closer to him."

"I didn't know."

She shrugged again. "I'm surprised to see you here, though. Is it helping? Talking to him, I mean?"

I shook my head and looked back to the smooth marble headstone. I traced the letters with my eyes. "No."

Kat didn't respond right away, but after a moment, she said, "Dad would have loved Lucy."

I stared at my sister.

"He would have," she said. "She's smart and funny and cute." She lifted an eyebrow. "And she loves you and Meri."

"She doesn't—"

"She does." Kat looked so sure of herself. "You know how I know?"

I blew out a breath. "Tell me."

"She never would have left if she didn't," Kat said simply. "Think about it. If she didn't care, if this was just a job to her, she'd still be here. But she's not, because she's hurt. And the only reason you get hurt is because you care. She loves you."

"Wow."

"Wow good?"

"Just, wow." I shook my head and let my sister's words sink in. "I love her too, you know?"

"I know."

I glanced at Kat in wonder, but she wasn't looking at me.

After a minute, I chuckled. "How did you get so smart?"

When Kat turned to face me, there were unshed tears in her eyes. "The same way you did, dummy. Mom and Dad."

Her words hit me in the gut, and I swallowed down the sudden lump in my throat.

"For the record, I'm jealous it was your turn."

Again, my sister surprised me. "Why on earth would you be jealous? This is hell trying to navigate whatever whims Dad had before he died. It's definitely nothing to be jealous of, Kat."

She stood and brushed the grass from her jeans. "I take it back. You're not smart at all." There was laughter in her voice. "You don't get it. First it was Chase, and then Charli and now you. You all got one last chance to have Dad on your shoulder, giving you advice and rooting for you."

That was not at all how I was viewing this experience. Not. Even. Close.

"And the letter…I can't wait to get my letter, too."

"Letter?"

"You got one, right?"

I'd forgotten all about the letter. Again. "I did."

She spun and faced me. "What did it say?"

"I didn't read it." I clenched my teeth together, the tension radiating up my jaw. "I don't need to know any more about how he thought I lacked as a father."

Kat smacked my arm. "Haven't you been paying attention, Craig? Seriously. He didn't think that. That's not what this is about. Think about it. Chase had to stay in Trickle Creek. Why? Because he needed to be forced to realize how important family and connection was. And Charli? She had to start a business from nothing and turn it into a success in only a few months. Why did she have to do that?"

She didn't wait for my answer.

"Because she needed to learn how to believe in herself."

I took a staggering step back as if I'd been struck.

Kat let out a long, low sigh. "Read the letter, Craig. And figure out what the hell it is you're supposed to learn before you lose everything."

Chapter Twenty-Six

LUCY

I'D BEEN HOME for three days. Only Vancouver didn't feel like home anymore. The city streets were too busy, full of anonymous people who were all hurrying to get anywhere but where they already were. I longed for the plaza and the friendly faces I was getting to know by name. I missed looking up and seeing the mountains right there. The long nature walks I'd take on the forest trails with Meri, where we'd count how many squirrels we could see and thrill when we saw the deer with her fawns.

I missed Trickle Creek.

But it wasn't just the small mountain town I missed.

I needed to go back. Even if I didn't know what I was going back to.

It was the right thing to do. I couldn't keep running away.

I was going to run out of places to run to.

After yet another night of very little sleep, I pulled myself off Mandi's couch and reached for my phone.

No new messages.

Not that I expected any.

When my friend had finally forced me to face my phone, I wasn't sure what I expected to find, or more importantly, what I'd been hoping to find. Part of me wanted Craig to have called and left a heartfelt voice message admitting that he knew how wrong he'd been not to defend me and claim our relationship. I wanted him to tell me how sorry he was and tell me how much he loved me and needed me and wanted me to come home.

Home.

But that hadn't happened.

There had been two missed calls from him. No voice messages at all. And one text message that asked if we could please talk.

That was it.

Had I been wrong to expect more?

Maybe I should have been the one to call. After all, I'd been the one to leave without notice. Did that mean I'd quit? How was Meri doing without me?

Before I could stop myself, I pulled up Craig's contact information, and my finger hovered over the button that would call him.

I squeezed my eyes and—

My phone vibrated with an incoming call. My eyes snapped open.

Charli's name flashed on the screen.

My hand shook as I took the unexpected call. "Hello?"

"Lucy. I'm so glad I got you. How are you?"

I swallowed hard and decided to go for honesty. "I've been better."

"I'm so sorry I haven't reached out until now," Charli said. "I wanted to give you some space, and Symon tried to tell me to stay out of it because it's none of my business. Whatever is going on with you and Craig, I…well…I guess he's kind of right. It's not really any of my business. But—"

"Thank you for calling, Charli."

I heard the other woman exhale. "Are you okay?"

"No," I said. "But I will be. How's Meri?"

"She's good. I think Craig told her you were on a holiday. But she misses you, Lucy."

I blinked back the tears that threatened. "I miss her, too."

"Look," Charli started. "I can't speak for Craig or what went on between the two of you."

I swallowed.

"And he'll probably get upset with me for calling you, but I don't care because I think there's something you need to know."

Whatever it was, I didn't want to know, but I couldn't find the words to tell her.

"I'm not defending my brother," Charli said. "Not at all, but I don't think he ever told you why he hired you in the first place."

I shook my head before realizing she couldn't see me. "No," I said softly. "He didn't."

"He had to hire you because of a stipulation our father put in his will. It's kind of complicated, but he's basically giving all of us a task for six months that we have to complete in order to keep our family's inheritance. It's Craig's turn."

"And he had to hire a nanny? That seems—"

"Strange?" Charli chuckled. "I would tend to agree with you, except my father definitely had his reasons for everything he did. And as upset as Craig is about it all, he knows it, too. He's just having a hard time seeing it."

"So he had to hire a nanny for six months? That's it?"

"I know it seems like a minor thing," Charli scoffed. "Trust me, compared to what I had to go through, I agree with you.

But for Craig, it was a pretty big deal to let someone else care for Meri."

I could see that. Craig was an excellent father, and everything he'd told me about Meri's birth mother and how he'd committed to raising her on his own showed me how proud he was.

"I'm only telling you this, Lucy, because I think that's why Craig tried to keep his feelings for you secret. He didn't want to risk anything blowing up before the six months were up and jeopardizing everything."

There was a silence while I ingested everything Charli had told me. Craig hired me because he had to. He'd hidden our relationship because he felt like it was what he had to do, and now it was all for naught because I'd left anyway.

"So you're saying that because I left before the six months are up, the entire family will lose their inheritance?"

Charli hesitated before speaking, and her pause told me everything I needed to know.

"That's not why I called," she said after a moment.

"Why *did* you call, Charli?"

If it were even possible, the conversation only made me feel worse. Not only was my heart broken, but now I wore the heavy cloak of guilt as well. The Carlson family, all of whom I'd grown to care about, would lose everything. All because I'd left.

"I'm calling because I've never seen Craig like this before, Lucy. I've never seen him look at a woman the way he looks at you. I've never seen him light up like he does when you come into a room. I know this didn't go the way anyone planned, but the only reason I called today was because I love my brother. I feel awful that I contributed in any way to Craig feeling like he couldn't tell us about his feelings for you, and I feel even worse that I didn't speak up in favor of it when I noticed. I'm taking the blame."

"It's not your fault."

"At least partly, it is."

There was silence on the line before she spoke again. "I wouldn't dream of telling you what to do, Lucy, and it's not my place to ask you for anything. But I value your friendship and more than that, I value what you've done for my brother and my niece. I guess I just called to tell you that. Thank you, Lucy. And no matter what happens, I'm sorry."

Twenty minutes later, I still hadn't fully processed the conversation with Charli. My first impulse was to call Craig and ask him about it, but I couldn't do that.

Instead, I took my time folding the blankets on the couch and tucked them away in the closet before packing up my things. I still didn't know what to do, but what I did know was that I couldn't stay on Mandi's couch forever.

I was in the kitchen, making a piece of toast, when the front door swung open.

"Hey. It's nice to see you out of bed."

I looked from my friend to my closed bedroom door and back. "What are…where…were you not here last night?"

Mandi laughed and moved past me to the fridge. Her short blonde hair was flat on one side, and the traces of last night's makeup were evident under her eyes. I leaned against the counter and stared at my friend as she drank orange juice straight from the jug.

"What?" Mandi wiggled her eyebrows. "I get that you're having an existential crisis and everything, but I'm allowed to have a life, you know?"

I shook my head and laughed. "You certainly are. What's her name?"

Mandi shrugged. "Does it matter?"

We were so fundamentally different that I couldn't help but shake my head, my own problems momentarily forgotten. "I guess it doesn't. But one day, it might be nice if you settled down with one person."

Mandi grabbed an apple from the bowl on the counter and flopped into the oversized chair. "With all due respect, I haven't seen that work out all too well." She took a bite of the fruit and waved toward the couch. "You seem different this morning. What's going on?"

"I'm going home."

I hadn't even realized I'd made the decision until I spoke it aloud.

Mandi almost choked on the apple. She sat upright and coughed. "Like, as in to your mom's?"

"Oh hell no." Even if my mom hadn't been out of town on a trip, it wasn't an option. There was no way I could explain to her that I'd dated my boss, who ended up being married, so I ran away from my life to an entirely different town and situation, only to once more date my boss and screw up a perfectly good job.

No. I didn't need to deal with that on top of everything else.

"So, if you're not going to your mom's…" Mandi raised an eyebrow. "Where *are* you going?"

I took a deep breath and exhaled slowly. "I'm going back to Trickle Creek."

"Did he call?"

I shook my head.

"Did you call him?"

"No. His sister called."

I spent the next few minutes filling Mandi in on my conversation with Charli. But even when I was finished explaining it, I wasn't any closer to making sense of anything. All I knew was there was a feeling deep in my gut to go back.

"Are you going back because it's what you want to do, or what you *think* you should do?"

I dropped my head back for a moment. "It's the right thing to do."

"Fuck that." Mandi shook her head. "That's not what I asked. What is it *you* want, Lucy?"

I couldn't remember the last time I'd been asked that question. What did I want?

I pushed my uneaten toast to the side. "It's stupid."

"I like stupid."

My lips twitched into a little smile, and I nodded. "I want the happy ending," I said simply. "That's it. I want the man, the family, the…I want it all."

"You want Craig and Meri."

It wasn't a question, but I nodded. "I do." I dropped my head and took a deep breath before standing straight and exhaling. "But I also know I deserve better than being treated like a dirty secret."

Mandi sat up and put her elbows on her knees. "I'm listening."

It was as if all the puzzle pieces had finally clicked into place, and for the first time, I could make sense of everything. "What happened with Ross screwed me up," I started. "Probably more than I knew until recently. I know what he did was wrong. But that made me wrong, too."

Mandi tried to interrupt, but I held my hand up to stop her.

"Maybe it wasn't my fault, Mandi. But I think, on some level, I knew something wasn't quite right. I'm not stupid. But I sure played the part. And I think, to some level, I did that with Craig, too."

The more I spoke, the more everything made sense.

"I was still messed up from everything with Ross that I didn't even realize I was letting myself fall into similar patterns."

"I haven't met him yet," Mandi said. "But Craig doesn't sound anything like the douche bag."

I chuckled. "Oh no. Don't get me wrong," I added. "They are nothing alike. Ross made his decisions selfishly. And Craig…" I closed my eyes for a moment. "He made the decisions he did out of love." I paused. "But the thing is, I let myself agree to less than I deserved by keeping our relationship a secret. That's on me."

"You care about him."

I looked my friend dead in the eye. "I love him."

"Yeah." Mandi shrugged. "I know. I just wanted to hear you say it."

"Well, I do. I love him, and I love Meri, and I love that little town and all the people in it."

Mandi clapped, and I laughed. A moment later, reality sank in, and I dropped my head into my hands on the kitchen counter.

"So what's the problem?"

"It's too late now."

"For what exactly?"

Reluctantly, I lifted my head. "If I had spoken up earlier and told him that I didn't want to be a secret, and demanded he tell me the real reason, then maybe…"

"No." Mandi put a hand on my shoulder. "His actions aren't on you. It's not your fault he didn't tell you everything, or that he thought it was a good idea to keep a secret, or even that he didn't stand up and claim you as his girlfriend and the love of his life when he had the chance. None of that is on you. Own your part, certainly. But do not take on his missteps as your own. I won't allow it."

I stared at my best friend and shook my head. After a moment, I smiled. "You really think I'm the love of his life?"

CRAIG

I found the note where I'd left it, stuffed under some books on my nightstand.

I unfolded the envelope and stared for a moment at my name written in my father's familiar scrawl.

Did it really matter what was written in the letter? Would it make any difference to my current fucked-up situation to find out that my dad had never believed in me as a single father, or that I shouldn't have attempted to raise Meri on my own?

No. It wouldn't make any difference to the mess I was in now.

Reading some stupid letter from my dead father wasn't going to bring Lucy back. It wasn't going to change the fact that I'd let her go. And then, instead of calling her and begging her to come back to me, I'd let days go by.

I groaned and shoved my phone away. I couldn't call her now. It had been too long.

I didn't deserve her. I'd demonstrated that clearly enough.

"You win, Dad."

I snatched up the letter and tore it open. I pulled the piece of paper from the envelope and before I could change my mind, I started to read.

> Dear Craig,
>
> Son. There is so much I wish I could tell you right now.
>
> The first thing I want to tell you is the one thing that I imagine you're doubting right about now. I believe you are an excellent father.

I sneered and immediately hated myself for it. This whole

experience was changing me, and more and more, I wasn't sure it was in a good way. I exhaled slowly and kept reading.

I know you're angry at me right now.

That made me chuckle.

Of course you are. I can see you sitting there, saying, "Yeah, right. Then why did you make me hire a nanny?" I know you, son.

Despite myself, I smiled.

I hope you know by now that I've always admired the way you stepped up and changed your whole life to be a father to Meredith. I never doubted for a moment that you'd be an excellent father. It's true that I was concerned. But not that you couldn't do it. No. I was worried that you would give so much of yourself to that little girl that you would forget about you and what you need.

And my worries were well founded. I've watched that very thing happen.

Now, I don't know when you'll read this letter, son. Perhaps Meri is a teenager already and if that's the case, you've probably found my request even more ludicrous. But there is a method to my madness.

And if you haven't figured it out already, let me lay it out for you.

Just because you can do everything on your own, doesn't mean you should.

No man is an island, Craig. It's not only okay to ask for help, it's a good thing. And you won't be the only one to benefit. Meredith needs it, too.

Being a great parent is important, but it's equally important to take care of yourself.

I hope by now the nanny you've hired has shown you this very thing. You can be a better version of yourself, and a better father, when you have time to breathe and hopefully even time to find yourself a bit.

There has never been one moment where I didn't believe in you, Craig. I hope you realize that wasn't what this was about. Not for a second.

My hope for you is that this exercise has taught you that you don't need to go it alone. Live a full life, son. Let others in. Trust them. Learn from them. And maybe even love them.

We weren't put here to do life on our own.

Life is rich and full when it's shared with someone else.

I hope that's a lesson you can pass on to Meredith as well.

All my love,
Dad.

Tears streaked down my cheeks by the time I finished reading the letter. I folded it and carefully put it back in the torn envelope.

"Dammit. Kat was right." I laughed at myself and wiped at my face.

The cat chose that moment to join me in the kitchen. With a loud mewl, Garfield jumped up first onto the chair and then on the table, where he flopped down on the letter and sprawled out in front of me.

"The letter from your dead parent will get you every time, won't it, buddy?" I ran my hand down the cat's furry belly. Garfield's purring filled the kitchen. "It sure got me."

I let myself drift into thought while I stroked the soft fur.

I'd been so caught up in what didn't matter that I'd missed all the things that did. And my dad was right. The last few months with Lucy had been amazing. I'd spent too much time trying to be everything to everyone that I hadn't seen what was missing from my life.

And now…

I exhaled slowly, suddenly exhausted. "What do you think, Garfield? Will she come back?"

The cat lifted his head and meowed before dropping it down again.

"I hope so, too, buddy. But in the meantime, I think there's something else we need to take care of. Something I should have taken care of a long time ago."

Meri held the stuffed unicorn with the purple cape that Lucy had given her for her birthday and stroked the pink tail as I spoke.

I hadn't wanted to waste any more time, so after our dinner of chicken fingers and fries, I sat my daughter down in the living room to tell her the truth about her mother.

"Do you have any questions?" I said after relaying all the facts.

She worried her bottom lip with her teeth for a moment before speaking. "My mom didn't want me?"

My heart squeezed.

I reached for her hand. "No. That's not it at all. Your birth mother wanted you very much. She wanted you to have the best life and be surrounded by people who loved you more than anything in the world. Like Auntie Charli and Auntie Kat. And Uncle Asher and Uncle Chase. And—"

"Lucy?"

I swallowed hard and nodded. "Yes. And people like Lucy."

Meri accepted that answer.

"It's important that you know how loved you are, kiddo."

"I do. But…"

I knew there would be questions. As ready as I thought I would be, there was nothing that could properly prepare a man for a situation like this.

"Why doesn't she want to love me?"

"I know this is hard to understand, kiddo. It's hard for me, too. But sometimes people know they can't be the kind of mother or father their kids deserve, so it's actually an act of the greatest love to make room for other people to do that loving."

"People like Lucy?"

I swallowed hard. "There are a lot of people like Lucy who have so much love to give."

Meri was quiet for a moment. She lifted her unicorn to her nose and held it there before lowering it again. "Okay," she said.

"Okay?"

Meri nodded.

"You know we can talk about this whenever you want to, okay? I promise I'll always answer your questions as honestly as I can. Deal?"

"Deal." She nodded again, and I gave her a hug and a kiss.

I held her in my arms and let all the love I had flow into her, hoping she felt it. That she always felt my love.

When I finally sat back, there was a new question on Meri's lips. "Dad?"

"What's up?"

"Can Lucy be my mom?"

I sat back with a chuckle and shook my head. I was about to open my mouth to tell Meri that it wasn't that easy, but I stopped myself.

Maybe it wasn't *that* easy. But why did it have to be hard?

I'd already screwed things up by complicating everything, keeping secrets and not being totally upfront with the woman I loved and the people I cared about. Maybe it was time to try a new approach.

"I would like that very much," I answered honestly.

Garfield jumped up on the bed and threaded his orange, fluffy body between us, giving me an idea.

"Meri? You know what? I think you've both given me an idea, because if we want Lucy to be your mom, we're going to have to ask her."

Meri bounced up and down on the bed.

I put a hand on her knee to calm her. "But we can't get ahead of ourselves, because first things first. Lucy's still, well…I think Lucy's pretty upset with me. And I need to—"

"What did you do?" Meri tilted her head, pressed her lips together, and looked so stern that I couldn't help but laugh. "Dad?"

"I made a mistake," I admitted. "But I'm going to fix it. At least, I'm going to try my hardest. I need you to know that even if she doesn't forgive me, that won't change how she feels about you, okay? Lucy loves you, and that won't change no matter what."

Chapter Twenty-Seven

CRAIG

AFTER MY CONVERSATION WITH MERI, everything became clear. My only regret was that it had taken me so long to get out of my own way and see things for what they were.

I loved Lucy.

I was in love with Lucy.

That was all that mattered.

It was that simple.

My dad was right. Life was meant to be shared. And that was exactly what I intended to do, if she would forgive me.

After I tucked Meri into bed for the night, I called her, but it went straight to voicemail. I tried again. On the third attempt, I left a message.

Lucy. It's Craig.

I was hoping you would answer, but I don't blame you for not picking up. I need to apologize to you.

For a lot of things.

The first and most important thing is that I'm so sorry for asking you to keep our relationship secret. That wasn't fair of me. Especially after you told me about your ex and how poorly he treated you. That was wrong, and I'm so sorry.

You deserve so much better than that, Lucy.

I thought I was doing the right thing for everyone, but I know now that I wasn't. I hurt you. And for that, I will be eternally sorry, because I never want to hurt you, Lucy. I…

I stopped myself before I told her I loved her. I needed to look her in the eyes when I said that for the first time.

I also need to apologize for not telling you why I hired you. I don't know why I didn't. I think I was ashamed to learn that my father thought I needed help after all. I was too proud to share that with you. I'm sorry.

I took a deep breath and exhaled slowly.

There's a lot more I want to say, and I really hope I get the chance to say everything in person. Please come home, Lucy. Meri and Garfield miss you. I miss you. A lot.

Come home.

I ended the call and stared at the phone in my hand, hoping she would listen to the message and call me back.

Soon.

I still hadn't moved from the spot on the living room floor when I heard the back door open a few minutes later. I jumped up and moved into the kitchen—and froze.

She stood there.

"You're back."

She wore leggings and an oversized T-shirt. Her hair was pulled into a messy bun, and dark circles sat under her eyes. I had never seen her look more beautiful.

Lucy dropped her bag at her feet and slowly looked at me. "I'm back."

I held up my phone. "Did you listen to…did you hear…" My words trailed off, because I knew there was no way she could have heard the voicemail if she'd been driving and I'd just finished leaving it.

"My phone is off."

I wanted to cross the room and take her into my arms, to tell her everything I'd finally figured out. Instead, I nodded stupidly. "I left you a message."

"Okay." She nodded and lifted her bag again. "I'm exhausted. I'm just going to—"

"I'm sorry I didn't call earlier. I just—"

The rest of my words died on my lips when she turned back to look at me. The pain in her eyes hit me like a punch to the chest, and I hated myself for being the reason it was there.

She shook her head and walked past me, toward her bedroom.

"Lucy?"

She stopped and turned. "Look, Craig. I don't know what you want from me right now. It's been a long day." She shook her head. "No. It's been a long week. I just... I came back for Meri. It wasn't fair to leave like that."

She adjusted the strap of her bag on her shoulder. "And I just want you to know that I'll stay. Your family isn't going to lose everything because of me."

LUCY

Seeing him again was harder than I expected. Not that I'd expected it to be easy, but I hadn't been prepared for him to be standing right there looking so...good. And hopeful.

I felt a little bad for not staying and talking to him when he so clearly wanted me to. But I'd been so caught off guard. And what was that about a voicemail?

The moment I closed the door behind me, I flopped down on the bed to pet Garfield, who immediately joined me for snuggles.

"I missed you, too, buddy."

The large tabby head butted me and purred in response.

"I'm sorry I left, but I know Meri took good care of you."

I pushed myself up to a seated position and pulled the cat onto my lap as I powered up my cell phone and pressed the button to listen to Craig's voicemail.

Come home.

His last words echoed in my ears.

Was Trickle Creek home?

Driving through the streets as I'd come into town had felt like coming home. Stepping into the kitchen and seeing Craig standing there...

I took a deep breath, and with Garfield still in my arms, I got to my feet and opened my door.

The lights were still on in the kitchen, and when I walked in, Craig was sitting at the table with his head in his hands, an untouched bottle of beer in front of him.

"Hi."

Craig's head shot up and he spun so fast, the beer bottle almost toppled over. "Hey. I thought maybe you were...it's okay if you...do you want a drink?"

I nodded, and he jumped up to get me a beer. "We have water or tea or orange juice if you'd prefer."

"Beer's fine." With Garfield still in my arms, I sat across from him and accepted the drink. "I listened to your voice-mail." I held a hand up to stop him before he interrupted. "Thank you for calling."

"I should have done it sooner. I was trying to give you your space and—"

"I could have called, too." I lifted one shoulder in a shrug. "I'm sorry I left the way I did. I should have said something."

"You have nothing to apologize for."

I laughed.

"You don't, Lucy. I was an asshole."

I smirked a little. "You were. But that doesn't mean it's all your fault." I exhaled, the exhaustion from not only the long drive, but the emotional weight of the last few days crashing down on me all at once. "When I took this job, I never expected any of this. And I wasn't ready for it." I shook my head. "None of it."

"And now?"

I looked down at Garfield, who mewled his response.

"Am I ready for it?"

Craig nodded. "I know it's not easy and I'm so far from perfect. Hell, I've screwed this up so much in such a short amount of time that I think it takes some sort of special skill to be this messed up."

I chuckled.

"But I'm learning and growing, Lucy. And sometimes that can be messy because I'm in completely uncharted territory here. I've never done this before." He pressed his hands on the table and looked me straight in the eye. "I've never felt this way about anyone before. And when you left the other day, I thought I'd ruined everything, and you'd never be back."

Garfield's soft fur kept me grounded as I listened carefully, hearing every word.

"I never want to keep anything from you again, Lucy. And I really don't want to hide how I feel about you from anyone. Never again." He took a deep breath and reached a hand across the table. "You know everything now." He dropped his head and shook it before looking up again. "No. That's not true. There's one thing you don't know yet."

I took his hand, warmth instantly flowing through me, steadying my nerves. "What don't I know?"

"You don't know how I feel about you."

My stomach flipped. "I think I do."

"Do you?"

I nodded, and he raised an eyebrow.

"Do you know that whenever I think about you, I smile?"

I tilted my head.

"Do you know that whenever I hear someone mention your name, my heart races? Or that the first time I kissed you, it was like magic?"

I swallowed hard.

"Do you know that when I'm with you, I feel like a part of me that's always been missing is complete again? Or that when I see you with my daughter, I can see my future? *Our* future."

A tear slipped down my cheek, but I didn't wipe it away.

"Lucy, do you know that the last few days knowing that I hurt you and thinking that I might never see you again almost broke me?"

"Craig."

He threaded his fingers through mine. "Most importantly, Lucy, do you know that I love you? And that I would give up absolutely everything, including my family's inheritance if that's what it took. Anything, as long as it meant you would be back in my life, because I cannot imagine spending one more day without you knowing just how much I love you and how you've changed every part of me."

Overwhelmed, I didn't know what to say. I just sat there, numb, staring at him.

"Lucy?"

Finally, I nodded.

"Please, say something."

Again, I nodded and glanced down at the cat, who looked up at me and let out a loud meow that broke the tension.

"Well, I guess we know how Garfield feels." Craig chuckled, and the cat, clearly offended, jumped off my lap and left the room. "But how do you feel, Lucy?"

He tugged gently on my hand.

"Craig, this has all been a lot." He opened his mouth, but I lifted a finger. "Let me finish."

"Of course."

I pulled my hand away so I could stand. Slowly, I moved until I was standing right in front of him.

"I think you know how I feel." I let one hand rest on his cheek. "But I think you're forgetting something."

"What's that?"

"You asked me earlier if I was ready for it." I waved my free arm around the kitchen, all of it. "If I was ready for this."

Craig stood so we were only inches apart. "And?"

I let the smile I'd been holding back since he said the word *love* finally break free.

"I've never been more ready."

He gripped my elbows. "Really? Does that mean—"

"I love you, Craig Carlson." Saying it out loud made my smile widen. "I love you so much. And I love Meri, and I love your crazy family and—"

My words were swallowed by his lips on mine.

The kiss was deep and desperate, filled with everything we'd both been holding back for far too long.

His hands cradled my face, as if he was afraid I might disappear again. But I wasn't going anywhere.

I was home.

Finally.

"Lucy?"

I spun around, instinctively starting to slip away from Craig's arms, but he held me close as we both turned to see a very sleepy Meri standing in the doorway. The unicorn I'd given her dangled from one hand.

She rubbed the sleep from her eyes. "You're home?"

Tears filled my eyes again, but this time they were different. I looked up at Craig, whose eyes were shining too, then gently pulled free and went to her.

"Hey, kiddo." I wrapped her in a tight hug. She threw her arms around my neck and clung to me. "I missed you so much, Meri." I swallowed hard against the tears that threatened.

"I missed you, too. And so did Garfield." She pulled back and nodded seriously. "But don't worry, I took really good care of him, didn't I, Dad?"

"You did a great job, kiddo."

Craig joined us, and we all sank down onto the kitchen floor together. Meri climbed onto my lap, and Craig wrapped his arm around both of us. For the first time in almost a week, I felt whole.

Still sleepy, Meri rested her head against my chest and looked up at both of us. "So, did you fix things, Dad?"

My eyes widened. *Fix things?* What kind of conversations had they been having while I was gone?

"I think I did, kiddo." Craig nodded. "And you know what else? I finally told Lucy that I love her."

My stomach flipped and clenched all at once.

"It's about time, Dad."

We both laughed, and Meri sat up again.

She looked at me seriously. "Do you love my dad?"

"I do." I nodded. "And you know what else? I love you, too. Very, very much."

She wrapped her arms around my neck again, and I buried my face in her hair, my heart overflowing with more love than I thought possible.

When she finally pulled back, her eyelids were drifting shut.

Craig stood and lifted her into his arms. "Time for bed, kiddo. It's been a big day."

"I'll see you in the morning, okay, Meri?" I pressed a kiss to her cheek.

She dropped her head onto his shoulder, and as they left the room, I heard her ask a question that shattered me in the best possible way.

"Dad? Does this mean Lucy can be my mom now?"

Epilogue

OCTOBER

CRAIG

IT WAS the kind of fall day where if I closed my eyes, I might have believed it was still summer. But the golden leaves decorating the trees and falling softly to the ground told a different story. Winter was coming soon, but it still felt a million years away.

It was perfect.

I walked through the plaza, leaves crunching under my feet, until I reached Alpenglow. Of course Charli's storefront was gorgeous. Pumpkins, dried wheat, and bright blooms she'd told me were called mums filled the space and made it feel warm and alive.

The bells over the door chimed as I stepped inside.

"I'm in the back!" Charli called.

A moment later she appeared, her ballooning stomach coming into view first.

"I swear, you get bigger every time I see you."

She shot me a look, but I caught her grin. "This baby is going to be a monster."

"You look like you're ready to pop, sis." I held up my hands. "No offense, obviously. But isn't that baby due soon?"

She groaned. "Not for a few more months still. But I'm not in a hurry. She'll come when she's ready."

"She?"

"Or he." Charli winked.

I shook my head. The whole family had placed bets on the sex of the baby, and I was convinced Charli and Symon already knew. If they did, they were keeping it to themselves.

"Today's the day, huh?" Charli leaned back against the counter and folded her hands over her stomach. "Six months."

"Exactly."

After Lucy came back to Trickle Creek—and as Meri put it, after I fixed things—everything had been different. Better.

For starters, there was no reason to hide our love anymore. And once it was out in the open, it only grew stronger. I hadn't known it was possible to feel so much for another human being beyond what I felt for my daughter. But what I felt for Lucy was different. Deeper. Something I wanted to honor properly.

Just as soon as I could.

Earlier in the summer, after Lucy returned, we'd held an emergency family meeting with William Evans and Steven Larson to make sure I hadn't breached the terms of the will. I'd meant what I said—I would've given it all up for her. I knew my family might've been upset. Very upset. But they would've understood if it was for love.

Thankfully, it hadn't come to that.

Lucy had insisted she not be the reason the Carlson family lost its legacy. And William Evans had agreed her trip to Vancouver was exactly what it was—a holiday. Not a breach of conditions.

For the last few months, Lucy had continued in her role as nanny. She'd even insisted on keeping a separate bedroom, which was slowly driving me insane. But I respected the boundaries she needed.

"I bet you've been counting down," Charli said with a laugh.

"You know I have." I shook my head. "I couldn't be happier to be done with this. Let it be someone else's turn. I've learned what I needed to learn."

The smile slipped from her face, and she grew serious. "I really think you have."

I had.

Despite my initial anger toward my father, I understood now that he'd been right. I'd spent too long thinking I didn't need anyone. Maybe Michael Carlson hadn't intended for me to fall in love with the nanny—but the lesson was the same.

Life was richer when you shared it with someone else.

"Honestly," I said quietly, "I hope I can be even half as wise as he was one day." I swallowed hard. "I never thought I'd say this, but I'm really thankful for the last six months."

Charli moved around the counter and hugged me as best she could with her belly in the way. "I know exactly how you feel. And I'm so excited for you today, Craig. It's going to be perfect."

"I sure hope so." I glanced at the time. Ten minutes.

"It will."

She moved toward the flower cooler along the side of the shop.

"I got what you asked for."

"Thank you."

The bells chimed again, and I turned to see Kat walk in right on time, maneuvering a large carrying case before setting it down with a thud.

She looked up at me and shook her head. "It's a good thing I love you and would do anything for you. Because you owe me after this."

"It'll be worth it," I said. "I promise."

LUCY

"It feels like summer." Meri grabbed my hand and swung it back and forth as we made our way through the plaza. "Doesn't it, Lucy?"

"It really does." It was such a beautiful day that I'd walked to pick Meri up from school. But as much as it felt like summer, it was most definitely not.

It was approaching the end of October, and that meant one thing.

Today was my last day as Meri's nanny.

Which was exactly why we were going to get ice cream to celebrate. We'd made it the whole six months. Even if it was a little touch and go for a moment, we'd made it. And that was worth celebrating.

Because now that we'd fulfilled Craig's obligations to the family, I could officially be just Craig Carlson's girlfriend and not the nanny. And that was going to feel really good.

Really, *really* good.

"Do you already know what flavor you're getting, Meri?"

"Of course I do!"

Next to me, Meri nodded and jumped up and down so much that I stopped under the gazebo in the plaza and laughed. "You're crazy."

She stuck out her tongue and waggled her hands next to her head, ramping up the level of goofiness that just made me laugh harder.

The last few months, living—mostly—as a happy family had been some of the best times of my life. I never could have imagined how much love I had to give and how much I could receive if I opened my heart and let it in.

I bent and gave her a big hug. "I love you, crazy girl."

"I love you, too, Lucy."

I squeezed her tight before she wiggled free.

"Come on. We need to go!"

I took her hand and let her lead me through the busy plaza toward the Sugar Shack. "Ice cream isn't going anywhere, kiddo. What's the rush?"

She broke away from my hand and ran toward the bright-blue door that led to the rental apartment that had been my very first stop in Trickle Creek all those months ago. I took a moment to take that in and remember just how far I'd come since I'd arrived in town. I smiled to myself, and it turned into a laugh when I looked down to see Meri crouching next to me.

"Meri, what on earth are you—"

"Lucy! Watch out!"

She pointed behind me, and I spun around just in time to see a giant orange fluff ball running at a speed Garfield didn't normally move at. I bent and grabbed him before he could crash into me. "What are you doing out here?"

"Good job, Garfield." Meri scratched his head and held out a treat that he quickly gobbled up.

"What do you mean, good job?" I looked at her smug little smile. "Meri, he shouldn't be out here and—what's this?"

Garfield was wearing a collar he never wore because he was supposed to be an inside cat. Attached to it was a little velvet bag. I looked at Meri and raised an eyebrow, but she wasn't helpful.

"Open it."

Somehow, I managed to detach the bag while juggling the large, wiggling cat. The moment I pulled the drawstring open and saw what was inside, I froze.

Garfield was lifted from my arms with a mewl of protest,

but I didn't look up to see who'd taken him. I couldn't. I only had eyes for the ring nestled inside the black velvet bag.

"Lucy Willis?"

I looked up to see Craig walking toward me with a bouquet of out-of-season tulips.

My favorite flower.

Behind him, a small crowd had gathered. I vaguely recognized friends and family, but I only saw him.

"What is…" I shook my head. "What's going on?"

He reached me and took the little bag from my hand. "This is where we met, Lucy. Do you remember?"

I laughed. "Of course I remember. Garfield…oh." I pressed a hand to my mouth.

"The day that fluffy orange beast crashed into my legs changed my life forever." With the ring in his hand, Craig dropped to one knee, and I sucked in a breath. "From the moment I met you, Lucy, I knew you were special. But I don't think I realized then just how much was missing in my life. Now, there isn't a day that goes by where I'm not thankful for you and everything you've brought into my life."

He glanced to his right, and a moment later, Meri joined him.

"Our lives."

Very seriously, she got down on one knee beside her dad and looked up at me.

I swallowed hard, tears already slipping free as she spoke.

"Lucy, I—" Her voice shook. She squeezed her eyes shut, then opened them again. "I think you're the nicest lady I know. You play with me and read to me. And you wear purple, just like me."

I laughed through my tears.

She looked up at her dad.

"Go ahead," Craig said gently.

She nodded and looked back at me. "Dad said that after

today I could ask you this." She took a breath. "Lucy, will you be my mom?"

"Oh."

Nothing could have prepared me for that.

My hands flew to my mouth as she waited patiently beside her dad.

"Oh, Meri." I nodded and looked to Craig, who had tears streaming down his cheeks. "There is nothing I'd like more in the whole wide world than to be your mom."

I stepped forward and pulled her into my arms, tears spilling freely as we squeezed each other tight.

Beside us, Craig cleared his throat. "I hate to interrupt," he said with a chuckle. "But I still have something I need to ask, too."

"Oh, sorry, Dad."

She untangled herself, but I kept hold of her hand as I turned back to the man I loved.

"I feel like this might be a bit anticlimactic now," he said. "But I need to ask." He held out the ring, sunlight catching the stone. "Lucy, will you please marry me and be my wife?"

CRAIG

The impromptu party in the plaza was a smashing success. With my new fiancée on my arm, I was on top of the world. Together, as a family, we made our rounds and accepted the well wishes of our friends and family, including Mandi and Lucy's mom, Audrey, who I'd arranged to come witness the special moment.

I was looking forward to getting to know them both better, but for now Charli and Annie had taken them under their wing and were making sure both women were being well cared for.

Asher had arranged for a few tables with bottles of champagne to be set up to celebrate, and somewhere along the way, someone had found a speaker and upbeat music filled the plaza.

"Congratulations, man." My best friend Andy appeared and handed us each a glass of champagne before giving me a quick hug and a slap on the shoulder. "And Lucy, I can't tell you how nice it is to finally meet you. I've heard so much about you."

"Is that right?" Lucy shot me a look, and I held up a hand in defense.

"Only good things, of course." Andy winked. "Kat told me from day one that she knew you were special."

"Oh, did she?" I raised an eyebrow at him. "You two are sure chatting a lot these days."

Fortunately for Andy, he was saved from answering when Meri barreled into him for a hug a moment later. "Uncle Andy."

"Hey, kiddo." He picked her up and twirled her around. "What's new?"

"I'm going to have a mom."

We all laughed.

"You sure are."

"And Garfield gets to live with us forever now."

I groaned, though truth be told, the cat had grown on me.

"Speaking of Garfield," Lucy said. "How on earth did you get him to do that? I've had him forever and he's never done anything like that before."

Meri pressed her lips into a thin line and looked Lucy straight in the eye. "I told him how important it was, Lucy. And we practiced. A lot." She rolled her eyes. "Remember what you said when I was trying to tie my shoes?"

Lucy laughed. "Practice might not make perfect, but it will make it better."

"That." Meri pointed at her, and we all laughed.

"Come on, kiddo." Andy lifted Meri onto his shoulder. "Let's go find your Auntie Kat. I think you deserve an ice cream."

I gave him the side eye again but brushed it off. Kat had always been the annoying little sister to both of us growing up. Something had obviously changed.

I focused on my fiancée and pulled her into my arms for a not-so-sneaky kiss for everyone to see. Just the way it should be.

"I love that you're going to be my wife."

"I love you." She smiled and touched my lips with her finger. "And for the record, this was all pretty perfect. Thank you for today."

"No, Lucy. Thank *you*. For crashing into our lives the way you did and for taking a chance on some random guy who hired you to be a nanny when all you wanted to do was scoop ice cream."

She tossed her head back and laughed. "I still kind of want to scoop ice cream."

"You do?"

"I mean, maybe once or twice." She laughed. "But I'm not worried about what comes next, Craig. Because the only important thing is that we're together. The three of us."

"Just three?" I wiggled my eyebrows. "Because I think maybe having a—"

"Simmer down." She smacked my arm playfully. "One thing at a time. We're barely even engaged. Besides, all the fun is in the practicing." She winked. "Come on, let's go mingle a little bit and then you can take me home for a little of that practicing."

I happily let her lead me back into the party.

"Like you said, sweetheart. Practice makes it all better."

Peak in on Craig and Lucy on a rare and sexy date night that includes some sweet dessert with an exclusive bonus scene. Click here to grab that scene!

Next up is Asher's Story in Because You Loved Me

And if you want even more romance…click HERE for an exclusive FREE novella that isn't available anywhere else!

Bonus Scene

DATE NIGHT

CRAIG

Date night was a rare occurrence when you had a six-year-old. A detail that had never been very important to me. Until recently.

As much as I loved hanging out with Meri and Lucy together as a family, I couldn't deny I'd like to have the opportunity to get my beautiful fiancée alone in our house a little more often.

Which is why when Charli and Symon offered to take Meri for a sleepover, I jumped at the opportunity and not just because it was probably the last time for Meri to spend some quality time with the two of them before the baby was born.

"Have I told you how beautiful you look tonight, Lucy?" It was such a mild fall evening, we'd walked to the Plaza for dinner and after eating an adult dinner of clam and mussel linguine, and sharing a bottle of wine, Lucy wanted to take her time walking home in the cool night air.

"You may have mentioned it once or twice." She twirled for me, her dress dancing over the tops of her thighs.

My cock twitched to life in my pants. I reached for her and pulled her in tight for a kiss. "Ummm." I pulled away and licked my lips. "Delicious. But not as delicious as the dessert I have planned."

"Ohh." Her eyes widened with anticipation. "Are we going to stop at the Sugar Shack for chocolate?"

I pulled her close again, and let my hands slide down her body before letting one hand inch its way up and under her skirt.

"Whoa!" She tried to pull away, but I held her tight. "You're being very cheeky, Mr. Carlson," she teased.

"I can't help it." I nibbled at her neck. "I need to get you home."

"What about dessert?"

I kissed her one more time before forcing myself to pull back. "Oh, we're definitely having dessert."

"Leave it to a man who owns an ice cream shop."

I licked my lips and left the counter top where I'd finished assembling my ingredients that included whipped cream, sprinkles and chocolate sauce. "You are going to be delicious, my love."

I kissed her slowly until her knees buckled a little. I traced a candied cherry along her lips, teasing her with the sticky sweetness until finally sliding it between her lips.

While the sweet treat exploded in her mouth, I unzipped her dress and let it fall to the floor before moving to her bra and panties.

When she was completely naked, I ran my hands down her body, leaving a trail of heat in my wake.

"Umm." I grunted with a shake of my head. "Suddenly, I'm ravenous."

Still in the kitchen, I grabbed the can of whipped cream and sprayed it over the top of her breasts. Her nipples puckered when the shock of cold hit. A moment later, my tongue traced the trail of cream, before I sucked one nipple in between my lips.

I took my time cleaning the first round of whipped cream from her body before once more reaching for the can.

"I was right." I wiggled my eyebrows. "You are absolutely delectable."

She laughed.

"Don't tell me you think it's funny that I find you delicious?" I pretended to look affronted and wielded the can of whipped cream. "Because I am nowhere near done with you yet." I took her hand and led her to the kitchen table. I put the can down long enough to lift her by the hips and set her on the table.

"What are you doing?"

"Trust me."

"Always."

I gently laid her back on the table before picking up the whipped cream again.

The cream was sticky and cool. I took my time, spraying it around each breast, topping each nipple with a large dollop.

"I can't resist." I winked and dipped my head for a quick lick that sent a shot of desire through her and straight between her legs. A moan slipped from her lips.

"You like that?"

She nodded and wiggled her hips a little.

"Then you're going to love this." I continued my work with the whipped cream. She squealed when I arrived between her legs and tried to squeeze her thighs together but I stopped her.

"Sweetheart. This is going to be the best part."

My eyes were clouded with desire, the other toppings

forgotten as I sank to my knees on the kitchen floor and began eating my dessert.

It didn't take long before the pressure inside her began to build. I held her in place while I licked, lapped and sucked and she came apart, exploding in a kaleidoscope of sensation as the orgasm took over her body.

When Lucy opened her eyes a few minutes later, I was hovering over her, licking my lips with a satisfied grin. "Umm. Just as I thought. Absolutely delicious."

She sat up and put a hand to my still-clothed chest. "But I haven't had dessert yet." She licked her lips and watched as my pupils dilated with desire. "And you are wearing far too many clothes for me to enjoy myself to my fullest."

Lucy slid off the table and reached immediately for my belt. I helped her and soon, my jeans and boxers were on the floor in a puddle. She slipped her hands up my hard chest and tugged my sweater up and over my head.

"Better." She bit her bottom lip and moved her hands down my gorgeous, hard body until her hands were wrapped around my long, hard length. I groaned and tipped my head back.

LUCY

I was tempted to skip the toppings altogether, but the prospect of indulging in a little extra sweetness was too good to pass up. I grabbed the can of cream and with my other hand, walked him backwards until I pressed him up against the kitchen counter, in close reach of the toppings.

With his cock fisted in one hand, I used the other to cover him in whipped cream. The sight of his hard dick covered in the sticky sweet stuff sent an unexpected thrill through me.

"Oh yes," I murmured. "I believe you're going to be very delicious, too."

But I wasn't done with him yet. I reached for the chocolate syrup and first dripped it onto his chest where I sucked and licked all the way up to his lips.

He reached out and captured my face in his hands, but I would not be swayed from my task.

"Don't try to get me to skip my dessert," I teased before returning to my task.

He groaned as I squirted the chocolate sauce over the whipped cream and then to add the finishing touch, sprinkled my *treat* with colourful candy sprinkles.

When I was finished, I stepped back to admire my work. I took my time assessing my handsome fiancé, and the dessert he presented to me before I slowly licked my lips and sucked my bottom lip between my teeth, the way I knew drove him crazy. "Oh yes, I'm going to enjoy every bite."

He groaned and braced his elbows on the counter behind him as I dropped to my knees in front of him. "I swear, this is the sexiest thing I've ever seen. Lucy, you are fire."

"Ssh." I looked up at him and winked. "It's time for dessert."

My tongue lapped slowly up his shaft, filling my mouth with cream and chocolate sauce. "Yum." I licked my lips and looked up, but Craig's head was tipped backward, his eyes shut as he worked to control himself.

I grinned to myself and resumed my attention on his cock. I licked up one side and then down the other, twirling my tongue around the head before I took his entire length in my mouth.

He groaned and his hands twined through my hair as I enjoyed myself.

The cream and chocolate were sticky and messy, but that

was the last thing on my mind when I felt every muscle in Craig's body tense moments before he too, took his release.

CRAIG

"You're right," Lucy said a few minutes later, once we had both recovered enough from our sexy, decadent desserts. "That was delicious."

She squealed as I grabbed her hand and spun her in for a kiss. Our bodies, still sticky, stuck together, but we didn't care.

"I love you." I released her. "How did I get so lucky?"

She turned around and winked at me. "You hired me, remember?"

"And it was the best decision of my life. My mom was on to something with the whole trust your gut thing."

"A mother's intuition should not be underestimated." Lucy paused, a rag in her hand. "Speaking of motherhood."

A jolt shot straight through me. I dropped the roll of paper towels I'd been holding and crossed the floor in a flash to stand in front of her. "What? Are you—" I tried to put my hands on her belly, but she swatted me away.

"No, silly. I'm not pregnant." Lucy laughed and grabbed my hands in hers. "But I did want to mention something."

I felt a flicker of disappointment, but it didn't last. We'd talked about it. We were on the same page. We both looked forward to adding to our family and giving Meri a sibling—when the time was right. For now, we were happy, enjoying each other and the little family we'd already built.

Lucy's face grew serious, and she squeezed my hand. "I have to ask you something. And I…well, it's…"

"Anything, sweetheart."

"Last night when I was tucking Meri in, she asked me something."

I knew exactly what was coming. Meri and I had talked about it earlier in the week. I nodded and waited.

"She asked me if it would be okay if she called me Mom."

My heart squeezed, just like it had when Meri had asked me the same question. I inhaled deeply. "And what do you think about that?"

"I think I would love it." Her eyes shone with unshed tears. "I love Meri and to be her mom…"

A tear slipped down her cheek, and I wiped it away without thinking.

"What did you want to ask me?"

"You know how much I love Meri, and yes, of course I want her to call me mom. But…" She looked down for a moment. "Once we're married, I would love to officially adopt her. She deserves a mother. In all the ways."

Emotion flooded me, and it was my turn to blink back tears. I pulled her close and held her face in my hands. "Nothing would make me happier, Lucy. Thank you."

"For what?"

"For loving my daughter the way you do."

"And you?"

I grinned. "And for loving me, too."

We kissed, soft and sweet, and when I pulled away, I shook my head in wonder. "Again…how did I get so lucky to find such an amazing person?"

She wiggled her shoulders and winked. "You're pretty amazing, too."

"Is that right?"

"Uh-huh." The seriousness of the moment faded as her eyes traveled down my still-naked body. "Oh yes. You are most definitely amazing."

She reached for me and ran one finger down my chest

before stopping abruptly and laughing. "But you are very sticky."

I laughed with her. "I know one way to take care of that."

The mess in the kitchen was forgotten as I led my beautiful, sticky, sweet fiancée to a hot, steamy shower—before taking her to bed. Exactly where I wanted her.

———

I hope you enjoyed Craig and Lucy's special date!

Next up is Asher's Story in Because You Loved Me!

About the Author

Elena Aitken is a USA Today Bestselling Author of more than fifty romance and women's fiction novels. The mother of 'grown up' twins, Elena now lives with her very own mountain man in the heart of the very mountains she writes about. She can often be found with her toes in the lake and a glass of wine in her hand, dreaming up her next book and working on her own happily ever after.

To learn more about Elena:
www.elenaaitken.com
elena@elenaaitken.com